GRAIL OF POWER

ORDER OF THADDEUS
BOOK 5

J. A. BOUMA

EmmausWay
P R E S S

Copyright © 2018 by J. A. Bouma

All rights reserved.

EmmausWay Press

An Imprint of EmmausWay Media Group

PO Box 1180 • Grand Rapids, MI 49501

www.emmauswaypress.com

No part of this book may be reproduced in any form or by any electronic or mechanical means, including information storage and retrieval systems, without written permission from the author, except for the use of brief quotations in a book review.

This book is a work of fiction. The characters, organizations, products, incidents, and dialogue are drawn from the author's imagination and experience, and are not to be construed as real. Any reference to historical events, real organizations, real people, or real places are used fictitiously. Any resemblance to actual products, organizations, events, or persons, living or dead, is entirely coincidental.

Scripture quotations are from New Revised Standard Version Bible, copyright © 1989 National Council of the Churches of Christ in the United States of America. Used by permission. All rights reserved.

PROLOGUE

GLASTONBURY, ENGLAND.
SEPTEMBER 1539.

A door at the back of the Lady Chapel of Glastonbury Abbey thudded loudly behind the last of Father Richard Whiting's parishioners, a widower who had stayed behind after Mass to offer the kind priest his confession. It was a small matter, something about a cross word he had had with his neighbor. But the elderly man of ninety years and two had been worried sick about the trespass.

Not to worry, Father Whiting had reassured him before praying over the dear man: "May our Lord Jesus Christ absolve you; and by his authority I absolve you from every bond of excommunication and interdict, so far as my power allows and your needs require." Then, making the Sign of the Cross, the priest concluded, "Thereupon, I absolve you from your sins in the name of the Father, and of the Son, and of the Holy Spirit."

Amen, the two said together.

The slight man had wheezed a sigh of relief and promised an extra shilling of alms for the poor as penance, then begged Father Whiting to yet partake of the host and chalice from the evening's ritual. He had forgone the spiritual sustenance in light of his transgression but wanted desperately for his soul to be fed by the body and blood of Christ himself. Whiting had been more than willing to oblige his most faithful congregant's request, as the host had yet to be retired to the tabernacle and the chalice cleansed.

After the man left, the priest attended to the Eucharistic elements, cleaning up after the sacred ritual. As he worked under the cover of dim candlelight, he wondered how much longer it would be performed in his land. Rumors had reached his abbey in recent days of the reforms wrought by King Henry VIII, and the violent cleansing his henchmen had undertaken for what he saw as abuses within the Catholic Church. That bloody German monk sure had lit a fuse that was burning the whole Temple of Christ to the ground, that was for sure!

Father Whiting stopped his work and closed his eyes. He took a breath and crossed himself, confessing his anger at the fellow brother in the faith known as Luther—even if he was a German nuisance turning the Church on end! He promised the good Lord a day-long fast on the morrow for his own dose of penance. The priest had certainly sympathized with the monk's disgust at the abuse of indulgences. But the German had taken his reformation too far when he had protested the veneration of relics, as well.

"It is claimed that the head of St. John the Baptist is in Rome," Martin Luther wrote in one work, "although all histories show that the Saracens opened John's grave and burned everything to powder. Yet the pope is not ashamed of his lies. So with reference to other relics like the nails and the wood of the cross—they are the greatest lies." He went on, writing in mocking tones, "Certain men have impudently boasted that they possess a feather from the holy angel St. Michael. The bishop of Mainz claims to have a flame from the bush of Moses. So in Compostella the banner is exhibited that Christ had in hell, and likewise the crown of thorns, the nails, etc., and also some of Mary's milk."

Whiting could feel the embers of his anger beginning to

rekindle. So he took another breath, sighed heavily, and went back to his priestly work. As he continued, the prized relic of his own abbey caught his attention, orange candlelight glinting off the surface of its golden reliquary. He finished clearing the host and cup, securing the remaining bread in the tabernacle and draining the fermented wine himself. Then he ambled reverently over to the table holding the holy object.

He stood silently before it, alone and consumed by its weight while contemplating its majesty and significance, the memory of the event contained within echoing in his very soul. As he venerated the object resting within, he thought about the lines of prose from his favorite of the Medieval romances depicting the holy relic:

> *And king Pellam lay so many years sorely wounded,*
> *and could never recover until Galahad the High*
> *Priest healed him in the quest for the Sankgreall.*
> *For in that place was part of the blood of Our*
> *Lord Jesu Christ, which Joseph of Arimathea*
> *brought into this land...*

He smiled proudly at the thought that Providence had chosen his lands to be the steward of what Joseph of Arimathea bore those many centuries ago—had chosen him and his parish as the final resting place of the Son's Holy Blood. He walked close to the container and lifted his robe, gently caressing and polishing the reliquary to a sacred sheen.

Suddenly, the double doors anchoring one side of the back end of the chapel burst open, thudding angrily against the cut-stone walls and sending a wave of air rippling across the candles near the high altar, their flames flapping in protest.

The priest spun around sharply. His breath caught in his chest and bowels went weak at the sight of six men of various ages and sizes, all dressed in dark brown hooded robes, rushing into the narthex and hustling through the nave toward him.

The man swallowed hard and braced himself as they approached closer. But then sighed with relief, realizing the intruders at that dark hour were fellow ministers of the cross, monks from the abbey standing ground next door.

Soon, however, it was clear all was not right.

"Brother Richard," the lead man said with purpose, his voice echoing off the vaulted ceiling, Christ himself staring down as a witness from his crucifix above to the urgency below.

Whiting took a hesitant step forward, and said, "Brother John, what stirs you six at this late hour?"

The others filed in quickly behind their brother as they hustled between rows of wooden benches toward the object of their urgent pursuit.

"The hour has come, I'm afraid."

No...

Father Whiting took a protective step back toward the holy relic, instinctively shielding it with his body.

"Henchmen are galloping toward Glastonbury as we speak," another brother said darkly, Brother Stephen.

"What news have you received?" asked Father Whiting.

"From Hailes, I'm afraid," Brother John said. "The abbey has been stripped bare of its precious metal and jeweled adornment and...dismantled."

"Dismantled?" the priest said, his face twisting with a mixture of confusion and appall.

"Ay," the man said, "the whole chapel torn down, stone by stone."

Whiting gasped and stepped forward, clutching his robe in front of his chest. He whispered, "What of the holy relic? The Holy Blood of Hailes?"

Brother John glanced at Brother Stephen, then he shook his head. "It is unclear what has befallen it. Which is why we have arrived, to secret the Arimathean treasure away before it is despoiled."

The doors at the back of the Lady Chapel thudded loudly again, causing the heads of all seven of the men huddled around the sacred relic to snap toward the narthex.

"They're here!" a young lad shouted, his voice cracking with urgency and brown robe flapping behind him as he ran toward the front of the nave. "Descending upon the abbey in droves, bearing torches and arms!"

Brother John's eyes, wide and frantic, met Father Whiting's own eyes, betraying an equal measure of fright.

"The king and his men, then?" Brother John asked.

The lad shook his head. "No. These men bear not the king's colors."

The monk stepped forward and narrowed his eyes. "Then it appears an ancient threat is bearing down upon the Church this dark hour."

Whiting swallowed hard and nodded knowingly. "Quickly, come with me. And you," the priest said pointing at the lad who had just burst into the chapel, "barricade the entrances. We're going to need every ounce of favor for the departure, whether natural locks or divine Providence."

As the one monk rushed back to secure the sets of doors, Brother Richard and Brother John worked to carefully extract the holy relic from its sacred home. Brother John opened a leather satchel and withdrew a purple cloth, at one point soaked in the sacred waters of the mighty Jordan itself, he said, the river in which Jesus was baptized.

A fitting shroud for the holy chalice...

They carefully wrapped the humble wooden cup in the garment and placed it securely in the leather satchel. The lad returned, and Whiting led them to a small door. He withdrew a large ring of keys and inserted one of them into the lock.

Beyond the narthex, there was a whine of horses and a

commotion outside. Then the doors on either end shook violently. There were loud, muffled curses, and then another assault on the ramparts to the Lady Chapel.

The sands of time had reached their end.

The priest twisted the lock and crossed himself, then flung open the small, sturdy door and ushered his brothers inside to a stairwell that descended beneath the sacred space. Before closing the door, he lit a torch from one of the altar candles. He hustled them inside and closed the door securely behind them then set the lock, forcing his mind to abandon any thought to whatever was about to occur in the holy sanctuary he had cultivated for a generation. He urged the monks downward to a chamber beneath the chapel, then took the lead to guide them through the darkened passage built for such a time as this.

Soon, they emerged at the far end to another set of stairs that took them back to the surface, arriving at the modest house anchoring the northeast corner of the abbey grounds beyond a wall of trees.

Whiting handed his torch to Brother John. He withdrew his ring of keys once more and thrust one into the complementary lock. He closed his eyes and held his breath, his heart pounding a mean rhythm as he waited—listening, discerning, praying.

Hearing nothing of import, he twisted the lock and eased open the door. The abbey abode was still, silent, but for a wicked menace raging several blocks west from whence they came.

The priest stepped into the darkened space growing brighter from an orange glow seeping in through small windows a few rooms down. He ushered his brothers inside and led them to a door that would take them to an adjoining stable.

They quickly saddled three steeds and mounted them as the revelry and mayhem continued desecrating the sacred space they had just fled. The men exchanged words with Father

Whiting; the priest blessed them for their journey and urged them to make haste.

As the sound of the galloping horses faded into the darkness, the corners of Whiting's eyes couldn't help but prickle with sorrow at the loss of the relic that thousands of pilgrims had venerated for centuries, including himself—the echo of its memory provoking within them a deep devotion for the Savior whose blood had been spilt into it.

The grail of power will live to see another day—provoking faith with its memory, nourishing souls with its blood.

DAY I

DECEMBER 17

CHAPTER 1

NEW YORK CITY. PRESENT DAY.

ive. Four. Three. Two. One.

In the next beat, every single one of the burnished bronze lampposts lighting Central Park flickered off. From the vantage point of the man with the mustache and slicked-back hair hovering high above, it looked as if the Universe itself made a wish and sent a lungful of air across them all, puffing them out like tiny birthday candles.

Joining the outage were several blocks along Fifth Avenue between 79th Street and 82nd Street. Apartments, office complexes, and retail shops, the whole lot of them dimmed down to nothing, like a replay of the great Northeast Blackout of 2003.

Including one building in particular, the target of the midnight spectacle.

Predictably, headlights and horns from the rat-pack of cars below responded with frustration. Voices, faint but distinct, rose upward with confusion, as if petitioning the gods for redress. The man could smell the fear high above, mingling with the urban stench of idling cars, fast food, and too many bodies emanating from the streets below. He swallowed hard, bile threatening to sideline him before the mission and embarrass him in front of his two companions.

How he hated America and everything it stood for. Especially that two-thousand-year-old faith, with all of its weakness and self-loathing and guilt-laden pity, its dead god and hypocritical followers, its easy-believism and cheap grace written in blood. His stomach clenched as another round of bile reached for the surface. Again, he swallowed.

Soon the world will experience the full weight of our confusion and reap the benefits of what we have to offer in place of the Church. But all in good time...

The mechanical bird swooped in from its perch high above in the low-hanging midnight clouds, coming in fast toward a rooftop garden on the southwest corner of the baroque-style building sitting on the eastern edge of Central Park along Museum Mile, one of the world's largest art galleries with over two million works. The New York Metropolitan Museum of Art. It also happened to contain a single object that would bring about a realignment of the religious faiths, as well as destruction to the bane of his and his spiritual order's existence.

The helicopter came in low and was brought to a sudden standstill. As it hovered, a rope was thrown from a side door, and three black-clad operatives shimmied down to the deck below. Within seconds the chopper retreated toward safer space back to its perch above while the trio ran to the elevator entrance leading down into the belly of the museum where their relic waited for them.

With the power cut, the man with the mustache took the lead by shoving a crowbar into the thin wedge running the length of the heavy metal doors. A second man helped him pry them open, while the other heaved one door in the opposite direction. With a little muscle the door gave. The mustachioed man dropped the bar with a clang and quickly positioned himself between the doors, arms pressing against both sides to shove them open. After they gave and retreated inside the wall, he clicked on an LED penlight and peered down into the abyss below. Thankfully, the carriage was down at ground level.

He nodded to the other two, stepped out, and grabbed the cable running from top to bottom. Then he descended into the darkness, emergency lights guiding his way until he thudded heavily on the roof of the elevator car. He moved to the side as the other two quickly followed behind him, stooping to open the ceiling trapdoor.

He hesitated before climbing down inside. It was dark and quiet. He let another three beats tick by. Satisfied, he jumped into the void. The others followed. The elevator doors stood open, a faint trace of white LED light from more emergency lighting deeper inside the museum casting eerie shadows toward the trio.

The man's heart began to gallop forward, the familiar coppery taste of adrenaline from similar missions offering a high to encourage him forward. He withdrew a weapon stuffed at the small of his back, a Heckler & Koch semi-automatic special forces handgun outfitted with the optional silencer and laser sight. His weapon of choice.

He glanced back to his two comrades who had also retrieved their weapons, suppressed submachine guns, both Heckler & Koch. As the head of the alt-spirituality's armory and commander of operations, he had spent years carefully assembling an arsenal built by the German defense manufacturing company, ensuring his soldiers would be armed with only the best engineering of his adopted homeland. Tonight they would need it. Nothing could go wrong. The Grand Master wouldn't allow any more mistakes after the disaster from earlier that fall.

The man with the mustache pivoted left and padded forward into the bare hallway, weapon outstretched and red dot leading the way. They passed a pair of restrooms on the left before entering the first gallery full of nineteenth-century sculptures. They moved quickly through the darkened room, passing a statue of white marble, a woman with long hair curled on either side of her face and a nearly-nude boy draped across her with a bowl spilled of its contents lying next to them. Europeans and their disgusting tastes in art! His people from the land of Persia would never create something so garish.

They continued on into the next room, where pale-white emergency lighting up ahead beckoned them and more European sculptures of stone and metal awaited. The man stopped short before entering, holding up his arm with a fist to instruct his men to do the same.

The space was larger and longer, a court with a high ceiling of glass built between two separate additions to the original museum. The vastness was bathed in faint white light, giving it an air of mysticism with its platoon of mythological and allegorical statues bearing swords, as if they were ready to go to their deaths protecting the treasured works of art within.

He held his breath—waiting, listening, intuiting. When he was satisfied they were safe to proceed, he stepped forward, leading his men toward their prize.

"I don't know what the hell is going on!"

The man stopped short and cursed under his breath, then retreated into the darkness.

The voice was gruff and gravelly, sounding forth from a man who knew how to carry himself, with steps that were heavy, purposeful. Not good.

The trio quickly, quietly retreated back into the gallery shadows as voices and footfalls echoed from the left toward them. The mustachioed man eased himself leftward, gripping his silencer-equipped HK close to his chest, the long cylindrical barrel pointing toward the ceiling but ready to do business. The other two had backed up away from the entranceway across from him, their own weapons ready for a fight.

"This is 2003 all over again," another man mumbled, pitch

high and heady. He was someone who would certainly fold without a fight.

"There goes our night. Shot to hell along with the power."

They were nearly at their doorstep. Literally. The man inched backwards as the voices came upon them. His breath was hot and heavy; he had always struggled with keeping his body under control during crucial missions. He cursed himself silently and willed the two men to pass.

"Did you hear that chopper earlier? Think it had anything to do with the power?"

"In this city? Choppers are a dime a dozen, zooming this way and that like flocks of geese!"

There they were. A few more steps and they would be upon them.

"True that I guess."

"Come on," the gruff one echoed toward them. "Let's see what's going on with that damn generator. Those cheapskate curators care more about their precious pieces of art and pottery than they do keeping the lights on!"

And then they passed, retreating farther into the space, arguing about the outcome of the recent presidential election before a door creaked open and clanged shut behind them.

The man with the mustache closed his eyes, then exhaled heavily. He lowered his weapon, nodded toward the submachine-gun duo across the room and hustled through the entrance and through to the other side past large doors of dark solid wood. The generator complicated things, but no matter. They would be long gone before then.

They continued onward through a lightless room with darkened walls of Sèvres-porcelain-mounted furniture. The French theme continued through two more rooms of various sixteenth-century tin-enameled earthenware dishes until they reached the main sculpture hall of Medieval art—the next-to-the-last stop until they reached their object of pursuit.

More of the same mystical faint light gently dappled the room in white from the room's four corners, this time aided by moonlight struggling for purchase through fourteen windows set high above. The clouds must be giving way, which would make their escape more difficult.

They pressed onward, a cadre of gargoyles and small Byzantine statues staring at them in a mixture of apprehension and appall as they prepared to do their deed. He glanced at one as he passed, a man standing and holding his head, a saintly Christian martyr perhaps. How appropriate.

They veered to the right, taking another darkened passageway filled with more Christian relics—a sarcophagus displaying the twelve apostles, crosses and censers for worship, Eucharistic instruments used to celebrate the body and blood of Christ.

Again, how appropriate.

Wait...

He nearly passed the object encased in glass had light from behind not glinted off its surface. It was so modest, so humble, so unlike what he expected given what it was supposed to have held.

Stuffing his weapon behind his back, he knelt on his haunches. There it was. The submachine-gun duo came up next to him as he examined it, verified it, even quietly venerated it.

If only you had known then what you'd be part of two thousand years later...

The man grinned widely, the caterpillar resting above his upper lip wiggling with approval. He snapped his fingers and pointed to the object. One of his two companions got to work, zipping down his black jacket and pulling out a device. A suction cup with a rod six inches long anchored on top, tipped with a quarter carat diamond. He held the device over the glass in front of the object the mustachioed man had pointed to, then gently pressed it against its surface. Kneeling, he eyed the object on the other side, then adjusted the length of the rod, sliding it a few inches to shorten its reach. Grabbing the head of the device and pressing it firmly against the glass, he began turning it in a circle. It squeaked in protest as he continued spinning it around, the tip of the diamond slowly cutting through the glass with each lap.

When he was satisfied, the man stopped spinning and removed the device with a *pop*. Then he pressed his gloved hand against the circle and began pressing into the glass, leaning into it with more of his weight—

Until it popped into the case with a gentle *ting*.

The man with the mustache snapped his head up, the caterpillar drooping with apprehension as the man scanned both sides of the corridor verifying they hadn't been heard or discovered. The power failure ensured not only the lights would be cut, but the security measures would be disarmed, as well.

He held his breath, continuing his search. No voices, no movement. Good.

He shoved the man aside and carefully reached his own gloved hand through the freshly-cut hole and grabbed ahold of the silver relic. He gently lifted it off the creamy velvet resting place, eyes darting this way and that as he eased it out of the—

What the hell?

It was stuck. He turned the object around in his hand, so that its base was at his palm, then tried sliding it out again. It wouldn't budge. He frantically repeated the process several times over, searching for a position that would offer a way out.

No way, no how.

He swung his head to the imbecile still squatting next to him, eyes wide with panic and mouth open with rage. The man shrugged silently next to him.

The man with the mustache gently set the relic back down inside the case, then slapped the man before pouncing on him.

His companion shielded his face for another blow, but the man whispered angrily, "Fix this!"

He climbed off of him. The man shuffled back over to the case, withdrawing the device again for another go. Precious minutes ticked by as he worked the diamond tip manually around the opening, trying desperately to undo his screw up, more squeaks setting the mustachioed man on edge as he waited for the solution to emerge.

A few minutes later, the man systematically cracked pieces of glass around the edge of the hole, enlarging it for the relic inside. Then he carefully reached inside and withdrew it before presenting it to the man with the mustache.

He smiled weakly and nodded as he took it.

Perfect.

Suddenly, the lights returned with blinding indifference to the six darkness-adjusted eyes below. The generator had saved the two Rent-a-Cops' asses after all.

Accompanying the lights was a deafening squeal, the echo of an alarm raging at their intrusion.

The man with the mustache mumbled a curse. Without confirming with his pals, he stuffed the relic under his arm like a rugby ball with one hand, reached behind his back for his weapon with the other, and took off back toward their landing zone.

"Radio the chopper," he growled back.

He ran past the headless martyr and back into the Medieval sculpture hall, stopping short in front of a statue of Madonna and the Christ child. Raising the arm cradling the relic slightly, he smiled knowingly, then pivoted left and started back through the galleries of French still life. Up ahead was the court of European sculptures.

And then the silhouette of a very large man.

On instinct, he outstretched the arm holding the Heckler & Koch and fired *one-two-three* into the dead-center mass.

The Goliath clutched his chest, offered a disapproving moan, then crumpled in a massive heap.

The mustachioed man ran faster, clutching the relic closer to his side. Just like the old days back in Iran.

Another man appeared, mouth agape. "My God in heaven!" he screeched, hands cupping his mouth like someone who had clearly never saw the other end of a barrel. He snapped his head up toward the French corridor, hands still covering his mouth. It was the last thing he saw before his head snapped backward, and he joined his fallen comrade on the floor.

The three men ran across the bodies with neither care nor respect for the dead, reaching the elevators at the far end and taking the resuscitated carriage up to the top. Awaiting their arrival was their helicopter, black and stealthy against the now-gleaming rooftop garden. It descended to accommodate the men, the two companions climbing in first in order to help the man with the mustache holding the relic inside.

The faint whine of sirens faded in and out above the din of thwapping blades as the chopper rose back into the sky, orbs of red and blue racing down Fifth Avenue toward the MET to protect its treasures.

Only they would fail.

And soon, so would the Church.

CHAPTER 2

PUNTA CANA, DOMINICAN
REPUBLIC.

I *could get used to this.*

Silas Grey gulped the last of his Mojito, savoring every last drop of the white rum, mint, lemon juice, sugar, and soda water cocktail as it gently slid into his still-full belly from the late-morning brunch of bacon, eggs, fried potatoes, and Jamaican Blue Mountain coffee. It was not even noon, and he had already imbibed two glasses of his favorite Caribbean drink. But, hey, it was Happy Hour somewhere, right?

"Another, señor?"

Silas squinted into the high-morning sun at the bronze young man standing at attention in a red-and-white striped collared shirt and white shorts, balancing a tray of empty glasses on his flattened palm.

He smiled and handed the helpful chap his empty glass. "Alejandro, my man! Don't mind if I do. Add extra mint, por favor. And a pinch more rum." He handed him an American ten dollar bill and winked.

The man smiled widely and snatched the incentive. He bowed, and said, "Sí, señor!" Then he hurried off through the powdery white sand.

"Muchas gracias," Silas mumbled as he closed his eyes and

settled back into the green beach lounger commanding Playa Blanca beach. Three Mojitos before noon. He could definitely get used to that.

And why shouldn't I after the hell-of-a-year I just went through?

Not only had he nearly gotten himself killed trying to prove the Church's central teaching, the resurrection of Jesus Christ. He was denied his life's ambition, tenure at one of the nation's most prestigious universities, and he was fired in the process. Then there was the matter of his brother, Sebastian. They had always had a rough go of it, being twin siblings and all and fending for themselves after their mother had died giving them birth and their dad was busy keeping America safe as a colonel in the Army. And when Dad died during the 9/11 attack on the Pentagon and Sebastian became hostile to all things Christian, their incommunicado routine became a staple of life. But his double betrayal this past summer and during the recent presidential election had breached a gulf that would be virtually impossible to bridge.

Silas sighed heavily at the memories pressing against him as the Punta Cana waves of aqua and turquoise and indigo gently rolled across sugar-white Punta Cana sand. He had struggled to make sense of it all, struggled to understand why the good Lord would allow—no *cause* his life to shift so dramatically, dismantling all that he was in the process of constructing after years of careful planning and not a small amount of elbow grease.

He had worked his butt off in the Army, racing to the nearest recruitment center after that fateful day on 9/11 and later being recruited as a Ranger, quickly rising to Sergeant Major with distinction before being discharged. Then there was graduate school at Harvard, where he graduated *magna cum laude*. As a professor of religious studies and church history at Princeton University, he had risen fast as one of the more beloved and distinguished faculty members. And as one of the foremost experts on relicology, the study of religious relics and icons, he had made something of a name for himself in the niche academic circles that cared about such arcane things.

All before it came crashing down in one fell swoop.

Of course, he wasn't entirely done for, just starting a new chapter in an entirely new volume of his life. A smile curled upward as he lay baking in the Caribbean sun thinking about the new adventure that would await him when he returned to the land of the living after his vacation break for Day One of his new gig with the Order of Thaddeus.

You sure got your way didn't you, Radcliffe?

Rowan Radcliffe was the Master of the ancient Order stretching back to the earliest days of the Church, formed by one of Jesus' disciples and the early Church leader Thaddeus, or Saint Jude as he is often known. As the patron saint of lost causes, he was acutely aware of the forces already pressing in against the Church and the teachings of the faith, which he wrote about in a letter to Christians living in Asia Minor. The heart of his epistle included in the canon of the New Testament reflected this urgency: *"Contend for the faith that was once for all entrusted to God's holy people."* Not only for the faith itself but the shared, collective memory of the faith.

The Order Master had been trying to recruit Silas all year as a member and special-ops agent for one of their more kinetic endeavors, Project SEPIO. A decade ago, the Order realized it needed to make a more deliberate effort in contending for and preserving the memory of the faith. In the face of a number of threats from within and without, the Church was quickly coming to a precipice unless they took measures to deliberately protect the once-for-all faith and teaching tradition. SEPIO was launched to spearhead that movement, the full acronym being: *Sepio, Erudio, Pugno, Inviglio, Observo.*

Protect, Instruct, Fight For, Watch Over, Heed.

The meaning of the Latin word *sepio* itself captured the project's mission perfectly: "to surround with a hedge." In the case of the Order's project mission, surround the memory of the Christian faith with a hedge of protection. Not only the dogma and doctrine of the faith, but also the Church's objects and relics containing the memory of the faith, exploiting them to inform and nourish the spiritual journeys of God's children —and keeping them safe from Nous, the archenemy of the Christian faith and scourge of the Church. Early in the life of the Church, Nous tried to undermine the essence of the Christian faith by destroying her teachings. The Order had been following the organization for generations, keeping tabs on it and keeping it at bay to preserve and contend for the faith— and stop it from destroying the Church.

Silas was their newest recruit, but he wondered if he was making the biggest mistake of his life. He was certainly qualified for the job, given his military training and academic background. But he never would have chosen such a line of work. And he knew why: not enough glory in it. Pride had always been one of his fatal flaws, so maybe that's exactly what he needed, a way to serve the Church without expecting anything in return. No glory, no accolades, no name-in-lights. Perhaps it was true, the maxim that God works in mysterious ways. He just wished he would take some time off from meddling in his life. Maybe kick back with a Mojito on a nice sandy beach in Punta Cana.

The bright sun dimmed as he continued contemplating the next leg of his life-journey, as if a large storm cloud had passed in front of the golden orb of Caribbean glory. Or, rather, someone was standing near him blocking the sun.

Mojito number three!

Silas's mouth watered in anticipation as he opened his eyes. Then he frowned. "You're not Alejandro."

"Ali-who?"

Standing at the foot of his green lounger was a six-four man built like a tank, sporting black swim trunks, black shades, and a sweaty, shirtless gut with far too much black hair. Not the view Silas had flown four hours to enjoy.

"Gapinski..." Silas moaned, sitting up and grabbing his t-shirt from underneath his lounger.

"Aloha to you, too," the SEPIO operative muttered. Matt Gapinski, God love him, was the last person Silas wanted to see. Not that he didn't like the guy. But his arrival meant there was trouble on the home front.

"Radcliffe said he'd give me two weeks to transition to my new gig." Silas looked down at a faded fake gold-plated Seiko watch clinging to his left wrist, a high school graduation gift from Dad. "I've still got ten days, twelve hours, and forty-two minutes left."

Gapinski wiped his forehead with his meaty palm. "Sorry, pal. Something's come up." He put his hands on his hips, stuck out his chest a little, and then smiled and nodded toward something in the distance.

Silas followed his gaze and saw a pair of college-age women in matching floral bikinis lotioning up, the look on their faces telling Gapinski all he needed to know: not a snowball's chance in Punta Cana, pal. The poor guy's face fell, and so did his chest.

He chuckled to himself, then stood and put on his shirt. "Big enough that Radcliffe flew you all the way down here to fetch me? Nothing a phone call couldn't solve?"

"Bigger than big. And you should know the drill by now. No cell phones for this kind of news when the stakes are so high."

He smirked. "Oh, yeah? How high?"

"Four words: Vatican and the New York MET."

"That's six words. And what could the Order possibly be interested in at the Metropolitan Museum of Art?"

Gapinski furrowed his brow and counted on his fingers,

then shook his head. "I didn't think the 'and' and 'the' counted for that sort of thing. Anyway, I'm not sure. The chief said we'd get the skinny on the situation when you and me connect with Celeste at JFK International."

Silas raised his head at the mention of Celeste. A boyish grin couldn't help but form itself as he thought about rendezvousing with her. He looked down at his lounger, back to his bungalow several yards up the beach, and back at Gapinski, then sighed and nodded.

Gapinski extended his hand. "Welcome to your first day on the job with the Order of Thaddeus, partner."

Silas took it and smiled. "Alright, partner. Let's roll."

They went to leave when he heard a voice calling after him.

"Señor! I have brought your Mojito, and with mucho menta and rum."

He looked from Alejandro to Gapinski and back to Alejandro, face falling with disappointment. He handed him a fifty to pay for his drinks and tip, and said, "Have one on me, amigo."

The man brightened. "Gracias, señor!"

Don't mention it.

CHAPTER 3
NEW YORK CITY.

A taxi, a Gulfstream, and six hours later, Gapinski and Silas touched down at JFK International Airport. Much to Silas's irritation, the bleach-white powder sand of Punta Cana was replaced by the dirty white powder snow piled high across New York City and elsewhere up and down the eastern seaboard thanks to the snowpocalypse assaulting the East Coast in his absence.

Oh, how he hated snow with a passion that burned bright and strong. With all of its coldness and wetness and slippery annoyance. Maybe it was because of the years he spent in the DC area surrounded by crazy people who couldn't drive worth a lick at the first sign of flurries. Or the early-morning runs with his father to keep in shape during basketball season for the Falls Church Jaguars. It was probably more about the fact he was never any good at enjoying it like Sebastian. While his brother had picked up skiing and snowboarding with ease, Silas could never manage anything more than a bruised butt and a broken arm from never being able to keep upright. No matter how hard he tried to match his brother ski for ski, he never did catch on.

The height of embarrassment came when their father

brought them along to a leadership training summit at the Air Force Academy in Colorado Springs when they were in high school. While Dad lectured young cadets, the brothers spent a day on Copper Mountain. Only Silas made the mistake of taking Sebastian's bet that he would never make it down a double black diamond course. The ski lift brought them both up to the top; the ski patrol brought one back down after he nearly careened off the side of the mountain. Sebastian still ribbed him about it.

While Silas took it in stride, it was hard to shake the embarrassment. Like a millstone around his neck, it served as a reminder of his failure to keep up. It was always a competition with them, be it studies or sports or spirituality. The latter had caused not a small amount of tension between the two, mostly because of how Silas had handled his own newfound faith after he had come back to the Church during an on-base chapel service.

The brothers had grown up Catholic, their father making it a point to take them each and every Sunday to Mass. Sebastian had always been the more spiritually sensitive and interested one, helping out at the parish soup kitchen and even playing the part of altar boy while Silas goofed off during Father Rafferty's homilies, throwing spit wads at unsuspecting girls and grannies. But in their teenage years, there was a marked change in Sebastian. It became a fight to get him to come to Mass. He no longer wanted to serve in the Christian celebration. He even dropped the soup kitchen, leaving behind the friends he had made who had been his weekly inspiration for giving up his Saturday mornings.

Silas never understood or discovered the reason, didn't much care at the time. Not only because church didn't at all interest him. But more because he was too wrapped up in his own self to inquire, a theme that would continue to cause him trouble with his brother—and the rest of the world.

Gapinski and Silas stood in front of the door to the private aircraft as it eased open, a rush of frigid air slapping them in the face and making Silas irritated he wasn't still baking on a beach a million miles away. The only thing that made up for it was the tall brunette with long braided hair draped over her shoulder getting out of the awaiting black SUV in the Order's private hangar.

Celeste Bourne, director of operations for SEPIO, a former MI6 agent Radcliffe had recruited to spearhead the renewed effort to contend for the Christian faith's memory using more muscular means. Silas had fallen for her, then nearly lost her during one of their missions a few months back. Now things were unclear where they stood. He was never one to mix work with pleasure. But for Celeste, he had debated whether he could make an exception.

Wearing a long cream-color trench coat and black boots that meant business, she marched over to him and his new co-worker as they descended the stairs, her full lips parting for a grin.

She extended her hand to Silas. "Welcome aboard, mate." That perfectly polished British English got him every time.

He took it. "Thanks, however, I'm not sure I'm even on the payroll yet since I wasn't supposed to start for another ten days."

"I think we can work something out. Come on. We've got work to do."

The three climbed into the waiting SUV driven by Greer, another SEPIO operative he first met earlier in the year, and then they headed toward the MET. Traffic looked like it was heavy and slow. The old cliché about molasses through the Arctic pretty much hit the mark. He felt himself getting cranky as he thought about the R & R he was missing out on, not to mention those Mojitos that would go to waste. Whatever it was that happened at the MET better have been worth dragging his

sunbaked body back to the States—and during a snowpocalypse, no less.

"First of all," Silas said as their ride eased onto I-678 toward
Manhattan, "good to see you again, Greer."

"You, too. How's it hangin' brotha?" the African-American
man asked, voice low and deep. "I would give you an official
'Welcome aboard,' but you're practically family by now, given
all you've been through with our crew."

Silas chuckled. "I guess you're right. Alright, you three,
what's this about that you had to cut short my recuperation trip
and drag my Caribbean-loving butt to this Arctic hell?"

"Told you he was in a bad mood," Gapinski said.

"Sorry to break it to you, Mr. Cheeky," Celeste said, turning
around with a slight grin to face Silas, "but your life is all orders
now. Or have you forgotten what life was like back in the
service when you worked for Uncle Sam?"

"Yeah, we own you, pal," Gapinski agreed.

"I'm fine with orders. Just not the kind that takes me away
from my Mojitos in the dead of winter. And besides, what the
heck does the Order have any business investigating some
keystone caper at the MET, anyway?"

"Yeah, what is that about?"

"Right, so about that," Celeste said. "While I don't have any
specifics, this one is coming to us straight from the top."

"You mean the Vatican?" asked Silas.

She nodded.

"I thought they were no longer our employer, that the
Order went all ecumenical."

"I meant metaphorically from the top. The Commandant of
the Gendarmerie Corps himself, the head of the Directorate of
Security and Civil Protection Services for the Vatican, contacted
Radcliffe to appeal for our help in getting to the bottom of the
theft."

"Which we don't yet know anything about?"

She frowned and shook her head. "I understand this seems dodgy, but they and the NYPD are keeping this one close to the chest."

Silas folded his arms and shook his head. "I don't know. I'm smelling a boondoggle, here."

"Trust me. If the Vatican is ringing, it's 100 percent legit."

After another hour of excruciating stop-and-go traffic, the trio reached the scene of the crime—and quite the scene it was. The entire section of Fifth Avenue between 79th Street and 85th Street was blocked to traffic, which was pissing off not a small amount of city slickers trying to do their New York City thing. What's more: not only was Fifth Avenue flooded with NYPD cruisers, the feds were making a show of force, as well. Which definitely spelled big trouble. News organizations from around the globe were also trying to muscle their way onto the grounds of the famous museum, but the boys in blue were unrelenting, maintaining a tight perimeter around the building and surrounding blocks.

After exiting FDR Drive onto East 96th Street and wading through more nightmare traffic onto 85th Street, their SUV pulled up to a checkpoint where a bulky man wearing thick bullet-proof padding, a helmet with pulldown visor, and an M4 carbine rifle stepped forward with raised hand commanding them to halt.

Celeste quickly rolled down her passenger window as Greer pulled to a stop and flashed something at the man. The officer looked at her and nodded, then made a motion to someone up ahead to lower a metal barrier placed in the middle of the road.

"What was that?" Silas asked as Greer drove through.

She twisted around toward Silas. "Credentials," she said with a wink.

"Remind me never to leave home without you."

Greer pulled up to the curb just in front of a pedestrian

crosswalk square sitting in front of two abandoned food carts with red awnings.

"Mmm," Gapinski voiced as they climbed out the SUV. "New York chili dogs."

He bee-lined it for one of the carts as Silas slid out behind him and closed the door. The man opened the little service window and stuck his head into the shack, standing on his tiptoes as he inspected inside.

"Gapinski!" Celeste yelled.

He startled, bumping the back of his head on the window. "Ouch!" He withdrew his frame, rubbing the back of his head. "What? Can't a guy stock up before jumping headlong into no uncertain danger?"

She made a face and motioned toward the street. "Look around, mate. I'm pretty sure we're standing in one of the most secure spots in all of New York with all of this firepower."

"But...New York chili dogs! Look," he said pointing to the food cart. "It says they're the best hot dogs in New York. We can't pass that up."

"Sorry, mate. Here." She tossed him an unopened packet of mini pretzels she swiped from the Gulfstream galley cart.

Gapinski caught it with one hand. Opening his massive palm, he said, "Seriously? You expect me to live on pretzels alone?"

"Cheer up, Charlie," she replied. "I'll buy you a basket of chili dogs when we're through."

"You better!" he called after her as she and Silas began climbing the set of stairs leading to the baroque-style building flanked by Corinthian columns and banners advertising the latest exhibition.

The trio was greeted with a flurry of activity when they stepped inside the entrance. Heavily armed NYPD officers were standing guard throughout the vast space, keeping an eye on the remaining valuables. Several agents sporting dark jackets emblazoned with yellow 'FBI' lettering were huddled in groups, others were pacing the length of the hall. Other unidentifiable men and women in suits were similarly working the hall and the surrounding galleries. Gapinski wasn't joking. This really was big. And clearly Vatican big.

Silas put his hands on his hips and scanned the area. "Where do we start?"

"That chap looks like he might have a clue," Celeste said, pointing to a tall, trim man with a crown of silver hair and dressed in a long black clerical robe, accented by red trim.

"If that don't scream 'Vatican,'" Gapinski said, "I don't know what does."

Celeste led them to the man who was in conversation with another man dressed in a charcoal grey suit with white shirt and skinny black tie leaning against a check-in desk in front of a central set of stairs leading up to the mezzanine level. The man was much younger, with wrinkle-free, tan skin and sporting jet-black hair styled to perfection. He was the first to notice them, eyeing the tall brunette in black boots coming his way with purpose.

"Excuse me," she interrupted.

The man in the suit broke off conversation, and said, "Can I help you?" The man in the black robe turned toward her, too.

"I'm Celeste Bourne." She motioned toward her companions. "This is Silas Grey and Matt Gapinski. We were dispatched by the Order of Thaddeus with instructions from the Vatican to assist in an...investigation."

"Ahh, yes," the older gentleman said, his voice soft and fatherly with a distinct Italian accent. "Saint Thaddeus' cavalry has come to lend a helping hand."

Celeste laughed nervously. "Yes, well, I'm sure whatever services the Vatican believes we can provide will be entirely supplemental to the sturdy, steady hand of New York's and the FBI's finest."

"Grazie, Madame," the man said, bowing slightly. "I am Monsignor Giacomo D'Angelo, with the Pontifical Commission for the Cultural Heritage of the Church." Turning to the man wearing the suit, he said, "And this is Michael Kline, the lead agent handling the case for the museum with the FBI."

Agent Kline offered a smile and his hand, and said, "Pleasure to have you on board."

Celeste took it. "Happy to be of assistance, but the three of us are still in the dark as to why the Order was summoned in the first place."

"I will leave that to Agent Kline," D'Angelo said.

Kline extended his arm toward a narrow exhibit hall to his left flanked by cases holding ancient objects, Medieval and Byzantine art by the looks of the sign above the doorway. "Shall we?"

Celeste nodded and led the way, followed by Silas and Gapinski, then Kline and D'Angelo.

Three more FBI agents were huddled around one case in particular up ahead. Another was on his knees carefully brushing some sort of powder on the glass. It wasn't until they came closer that Silas could see a hole the size of a cantaloupe with jagged edges etched into the glass. Presumably, the crime scene's ground zero.

Kline introduced the three newcomers to the four other agents and asked for space to walk them through the events. They obliged and walked away.

The group moved closer to the case, the agent and the monsignor on either side of the trio. Celeste and Silas folded their arms, waiting for the story. Gapinski crouched low. Eyeing the glass, he whistled. "So what was in there, some saint's right knuckle or something? Must have been something good with all the feds lurking about." He turned to Kline. "No offense or anything."

The man smiled weakly but said nothing.

"So what was resting in the case, Agent Kline?" Celeste asked.

He took a breath. "The Antioch Chalice."

"Come again?"

The monsignor cleared his throat, and said, "The Sanctusque Calix."

"Sancti-whatchamacallit?" Gapinski said.

Silas dropped his arms—and his jaw. "The Holy Grail."

Gapinski stood shaking his head. "Always something."

CHAPTER 4

"You can't be serious," Celeste said, face twisting in disbelief. "The chalice purported to be the cup from which Jesus Christ drank at the Last Supper when he instituted the Eucharist, the one believed to have held his blood? Here, in this case?"

Agent Kline smiled sheepishly, then looked down and rubbed his neck. "That would be the one."

"Didn't we just replay one of Indiana Jones's plots a few months ago?" Gapinski said.

"And me without the fedora Radcliffe gifted me," Silas mumbled.

"Yeah. Wait." He turned toward Silas. "Radcliffe gave you a fedora?"

Silas shrugged. "Well, I ended up losing it in Luxor."

"Boys..." Celeste mumbled.

"Radcliffe never gave me any gift," Gapinski complained under his breath.

Celeste stepped toward the monsignor. "But I understand the Church has disavowed any claim to the Holy Grail, writing it off as a Medieval myth devised by French and English romance writers during the twelfth century."

"It has," D'Angelo said. "But the myth has endured through the ages, nonetheless, seemingly carried along by every wind of fanciful conspiracy theory. Certainly, it is a construct of the creative imagination, but many within Christianity have viewed it as an embodiment of the highest Christian ideal and experience: the Eucharist."

"Then for heaven's sake, why would anyone have reason to steal it—if it is merely a construct of the creative imagination, as you say, Monsignor?" Celeste asked. "And what is the Antioch Chalice, anyhow?"

Kline answered, "Apparently, a silver chalice discovered in Antioch at the beginning of the twentieth century by a one Gustavus Eisen. He dated it to the beginning of the Christian era, suggesting that the elaborate outer silver shell protected a more plainspoken inner cup. Which he identified with the Holy Grail. He claimed the elaborate footed shell enclosing the interior bowl was made within a century after the death of Christ to encase and honor the so-called Grail."

"But most well-respected relicologists have never sustained the identification of the chalice with the Holy Grail," Silas responded. "In fact, its authenticity has at times been challenged, instead being pegged as a sixth-century chalice for Eucharistic use. Ancient, yes. But not first-century ancient. And besides, its shape has been recognized as more closely resembling sixth-century standing lamps than a traditional dinner chalice. Perhaps in recognition of Christ's words 'I am the light of the world' from John's Gospel."

The monsignor turned toward Silas and nodded. "Impressive. You wouldn't happen to be the professor Silas Grey from Princeton, would you? The fellow whose groundbreaking work on the Holy Shroud of Turin authenticated the Church's central teaching on the resurrection of our Lord, that Grey?"

Silas felt his neck and cheeks grow warm with embarrassment from the spotlight, however pleased he was at the recognition. "Yes, well, former professor."

"I'm sorry," Celeste interjected, "but back to the task at hand. Are you suggesting some thieves of unknown origin stole themselves into the MET to swipe a goblet of questionable origin, all because it has been purported to be the cup that Christ bore at the Passover meal before his death, and then was later used to catch his spilt blood? Am I to understand that is the long and short of it?"

Kline tilted his head to the side. "Well, yes. Nicely put."

Silas snickered. "Are you kidding me?" The other four turned toward him. "We're to take this seriously, that someone infiltrated an art museum simply to swipe a silver dish—"

"Not just any dish, as you put it, professor," Monsignor D'Angelo interrupted, "one thought by some to be the Holy Grail."

"But as you yourself said, monsignor, the Church has always disavowed such nonsense. So why has the Vatican jumped at this latest episode of urban thievery?"

"Because, professor, another similar dish was absconded with the previous evening from a cathedral in Genoa."

That bit of revelation seemed to change the dynamics in the room. Gapinski grunted in surprise. Celeste brought her hand up to her chin in contemplation and folded her other arm across her stomach. Silas folded his arms, leaned back against a case opposite the crime scene, and looked at the floor shaking his head. It was all too fanciful to take seriously. Especially for SEPIO and the Order of Thaddeus to take seriously.

The group stood for several seconds, considering the revelation and taking in the duo events, that two chalices claiming to be the Holy Grail were stolen within twenty-four hours of each other.

"So how did it happen?" Gapinski asked, breaking the silence.

"Excuse me?" Kline replied, looking up from the floor.

He motioned toward the case with the hole in the glass. "All of this, the hole, the missing Sancti-whatchamacallit or Holy Grail or whatever. Can't believe it's easy to walk off with something like that in this sort of place."

The agent shook his head. "No, it normally isn't. But around the time of the theft, the city experienced an isolated blackout, in Central Park and along Fifth Avenue around the museum. Normally, a generator would have kicked in, but something went wrong. Anyway, witnesses described a helicopter coming in and hovering over the southwest quadrant of the building, a rooftop garden. From what we can gather, they made their way down inside the museum from the rooftop elevator, climbing down the shaft and entering in through the elevator ceiling trapdoor. Then they made their way to the gallery with the chalice, used a circulating diamond cutter, one of those hand-held devices, and swiped the thing. Two security guards eventually restored power. When they did, an alarm sounded, scaring off the intruders. Unfortunately, the guards didn't make it. The thieves took 'em right out after they stumbled upon them making their escape. The helicopter returned roughly an hour later, and then retreated."

Silas said, "Sounds like a major operation with major special-ops know-how and major backing if they can take out the power along several blocks in New York City and have access to a chopper."

"Absolutely. Obviously, we've dusted for prints and have been scouring every inch of the MET for evidence." Kline sighed heavily and shook his head. "But so far, we've got nothing. I've got agents searching through FBI databases trying to find some sort of connection with known terrorist networks and cells that would have interest in this sort of thing, high-level dealers in art or antiquity. But again, the same result. We can't find anyone or any organization that might have been able to pull something like this off, no one that has interest in something of this sort, some ancient tin can. It makes no sense."

Celeste asked, "Was anything else stolen?"

Kline shook his head. "Zip. Zero. Zilch. Only the silver chalice. They clearly knew what they were after. God only knows why."

Silas glanced at Celeste, catching her eye, wondering if she was thinking what he was thinking about who or what might be behind it, given the unique nature of the object.

"You said the power came back on, then scared the hostiles off. Is that right?" Gapinski asked.

"That's right."

"So that means the security cameras would have come back online when the power was restored. Correct?"

Kline nodded. "We've been through the footage, running facial recognition software on every cotton-picking frame. But we've got nothing. Absolute nada."

Gapinski looked to Celeste, then back to Kline. "Mind if we have a look?"

Kline shrugged. "Be my guest."

The agent brought the group to the main offices on the fifth floor of a newer section of the museum, then led them into the security office with banks of monitors showing the same kind of agents and heavily-armed officers the group had seen in the great hall. He instructed one of the agents to bring up the footage from the night. Within a few minutes, all of the monitors were showing the events around midnight and the hour beyond, glowing black and white before skipping ahead in time when the electricity rendered the cameras useless and then popped back on again when the power was restored.

Gapinski, Celeste, and Silas all stepped closer to the array of monitors once the documentary on the midnight raid started.

Three men were huddled around the same case they had

just been standing around. One of the hostiles was down on his knees before jolting upright, clearly startled by the sudden onset of lighting. Unfortunately, the angle of the cameras gave no good angle on his face or the others. Then the man in the middle clenched the chalice to his side and took off stage right. He continued through a series of monitors, his two companions following close behind, stopping momentarily before what looked like a statue of the Virgin Mary and Jesus before heading back toward their exit. Again, no good angle. Then the two guards appeared, one went down in a heap, the angle of one camera catching a glimpse of three pops to the chest without much reaction from the weapon itself. Then the second one went down, the three hostiles running on top and over them to make their escape.

As they flashed across a monitor, Silas wondered about their identities. Particularly if one of them were his brother, Sebastian. The revelation from a few months ago that he was somehow working with Nous still haunted him, and the thought of it made his gut clench with revulsion.

"Wait just a minute," Gapinski said suddenly, stepping closer to the monitor. "Right there, pause it." Kline obliged.

"What you got, big guy," Celeste asked stepping closer to the monitor herself.

He pointed to the black-and-white image of the man holding the chalice, mid-dash. "Can you give us some zoom love, my man?"

"You got it." Kline worked some controls and brought the image in closer.

"Now sharpen it a little...There!" He clapped his hands together, and exclaimed, "I knew it!"

"Knew what?" Silas asked coming up next to Celeste.

"Mr. Mustache," he growled.

"Who?"

"The little weasel who orchestrated the whole blasted theft

of the Passion relics a few months ago. Here he's got this weird Backstreet Boys hair thing going on that died with the '90s, but it's him. Definitely him."

"Farhad," Celeste said.

He nodded. "Farhad. Member of the Thirteen, the upper echelon of nefarious ne'er-do-wells we've affectionately come to know as—"

"Nous," Silas and Celeste said in unison.

"Exactly." He turned toward the monitor again and folded his arms.

"Wait a minute," Kline said holding up a hand. "You know who this is? Who did this? And what the hell is Nous?"

"But you're sure, are you?" Celeste said to Gapinski, ignoring the agent's questions and stepping in for a closer look. "The picture isn't exactly Kodak quality."

"I'd bet my bottom dollar it's the slimy sonofa—"

"Gapinski," she said cutting him off. She cocked her head. "It sure looks like the man, aside from the hair. But we mustn't speculate. We have to be sure it's him and Nous before forging headlong into a fox hunt."

Kline went to say something, but an agent suddenly came through the entrance and hustled up next to him, one of the four who had been huddled around the crime scene. He whispered something into his ear. The agent startled, furrowing his brow, then turned and walked toward the exit.

"What's going on?" Celeste asked.

"Something's happening," he said without going into detail, leaving the four behind as he and the other agent left.

CHAPTER 5

The three SEPIO operatives followed Agent Kline back into the great hall, the monsignor not far behind. A laptop had been placed on the check-in desk where Kline and D'Angelo had been in conversation earlier. Several agents were huddled around it. Kline pushed past them, face scrunched up with clear concern. The four pushed through next to Kline.

On the laptop was the image of a pale man from the chest up, face framed by shoulder-length greasy black wavy hair with piercing blue eyes, bulging and haunting, cheekbones high and angular, mouth plump and focused. He had aged well, looking as if he were still in his twenties, but crow's feet at the eyes and dark age spots dotting his fair skin betrayed his youthful look. He was sitting in a darkened chamber, on a stone chair flanked by similar ones on either side, though empty. Torches flickered behind him, illuminating the dark stone. It could have been anywhere. At the moment, he wasn't doing or saying anything. Just sitting, staring, waiting.

"This is playing all over the world?" Kline said to the agent who had alerted him.

"YouTube, Facebook, Snapchat. Somehow the man and his

org hijacked the internet. News agencies have picked it up and are broadcasting it now, too."

"And we can't shut it down?"

The agent shook his head. "We've tried. We're trying," he corrected himself. "But the redundancies on his brute force—"

"I don't need a damn technical discussion, agent. I need results! And who the hell is this guy, anyway?"

"We don't know. We're trying—"

"Shut up and go get me answers!"

The man took in a breath, nodded, then left. Agent Kline returned to the laptop, one hand on his hips and the other rubbing his forehead.

"Do you three know who the hell this is?"

Celeste looked to Silas and Gapinski. They shrugged. "Sorry. We haven't a clue. Never saw the man before."

"Just great..."

"Looks like we're about to find out," Silas said as the man on the internet shifted in his seat, then opened his mouth to begin speaking.

"Greetings," he said forcing a smile, his accent thick and Germanic-sounding but pleasant and inviting. He held up one hand to accompany his greeting, the underside of this arm bare and white except for an unmistakable set of markings. Two intersecting lines bent at either end, one set inward, the other in the same direction toward his hand.

Silas breathed in sharply at the sight, instantly recognizing the symbol. "Are you kidding me?"

"Crapola," Gapinski whispered in recognition.

"So it's true..." Celeste echoed.

Agent Kline pivoted right, brow wrinkled with confusion. "What's true? You know who this is? What's going on?"

"Nous," the three said again in unison.

"That name again!"

"Not a name, agent," Celeste said. "An organization. While

we don't know who this is, apparently he is their representative."

"And what the hell is—"

"He's speaking again," Silas interrupted.

"We are on the cusp of a new dawn," the mystery man intoned, "breaking through the unenlightened Dark Ages of religious superstition stretching from millennia past in order to empower the individual rational human to progress to feats not before imaginable."

The man paused, then smiled. "My name is Rudolf Borg, and I am here to take you there."

Silas's eyes widened. "No way..."

Celeste turned to him and whispered, "You recognize that name?"

"From this summer, when I was at that godforsaken compound north of Rome working on the Judas Gospel. That name had been thrown around. Seemed like a guy with power. Eli Denton had used it to get his way a few times. Used it to get me in the door and on the translating team." His gut twisted with regret at the thought of his old war buddy.

"Interesting..." she said turning back to the laptop.

Borg continued, "It is a known fact that the major religions of the world have one thing in common. War, violence. Jews killing Muslims and vice-versa. Hindus persecuting Muslims. And don't even get me started on the Christian Crusades and Inquisition!

"Then there is the continued ignorance of science and all the power and potential that it holds, and the bigotry at various expressions and presentations of the rainbow of the human race. While all of the religions are to blame for such folly, we blame one above all. The Church, with its history of geocentrism, that foolish insistence on the earth as the center of the universe; its denial of our collective origins, suppressing irrefutable proof of our development from nothing into something; its refusal to acknowledge the progress and evolutionary trajectory of the race toward greater heights of expression and enlightenment."

"Sounds like my Southern Baptist grandpappy up at the pulpit," Gapinski said.

"The man sure is preaching, that's for sure," Silas agreed.

Celeste added, "But toward what end? Stuff and nonsense, this is."

The pale-complected man on the screen continued his sermon. "And then there is the greatest sin of all, the one that Christianity has perpetuated from its start, with all of its nonsense about serpents and apples and short-tempered, self-absorbed gods. What is that sin you ask?"

Borg waited a few beats, head cocked, as if there were a true preacher-parishioner relationship that had formed through the internet. He leaned in closer, his dark locks falling forward. "The suppression of our self-consciousness, our self-determination. From the beginning, the Church has sought to suppress our highest human potential, obscuring and obliterating our god-consciousness in order to shackle us to guilt and shame for simply following the impulses that nature has forged within us, the ones that make us human in the first place. All of the passions of the flesh.

"And from the start, the Church got wrong its greatest asset in helping humanity rise and progress to its greatest potential, the humble peasant prophet. Jesus of Nazareth. Yes, they've got their Christ of faith, that dastardly creation of the Church nullifying and obscuring his true beauty and potential. But the Christ of history is far more fascinating, his blood far more powerful than a down payment on some heavenly flat in outer space!"

"What's he getting at?" Celeste asked in wonder, transfixed on the screen.

"The guy is definitely cuckoo for Cocoa Puffs," Gapinski grunted.

Silas answered, "Sounds like he's been drinking the Kool-Aid of too many dead German theologians. This whole Christ of history, Christ of faith bull is just rehashed liberalism from, like, fifty years ago."

"Then why take over the internet? What's he getting at?" she asked again.

Silas shook his head. Gapinski folded his arms. All three were transfixed on the laptop screen.

The man stopped, leaned back, and took a breath. He continued, "What we need is a new way forward. No," Borg said shifting in his seat and shaking his finger, "we need *someone* to show us a new way forward. To show us a better way of living and being human by rising above the ignorance and bigotry, to progress our race forward by revealing to us the universal ideal in a way that makes sense to our twenty-first-century human condition."

The man pushed back a lock of dark hair that had fallen across his face and smiled. "That day has arrived. Or, rather, it will arrive." He reached for something off-camera. When his arm returned, he was holding a surprising object.

A silver-looking chalice wrapped in an intricate pattern of vines with a ceramic inner bowel.

The room erupted in a murmur of protest.

"Bloody hell..." Celeste said.

"That's my Grail!" Agent Kline exclaimed.

Borg held it and smiled, seeming to marvel at the ancient relic. He said, "Then he took a cup, and after giving thanks he gave it to them, saying, 'Drink from it, all of you; for this is my blood of the covenant...'" The man trailed off, setting down the chalice, then looked back at the camera. He bowed his head slightly, the lights above accentuating the sharp angles of his face, his bulging eyes transfixed. A smile spread below them.

"In four days' time, the power of those words will be realized and unleashed for the full benefit of all humanity—commencing the dawn of the Republic of Heaven."

With those parting words, the feed cut to black, then to television color bars.

THE ROOM WAS QUIET. No one said a word for what seemed like several minutes.

Agent Kline leaned over to an agent and whispered something to the man. He nodded and hustled away. Then Kline turned toward the three SEPIO agents. He snapped his fingers and pointed to them, and said, "You three, with me. Now. You're welcome to join us as well, Monsignor."

D'Angelo nodded and joined the pack as it weaved its way through the crowd of dark suits back to the security office. When they all arrived, Kline shut the door with not a small amount of force. He turned to the trio of Order operatives, hands on his hips, jaw clenched.

"Alright, time for answers."

Celeste replied, "What would you like to know, agent?"

"Let's start with this Nous organization. What's its nature? What's its agenda? Where is the blasted thing?"

"The archenemy of the Church."

"Excuse me?"

She smiled and chuckled to herself at the skepticism lacing the man's voice, a typical response of people in a world primed by religious conspiracy thrillers. She explained, "For centuries, from the very beginning of the Church's existence, Nous has manifested itself in various ways but with the singular agenda of undermining and destroying the Christian faith."

Kline folded his arms and tilted his head. "How so?"

Silas stepped forward to take on the man. "Nous is a Neoplatonic concept of divine reason stretching back to Greek philosophy. The concept is considered to be the original divine principle, the eye of reason for comprehending the divine, leading to higher knowledge and salvation."

"Think the hippy New Agey mumbo-jumbo from the '70s," Gapinski offered.

A small grin splayed across the agent's face. He was clearly amused and not buying it.

"Or how about Star Wars, and the whole 'May the Force be with you' mantra."

Silas continued, "Gapinski's not far off the mark. The essence of its worldview is ancient Gnosticism, the root of the Church's earliest heresies, teaching that salvation was reserved for the select few who could reach spiritual enlightenment and progress and push the human race forward through self-salvation. The central kernel of their teaching begins with the assumption of the divinity of the individual, a God-consciousness and God-in-hiding that every person bears to greater or lesser degrees."

"Sounds like Oprah," Kline chuckled.

Silas considered this. "You're right, it is. Much of what passes these days from those Hollywood guru types mirrors Nous dogma. There is no sovereign deity, but lesser spirit-deities. Pantheistic to the core, Nousati believe the Divine invades all things, living and non-living. And they assume that pre-historical humans enjoyed uninhibited access to the kind of spiritual truth that would bring about a humanistic salvation. So there's the angle of returning to our more pagan spiritual roots that undergirds Nous's agenda."

"You a religious man, agent Kline?" Celeste asked.

He unfolded his arms and shifted his weight, then reached behind his head and rubbed his neck. "Ah, not really. Grew up Lutheran, but it didn't much catch."

"No worries. I only ask, because there's a story in the first book of the Bible, Genesis chapter three."

"The one about Adam and Eve and that serpent?"

She grinned knowingly. "I thought you said it didn't catch?"

"Not much did. But growing up I was petrified of snakes. Still am. That story caught for sure."

"So you know the serpent tempted Eve to eat the fruit, claiming she would be like God, knowing good and evil."

Kline nodded his remembrance.

"You could say the kernels of early *gnostikos* were forming in the Garden of Eden. For the promise of their pseudo-spirituality is what the German philosopher Friedrich Nietzsche himself offered, the Übermensch."

"Uber-what?" the agent said shaking his head, his face twisting in confusion.

"The Overman or Beyond Man, as it's translated," Silas added. "Their whole dogma empowers the individual to become like God—not only knowing good and evil but deciding it and transcending it. Transcending this world and armed with the knowledge to determine good and evil, is the essential aim of the Nousati, to hammer and hone reality into the *imago homo*, as it were."

"The Image of Man," Kline added. "As opposed to the *Imago Dei*, the Image of God, is that what you're saying?"

Silas smiled and nodded. "I'd say more stuck than you give yourself credit for."

"Thanks, professor. But what the hell does any of this have to do with that blasted stolen chalice and the sermon that hijacked the internet?"

The three fell silent, considering the question. Celeste spoke first. "Nous is the organizational embodiment of this ancient worldview—an organization that's laid hidden in the shadows of history, until now. There is a militancy about Nous that has always threatened the Church and the faith. However, in recent months it has resurfaced with a vengeance. Early in the life of the Church, Nous tried to undermine the essence of the Christian faith by destroying her teachings. Its power and influence has waxed and waned over the centuries and manifested in various ways. And the Order of Thaddeus has been following its movements for generations, keeping tabs on it and keeping it at bay to preserve and contend for the faith. But this year there has been a marked increase in activity."

The agent folded his arms back into place, leaned against a wall, and furrowed his brow, seeming to consider this revelation "How so?"

Silas said, "Earlier this year, they made a play for taking out the Shroud of Turin."

Kline unfolded his arms again and pushed off the wall. "The burial cloth of Jesus Christ?"

"That'd be the one. And then they tried undermining the story of Jesus with a false gospel and then hunting down and revealing the fabled Ark of the Covenant."

"I heard something about that on the news. That was Nous?"

Silas nodded. Celeste added, "And that means if Nous is involved in the Antioch Chalice absconsion, and apparently another in Genoa, as you pointed out, monsignor, then there is something bigger going on here than simply a missing silver goblet. Which means we've got work to do, agent."

"I agree," Kline said, turning toward the door.

"And by *we*, I mean the Order."

He whipped back toward the trio, face twisted with irritation. "Whoa, whoa, whoa. What do you mean, *you've* got work to do?"

"The Order has a vested interest in seeing that Nous and whatever plans for which it is laying the groundwork do not in any way threaten the historic Christian faith. That chalice and that speech is evidence of a clear and present danger."

"And the FBI has a vested interest in retrieving that stolen chalice that turned up in that blasted internet speech!"

"And have at it, agent," she said smiling, her face remaining set as flint. "I sympathize, I really do. When I was with MI6, I probably would have responded in a similar manner. But my loyalties lay elsewhere. And we have our own work to do in light of the propaganda piece just broadcast around the world."

Kline stepped forward, his face hardening. "The FBI is handling this investigation. You were only brought in as a courtesy for the monsignor. He said you might be able to offer some information."

"And we did. Loads."

"She's right, pal," Gapinski added. "We did give you Nous."

The man glared at him, then growled, "This is our case. Don't get in the way."

"Not to worry, agent," Celeste responded. "We'll be sure to share with the feds anything relevant we may stumble across in the course of our investigation."

The duel finally seemed to end in a draw, stalemating between two hardened directors of operation. Kline finally offered a weak smile, thanked Celeste and the other two SEPIO agents for their help, then left the room.

"That was awesome," Gapinski said slapping Celeste on the back.

"Now what?" Silas asked.

"Now, we return to headquarters and plot our next course."

Silas sighed. "My first day on the job and it's a mission to hunt down the Holy Grail. What have I gotten myself into?"

Gapinski added, "Let's just hope we're not asked the airspeed velocity of an unladen swallow."

DAY II

DECEMBER 18

CHAPTER 6
WASHINGTON, DC.

There she is. My new 'home sweet home.'

As the Gulfstream came out of the low-hanging clouds for its final descent and began hugging the Potomac River for its final landing, Silas caught sight of the familiar pale Indiana limestone spires of the Washington National Cathedral reaching up through the onslaught of snow toward the heavens, the headquarters of the Order of Thaddeus and Project SEPIO, the new place of his employ. They continued following the snaking river below, and he could see Georgetown University, its red-brick Dahlgren Chapel peeking through naked twig-like trees, a reminder of how his whole complicated relationship with the Order began in the first place.

Then they passed George Washington University. Silas wondered whether Sebastian was tiring himself on his latest conference presentation or journal article, perfectly polished in his suede shoes, flat-front pants, and trademark bow tie. Or, was he snuggled up with mulled wine in his renovated row house in Adam's Morgan, fire crackling away in his fireplace and Dizzy Gillespie spinning on his turntable? He smiled at the thought of the latter, the love for jazz about the only thing the two had in common anymore.

The two had been well-schooled in the finer art of high-fidelity and high-quality music by their father, who boasted three record players, their amplifiers and pre-amps all vacuum-tube powered, and a collection of two thousand records, ranging from the original jazz and blues heavyweights to orchestral and symphonic to the rockabilly and rock-and-roll superstars of the mid-twentieth century. When he passed, surprisingly Silas and Sebastian maintained the peace of what could have been a contentious contest of wills as they divided his collection and equipment. Since then, their individual growing collections were another source of competition, each trying to one-up the other with original finds and discovering obscure artists.

The thought of his brother made him sad as they continued gliding past the city toward Regan National Airport in Alexandria, Virginia. Oh how he often wanted to wring the man's neck with that bow tie of his, given how oppositional and combative and pig-headed he could be about, well, everything. Lately, he just wanted to give him a hug, tell Sebastian how sorry he was for how he had treated him—how oppositional and combative and pig-headed he himself had been, especially with issues of faith. As they came in for a landing, Silas wanted nothing more than to get an Uber and drive over and pound on his door to reconcile. The alienation from years of their relationship fraying and the recent betrayals were strumming an angry tune that was eating at him. Maybe someday.

They hit the landing strip hard, bounced, then seemed to slide for a few seconds as the bird tried gaining purchase to bring itself to a halt. When it did, Silas sighed heavily, then realized he had been gripping the armrest as if his life depended on it. He took a breath, let go, then flexed his fingers stiff with fright. He thanked the good Lord for bringing them in safely. And he added a separate request: that he would somehow move heaven and earth to repair the breach in his relationship with Sebastian. He knew it was a big ask. But if the good Lord could turn water into wine, then he could surely turn a bitter relationship into a better one.

Blizzard Brutus, as the Weather Channel had named it, was as brutal as its name sounded. Snow sat piled high like snow cone balls at the outer edges of the airport's runways. Yellow Caterpillar snowplows with mouths wide and dutiful were trying their best to keep up with the continued snowfall but falling behind as the Order-issued Gulfstream taxied into a covered hangar. It was a miracle the airport was still opened, considering the relentless pounding DC was still experiencing.

A black Escalade was waiting for them, running and warm. Greer took command of the driver's seat, and soon they were zooming through deadened DC streets covered in packed snow and more piled to the sides. Soon the Cathedral was visible, sending a jolt of excitement and anticipation through Silas. Soon they would be huddled in Rowan Radcliffe's study deep beneath the sacred building plotting their next moves. He wouldn't have chosen the myth of the Holy Grail as his first mission, but he sure was thrilled to get back into the saddle of researching and figuring out a good relic mystery.

After the SEPIO operatives had finished with Agent Kline, Celeste had contacted Radcliffe with details of the theft as they made their way to JFK International to head back to Washington. However, Brutus grounded them for the evening and into the night. They had to wait until the next day to launch their expedition full-bore.

It was clear why the Vatican was so interested in the case: the purported Holy Grail was stolen, putting into play the mythic legend of the chalice that held Christ's blood. Radcliffe had scoffed at the notion. But given he and other SEPIO operatives back at the command center had seen the same internet live stream event the three operatives in New York had, Radcliffe couldn't easily dismiss the event. All hands were on deck after the charade, especially after the Nous tattoo reveal. But facts were pretty thin in terms of the who, where, and why, and SEPIO needed to get to work—and pronto.

Celeste was able to confirm the Farhad find from the surveillance footage, which both intrigued Radcliffe but also ratcheted up his concern for what Nous was planning. He was emphatic: if a member of the Thirteen was involved, the stakes for the Church were indeed grave. And given Borg's public propaganda piece, it was clear Nous was entering into a whole new level of engagement at trying to destroy the Christian faith. He was eager for SEPIO to hit the ground and stop "whatever in the bloody hell Nous is planning," as he put it.

As they trundled up Wisconsin Avenue through the snow-packed street, Greer took a side street that brought them through a tree-lined neighborhood of red-brick and white-paneled houses stretching back to the nineteenth century. Then he took a sharp right that brought them into a drive entrance near the base of the north transept, the sacred structure looming large through ribbons of fluffy snowflakes. The van disappeared through the black maw of a parking entrance and took a dip, moving swiftly underneath the national Christian architectural icon.

The edge of the narrow drivable passage was lined with LED lighting, showing the way downward and forward under the massive building. Old stonework shone in the faint light, before curving into a spiral that revealed newer masonry. Now they were turning ever downward, seemingly forever beneath the stately structure. The light noticeably brightened into a dim white, shining through a large carpark of gray cement. Several cars, all black, were docked in parking spots, as well as a few more vans matching their own military-grade one. It was just as Silas remembered it the first time he was ushered inside during the dead of night. He was glad it was on happier terms, but he feared the stakes were just as high as the first time around.

The four got out of their vehicle, their breaths steaming against the frigid air. Silas shivered in his long sleeve t-shirt and light jacket as they walked toward the entrance into the Order's headquarters beneath the stately sacred building, his winter clothes still tucked away in Princeton. Glass doors up ahead whooshed open. A tall, portly man with grey, thinning hair wearing a black cassock, neck ringed by a white clerical collar, stepped out into the underground garage. He wore a tired, if not determined look, as if the future of the world rested on his shoulders. His long black cassock swished as he hustled to meet the arriving party, the carport light glinting off golden buttons. Rowan Radcliffe. Silas smiled. It sure was good to see the man.

"Thank God you made it safe and sound," the man said in the same English-accented voice as Celeste's. "I've been fasting all morning, praying Regan would remain open and you all would arrive unscathed. Appears my self-denial worked." He embraced Celeste loosely, gently kissing her left cheek. She received it and kissed him back.

He turned toward Silas, grinning and opening his arms. "My boy, Doctor Grey," he said as they embraced. "Terribly sorry for cutting short your holiday, especially given the snow-pocalypse outside, as the kids are calling it these days. And sorry this business with the Grail is to be your first official assignment with the Order. But, as those same kids say, 'Go big or go home,' right?"

Silas chuckled. "Better that than sink or swim."

"We shall see," Radcliffe grinned knowingly, then winked. He patted him on the back and walked toward the glass entrance, and said, "Let's get to it, shall we?"

The four followed him as the glass doors gently swooshed open, the scent of sanitized air flooding Silas's senses. The slate-gray hallway was washed in the same dim white light as the garage, and quiet. Which made sense given the blizzard. As they came to a T-juncture, Greer left them, needing to follow up on the intel gathering process. The others followed Radcliffe to the right. The hall was lined with windowless, nondescript doors, each armed with a keycard entry pad. It was as secure as any of the military installations Silas had worked in through his military career before joining Princeton. And below one of the most important religious buildings in America.

They arrived at a set of double doors at the end of yet another hallway. After Radcliffe placed his hand on an entry pad, it pulsed a light blue hue before turning a solid green. The doors opened, revealing a vast room clad in dark cherry wood. It was lined floor to ceiling with bookcases. At one end was a large fireplace, the kind a person could walk into if they desired. A fire was crackling away, much to Silas's relief given the chill that still ran through his bones. At the other end was a large wooden desk, ornately designed with pillar legs and wooden sides. Behind it was a series of monitors, all dark and hiding their purpose. The center of the room was commanded by a large Persian-style rug with two burgundy leather couches, complemented by well-worn over-stuffed burgundy leather chairs. Rowan motioned for them to sit.

"I've got hot cocoa at the ready," the man said as he walked over to an alcove in-between two bookcases. "Anyone care to imbibe?"

The three gave a unified "Yes!"

He chuckled. "Thought so." After making preparations, he shuffled over holding a silver tray with three mugs and a pot of hot milk. Silas took a mug, as did the others. Inside was a mix of brown powder and white crystals, the distinct sweet-and-earthy scent of cocoa making him dizzy with delight.

"What, no whipped cream?" Gapinski complained.

"Beggars can't be choosers, Matthew," Radcliffe retorted. "And besides, a little less cream would probably do the body good, wouldn't you say?"

Gapinski frowned and looked at his bulging stomach. "Padre, how many times have I told you? I'm big boned, alright."

The old man raised an eyebrow. "If you say so," he mumbled as he settled into one of the overstuffed chairs.

"Right, let's get down to business." Gapinski was sprawled on the couch to his left, downing his hot cocoa. Celeste to his right in the other couch poured hot milk into her mug. She handed the pot to Silas. After pouring in the steaming white liquid, he stirred it to a familiar muddy brown of childhoods past, then took a sip.

Heaven.

"I have the same question I had back in New York City," Silas said from the chair across from Radcliffe.

"And what is that?"

He finished taking another sip of the hot drink then smacked his lips at the cocoa nectar. "The Church has always disavowed the nonsense of the Holy Grail. So why has the Vatican jumped at this chalice theft? And why is the Order and SEPIO giving it a shred of credibility by investigating it?"

"You saw the man yourself, Silas," Celeste said. "He was clearly sporting the Nous symbol on his forearm. That detail and Farhad's identification makes it clear Nous is involved with this theft. And it's no coincidence the next afternoon their purported representative or leader or whomever launched a propagandistic tirade against the Church. Whenever and wherever Nous is up to no good, SEPIO will be right there to answer, blow for blow."

"Can't argue with that," Silas said. "But the idea that we come answering some quest for the Holy Grail...I'm sorry it's just so preposterous, given that no one in the Church has ever offered any sort of proof for such a relic."

Radcliffe cleared his throat and crossed his legs, pitching his fingers together like a tent. Then he revealed, "That's not entirely true..."

CHAPTER 7
WEWELSBURG, GERMANY.

The chill of the stone sank deep into Rudolf Borg's feet with each pad up the stairs through the ancient castle of dark stone. He pulled his wool robe tighter against his body, but he relished the sensation against his bare feet as he made his way back to his study. He needed his wits about him. The next few days demanded it. The frigid, drafty stairwell would keep his senses taut for the battle that lay ahead.

He paused at a window embedded in the castle turret, glimpsing through the frosted panes the spire of his childhood church reaching toward the heavens. His stomach still turned at the thought of the memories bound up with that building, the sermons from that preacher and the physical revulsion he felt from peering up at that dreadful cross hanging behind the pulpit.

Tendrils of smoke joined its upward reach from countless village homes seeking relief from the winter wonderland outside. One of those was probably from his childhood home, the one where he first began to experience the compulsions and the possessions. The one he was forced to leave after the incident with the exorcist, and his parents could no longer stomach him.

He spotted something else, too, a massive evergreen commanding the center of the quaint German town crowned with a golden star, carrying on the Christmas tradition that first began with his homeland five hundred years ago. Borg recoiled from the window at the sight, the religious symbol serving as a sign of remembrance for the death of the so-called King of the Jews. What those poor, pathetic peasants forget, and their people had long forgotten, was the pagan roots to the symbol. No thanks to those scheisse Protestant Reformers who first used it as such! Thanks to them, it had been transformed from the celebration of all that the earth has to offer and the impending dawn of new life from spring into the birthday of a god-man offering the promise of celestial abode from some Bearded Being in outer space!

No matter. Soon that King would be co-opted for a different kind of kingdom. A republic. The Republic of Heaven!

Borg continued his journey upward, relishing the sensation that was sent from the cold stone through the bottoms of his bare feet up through his legs with every step. He also smiled at the concept he had been developing recently. It was a perfect, fitting label for what Nous was working toward.

What happens to the Kingdom of Heaven when the King is dead, murdered at the hands of sensible adults? What else but the complete transformation of the Kingdom into a Republic, governed not by the whims of a self-centered, self-indulgent, needy Bearded Being in the sky, but by the enlightened ones grabbing reality by the horns and transcending it to greater heights of purpose.

He relished in his genius as he reached his study. He opened the door and was hit by a wall of warmth thanks to a fire barely crackling in the hearth but its warmth still humming within the walls of stone and walnut. He padded across the warm stone and onto a bear rug commanding the center of the room. The space was a welcomed relief from the chill. He ambled over to a bookshelf anchored next to the fireplace and pulled down a weathered volume. *The Gay Science*, from the prophet of his people who died far too soon, a voice crying in the wilderness before his time making straight the paths of Gnostic enlightenment. Friedrich Nietzsche.

He caressed the soft, evergreen cloth cover, a companion from his adolescence. He opened it, its stiff creamy pages emitting the heavenly scent of musky paper and ink and age. He thumbed through the book, finding what he was searching for. The Parable of the Madman.

A smile crept across his face as he remembered the first time he had encountered the prophetic words that gave sight to his blind eyes. The local library had a copy, which he promptly swiped after discovering the diamond amongst the trash heap of town literature and hid it under his bed. It would prove to be the spark of enlightenment that set the rest of his life's course.

He started reading the parable, mouthing the words as a reminder of what he was undertaking:

Have you not heard of that madman who lit a lantern in the bright morning hours, ran to the marketplace, and cried incessantly: "I seek God! I seek God!"—As many of those who did not believe in God were standing around just then, he provoked much laughter. Has he got lost? asked one. Did he lose his way like a child? asked another. Or is he hiding? Is he afraid of us? Has he gone on a voyage? emigrated?—Thus they yelled and laughed

The madman jumped into their midst and pierced them with his eyes. "Whither is God?" he cried; "I will tell you. We have killed him—you and I. All of us are his murderers."

Damn right we have, he thought as he continued reading. Oh, that Bearded Being upstairs still popped up on Earth here and there with every suicide bomb and on those crazy religious cable television shows. But through science and brute force, humanity has finally begun to transcend its baser religious selves, rising to become like the gods—not merely knowing good and evil, but *deciding* what is good and what is evil.

He continued reading, coming to the line in the prophetic utterance that got him every time. "God is dead. God remains dead. And we have killed him."

A corner at one end of his mouth curled upward. He read it again: *God is dead. God remains dead. And we have killed him.* Then again.

And we have killed him.

But then he frowned. *Not quite, Prophet Nietzsche. Not quite.*

The Church had remained surprisingly resilient through the onslaught of modernity and the rise of post-modernity, that human feature of the twenty-first century age that has torn down all of the authorities and placed the individual rational human at the center of it all.

All in due time...

He was especially encouraged by Nous's most recent scheme. He checked his watch. The man with the bow tie should have been there by now. He huffed, then kept reading.

"How shall we comfort ourselves, the murderers of all murderers?" Borg mumbled. And then he grinned, reading the prophet's response: "Must we ourselves not become gods simply to appear worthy of it? There has never been a greater deed; and whoever is born after us—for the sake of this deed he will belong to a higher history than all history hitherto."

Amen and amen!

Borg drew his finger to the book, tracing the parable's final two paragraphs:

Here the madman fell silent and looked again at his listeners; and they, too, were silent and stared at him in astonishment. At last he threw his lantern on the ground, and it broke into pieces and went out. "I have come too early," he said then; "my time is not yet. This tremendous event is still on its way, still wandering; it has not yet reached the ears of men. Lightning and thunder require time; the light of the stars requires time; deeds, though done, still require time to be seen and heard. This deed is still more distant from them than most distant stars---and yet they have done it themselves.

It has been related further that on the same day the madman forced his way into several churches and there struck up his requiem *aeternam deo*. Led out and called to account, he is said always to have replied nothing but: "What after all are these churches now if they are not the tombs and sepulchers of God?"

Yes, Prophet Nietzsche. You were right: you were early. The world was not yet ready. The world was not worthy of your revelations.

Until now.

He closed the book and slid it back into its space on the shelf.

"The King is dead," he said loudly as he sauntered over to a well-worn leather chair in front of a large walnut desk. "*We have killed him—you and I. All of us are his murderers.*' Long live the Republic!"

The Republic of Heaven.

The metaphor had come to him in recent months through one of his blood-letting sessions, the dizzying effect of the ritual sending his mind into an ecstatic state that envisioned a world devoid of any reference to any deity—especially the Christian one. He wondered what it would be like to live as if the King of the Jews really had been dethroned and deposed of. That the King of the Kingdom had been killed, as the Prophet had suggested. That's when the notion of a republic hit him—a metaphor for the state of existence in our this-life reality when the collective humanity transcends their brutish nature and baser selves, while approaching the universe with curiosity and wonder and transcending the current human condition through enlightened reason.

They were so close he could taste it. Just a bit more time and he would have all he needed to take his own place amongst the great prophets of the ages, extending the great work of Prophet Nietzsche to become an embodiment of another Prophet, a so-called Messiah, even—

A knock interrupted him.

"Enter," he grunted. Someone did, the man with the bow tie. Borg was fond of him, not only for his resourcefulness and what he had been able to accomplish for Nous, but also for what he symbolized for his enemy.

He smiled and motioned for the man to sit in an empty chair near the fire in front of his desk. The man entered bearing a black case.

Borg's eyes widened with greed, his smile growing wider with anticipation. "Are these the other two?"

"That they are." The man set the case on the top of Borg's desk, handle facing him and ready to open.

Borg stood, his mouth gaping with glee. He flipped the two latches up on either side of the handle and opened the case. Inside were two chalices: the first, the *sacro catino,* a shallow green hexagonal dish known as the 'emerald' vessel of Genoa; the other, the *sacro caliz,* a small agate bowl from the Valencia Cathedral. The second and third chalices believed to be the Holy Grail.

His breath caught in his chest as he gently caressed them with both hands, sending a jolt of excitement coursing from his arms and through his body. A drunken giggle escaped, and a sudden sanguine urge began to bubble up within his belly to open up his veins and drain his own life-force into one of the precious vessels, mixing his own blood with that of the supposed Savior. But which one was anyone's guess. Which was why he was set on acquiring all of the so-called Holy Grail relics.

He licked his lips and swallowed, the anticipation triggering his salivary glands, filling his mouth with lust for the others that remained. His forefathers had borne the same unholy urge, seeking out the locations of the sacred vessel from legends past. He wanted nothing more than to fulfill the longings of what his great uncle had been unable to accomplish, but seemed so close to acquiring for the good of his *völk*, his people, his nation.

But where his concerns were far too narrow, given the crowd he surrounded himself with, Borg wanted nothing more than to leverage his discoveries for a worldwide revolution in support of his emerging vision of a Republic of Heaven, infused with the blood of power that had captivated so many for so long.

The clearing of a throat snapped Borg back into the moment. He realized he was staring at the vessels, hands cupped around them like a woman's bosom, mouth still agape. He clenched his jaw and slowly withdrew his hands, their power still tickling his belly. He slumped back into his chair and crossed his legs. Then he pushed his hair behind both ears and propped both elbows on his desk, interlocking his fingers and saying, "How are we progressing with the rest of our plan?"

"Swimmingly!" the man with the bow tie said.

"Good. Is everything in place for the next phase? Which I understand you are to lead, is that right?"

"Yes, that is true. Farhad thought it best. I'm leaving for the next chalice shortly."

"And what of the final Grail? I understand you've had some trouble determining its location. My great uncle had similar problems, and I will not be resigned to a similar fate."

The man with the bow tie shook his head. "Not to worry, Master Borg. I will not fail."

Borg grunted. "You better not." Then he placed both palms on his desk and leaned forward, his greasy black hair falling to the sides of his face as he transfixed the man with his bulging eyes. "We cannot afford a single problem to arise. For soon, a new dawn will emerge with the birth of a new prophet for our age. One who will empower the individual rational human to fully live up to the universal human ideal."

The man's eyes widened slightly, then he licked his lips and nodded. He got up from his chair, bowed slightly, then left.

Borg turned his gaze back to the emerald and agate vessels still nestled in the black foam insulation in the black case, one end of his mouth curling upward with satisfaction, with desire.

Three down, two to go.

CHAPTER 8

WASHINGTON, DC.

S
ilas was thrown by Radcliffe's comment. *Not entirely true? What the heck does that mean?*

His brow wrinkled with confusion, he sat straighter and asked, "What do you mean by that? I've never heard of a Grail tradition within the Church."

"Oh, but there is," Radcliffe said.

"There is?" Gapinski said sitting up himself. "So Monty Python really was on to something?"

Radcliffe turned toward him, then shook his head and cleared his throat. "As I was saying, there were three major relics from the Medieval era which claimed to be the chalice used by Christ at the Last Supper. The earliest one of these relics was recorded by a pilgrim who traveled from the British Isles to the Holy Land during the seventh century, a fellow by the name of Arculf."

He hoisted himself up out of his chair, grumbling about his old, aching bones. Then he shuffled over to one of the large bookcases that commanded the right side of the massive fireplace. He spent a minute searching its shelves, running his index finger along the spines of the vintage hardbacks and newer paperbacks that had informed the man's faith and served as intel for SEPIO's missions.

"There you are, you little rascal!" Radcliffe said from the other side of the room. He snatched an aging volume with fraying edges then shuffled back to his chair and settled back into it.

"Listen to this account our pilgrim Arculf gave of his adventures, a most enlightening account." He read from the book:

Between the basilica of Golgotha and the *Martyrium*, there is a chapel in which is the chalice of the Lord, which he himself blessed with his own hand and gave to the apostles when reclining with them at supper the day before he suffered. The chalice is silver, has the measure of a Gaulish pint, and has two handles fashioned on either side...After the resurrection the Lord drank from this same chalice, according to the supping with the apostles. The holy Arculf saw it, and through an opening of the perforated lid of the reliquary where it reposes, he touched it with his own hand which he had kissed. All the people of the city flock to it with great veneration. Arculf saw the soldier's lance as well, with which he pierced the side of the Lord when he was hanging on the cross. This lance is in the porch of the basilica of Constantine...

"And then it goes on." He closed the book and tossed it on a walnut coffee table in the center of the meeting area.

Gapinski grunted. "How do you like that? Good ol' George Lucas wasn't that far off the mark. Except his chalice was a simple stone cup, if I remember my fav childhood '80s flick right."

Silas added, "And the one stolen from the MET, while silver, didn't have two handles. And Arculf didn't call it a Grail in the way we think of now."

"True," Radcliffe admitted. "But the origin of the term certainly matches the description of the relic as a chalice. Besides, what's important is that this account shows there was at least a Grail tradition related to the chalice Christ bore at the Last Supper stretching back to the earliest centuries of the Church. Albeit from one bloke who claims to have seen it for himself being venerated as such in Palestine."

"And in a chapel next to Golgotha, no less," Celeste added.

He nodded. "Indeed."

Silas considered this. He couldn't argue with that.

Celeste shifted in her chair, and asked, "But why, then, is there no tradition in the Church itself? Not like the True Cross or Holy Shroud, for instance? Is there any mention of this silver chalice before or afterward?"

Radcliffe shook his head. "No, nothing is heard about the vessel after the seventh century. However, there is a reference to a Grail at Byzantium that was apparently looted from a church in the city during the Fourth Crusade early in the thirteenth century and then brought to Southern France."

"Is that the only other reference?"

"Well, there are other vessels with claims to being the Holy Grail. However, the certainty and veracity of their providences are not at all clear."

Silas said, "Such as the Antioch Chalice from the MET and the other one from Genoa, the one the monsignor mentioned also being stolen?"

"Yes, as well as—"

A buzz sounded from a phone on an end table next to Radcliffe, indicating an incoming call. "Hold that thought," he said as he put the call on speaker. "Yes?"

"Rowan, it's Zoe."

Silas smiled at the sound of the Order's resident techie sporting those cool baby-blue thick-rimmed glasses he liked. She had helped save not more than a few missions with her tech wizardry. She was a genius when it came to research, finding and making connections that had been crucial to their success foiling Nous plots.

"Yes, my dear. What is it? We're in the middle of it here."

"And what you're in the middle of has gotten a little more complicated."

Radcliffe sat forward, leaning closer toward the phone. So did Silas and Celeste.

"This doesn't involve the Knights Who Say Ni, does it?" Gapinski groaned.

Silas smirked and playfully slugged the guy in the arm for yet another Monty Python reference. Celeste threw him a look and shushed him.

Radcliffe was either ignoring or didn't hear him. He said, "Complicated? What do you mean complicated?"

"Another chalice was just reported stolen by the Vatican."

"What?"

"Where, Zoe?" Celeste asked.

"Valencia."

"Spain?" Gapinski said sitting up.

"Yes."

"Bullocks," Radcliffe cursed. "Any details on the theft?"

"Just that it was another night job, like the MET. I asked for server access to the Valencia Cathedral to, you know, comb through their surveillance. But..."

"It's a historic cathedral without need of such modern trappings?"

"Bingo."

"So no footage of the theft," Celeste said, sighing and sinking back into her chair.

"Unfortunately, no."

"Not like we need it anyway," Silas said. "With what we've been able to discover, the odds of this being another group or individual not connected to Nous is pretty much nil."

Radcliffe turned to Silas and nodded. "Thank you, Zoe. Keep us informed with any further developments." He disconnected the line and sank back into his chair.

Silas said, "Three chalices purporting to be the Holy Grail, all stolen in the span of a few days..." He settled back into his chair, as well. "And less than four days to get to the bottom of it all."

"I've got a bad feeling about this," Gapinski said.

They sat silently, the fire popping and sizzling in the background as they contemplated the turn of events and the continued mystery surrounding the mythical Grail. And what, if anything, it meant for the Church and Christian faith.

"Four days," Radcliffe finally said. "What's that you say?"

Silas looked up from concentrating. "Just, we've got four days to figure out what the heck Nous is up to."

"Why?"

"That's right," Celeste said. "Before he ended the feed, Borg mentioned something about the full power of the chalice being understood in four days' time. I presume that's when he and Nous will broadcast their exploits for all the world to see."

"Which doesn't give us much time to figure this out," Silas added.

Gapinski settled back into the couch, legs outstretched. "But why four days? Why not ten or three? Why not tomorrow? Why wait?"

Silas cocked his head, looking off as he calculated the timing. "Four days puts the deadline at, what, December 21?"

"December 21..." Radcliffe echoed, mumbling under his breath.

He suddenly sat up straight. So did Silas. They looked at each other and nodded, saying together, "The Winter Solstice."

"The Winter Solstice?" Gapinski asked. "As in, like, Stonehenge and fruit bathing?"

Silas turned to him. "Fruit bathing?"

He shrugged. "It's a Japanese thing."

"Boys, let's focus, shall we?" Celeste said. "Why do you suppose the Winter Solstice is so important to their unveiling?"

Radcliffe shook his head. "Can't say, my dear. But it's obviously significant since they clearly chose that specific day."

"Isn't the Winter Solstice the start of the solar year," Gapinski said, "and some sort of celebration of the rebirth of the sun? And isn't there a connection with Christmas?"

"Basically," Silas replied. "The Roman emperor Aurelian established December 25 as the birthday of the 'Invincible Sun,' as it was called, in the third century as part of Roman Winter Solstice celebrations. And then the Church selected this day in AD 273 to represent the birth of Christ. Fifty years later, under the direction of the new Christian convert Emperor Constantine, the Roman solar feast day was Christianized."

"No way it's a coinkydink that Nous is dropping some new spiritual revelation about the Holy Grail that close to Christmas," Gapinski said shaking his head.

"Agreed," Celeste said.

"But what's the link," Silas wondered, "other than the obvious with Christ's birth?"

The four sat in silence, considering the connection.

"I wonder..." Radcliffe finally said.

"What do you have?" Celeste asked.

"Well, one of the more interesting aspects of Grail lore is that it has been linked to the story of Joseph of Arimathea."

Silas looked up. "Joseph of Arimathea? The man who retrieved Jesus' body from Pilate to lay in his family tomb for burial? That Joseph of Arimathea?"

"Indeed. And actually, a Protestant, the Archbishop James Usher, linked the particular Grail story of Arculf to the story of

Joseph of Arimathea during the seventeenth century. And many of the original Grail stories stretching back to the twelfth and thirteenth centuries carry with them an Arimathean tradition, as well."

"You seem to know a lot about this Holy Grail stuff, chief," Gapinski said.

Radcliffe smiled. "Tales of King Arthur and Merlin and the Knights of the Round Table were the stuff of my childhood back home in England. And in university, a class on Medieval literature set my heart delighting in the grail romances of Chrétien de Troyes and Robert de Boron and Sir Thomas Malory." He closed his eyes and patted his chest, as if reliving the thrill of those literary memories.

"And what were those tales," Silas asked, "the ones about the Grail specifically?"

"The grail romances, as they were known, were part of a wider set of literature in the Middle Ages on King Arthur and his knights. Germane to our investigation is what began with Chrétien de Troyes, a French poet who was instrumental in crystallizing the legend, presenting the Grail as a means of not only examining the chivalric ideal but also the spiritual one. This remained core to subsequent tales, in which knights search for the legendary chalice. He introduced the symbol in his final tale, *Conte del Graal*."

"Story of the Grail," Silas said.

Radcliffe smiled and offered a short nod. "Bravo. You know your French. At any rate, a Welsh lad named Perceval undertakes a series of quests to become a knight in Arthur's court—one of which lands him at a castle where he encounters the mysterious Fisher King, who is wounded and offers a sword to the lad as a gift. Afterward, the Grail Procession commences, made up of a young man bearing the bleeding lance, later understood to be that of the centurion who pierced Christ's side; a young woman bearing a gleaming Grail made of precious materials, gold and stones and the like; and finally, a young maiden with a carving dish. Although the lad initially fails the quest for neglecting to ask the ritualistic question that would have healed the suffering king, this failure and a confrontation undressing him as an unworthy, wicked man spurs him on to devote his life to serving God and finding the Grail again. Subsequent romances would build upon this narrative, but the basic scaffolding of the story remained unchanged."

The Order Master paused to catch his breath, then continued, "Now at this point, the Grail isn't an explicitly Christian artifact, although the story is thoroughly Christian. Robert de Boron's *Joseph of Arimathea* would cement the Grail legend into an explicitly Christian symbol, specifically as the cup Christ bore at the Last Supper, and the chalice Joseph of Arimathea used to catch Christ's blood at the cross. This is then connected with the tradition surrounding the man who claimed and buried Jesus' body in the tomb."

Celeste said, "So what is that tradition, the one about Joseph of Arimathea and the Grail?"

Radcliffe crossed his legs, and said, "Well, as the legend goes, which let me make clear I believe to be very much a legend. Although, as I said with Arculf, perhaps the legend carries with it shades of an actual tradition. At any rate, the tradition first surfaces with Robert de Boron's version of the Grail story, in which he recounted the tale of Pontius Pilate presenting the cup used by Christ at the Last Supper to Joseph of Arimathea, who in turn was said to have collected Christ's blood from the gaping wound in his side made from the lance of the Roman soldier Longinus."

"Wait a minute," Silas said. "Didn't Arculf mention that same lance?"

"Indeed. In his account, Robert de Boron drew upon an Apocrypha text in a section of the so-called *Gospel of Nicodemus* known as the *Acts of Pilate*, in which Joseph was imprisoned by the Jews after Jesus disappeared post-resurrection. Now, in the original version, the Grail itself is not mentioned, only that Joseph's faith was miraculously sustained. However, in Robert de Boron's retelling, Christ himself appeared to the man in prison bearing the Grail and instructed him to celebrate Mass in commemoration of his death on the cross."

"Celebrate Mass?"

He nodded. "The Eucharist has been closely bound up with the Grail. In fact, Chrétien's account climaxes when *'Perceval came to recognize that God received death and was crucified,'* as he wrote, *'And at Easter, most worthily, Perceval received communion.'*"

"Now that's interesting, given what was happening around that time." Silas looked off and grew silent.

"Care to share, professor?" Celeste asked.

Silas shook himself out his contemplation and smiled. "From the start, early Christians took seriously Jesus' exhortation to remember the new covenant made possible through the blood he shed and the violence his body endured for our sins by drinking the cup of wine and eating of bread."

"Or, in my case, Welch's grape juice and saltine crackers," Gapinski complained.

"To each his own, I guess. Anyway, the Eucharist or Holy Communion symbolized his act of sacrifice on the cross. And from the fourth century through the twelfth, the role and meaning of the Eucharist developed and changed considerably. A belief began to emerge that the consecrated bread and wine actually became the body and blood of Christ."

"Transubstantiation, right?"

Silas nodded. "Exactly. This doctrine became an essential and rather dramatic ritual at the heart of the Roman Catholic Church at the time. Still is."

Radcliffe added, "And those themes of Christ's sacrifice central to this ritual—his death and resurrection and the implication of the same for the believer with salvation and eternal life—are also central to the Arthurian romances of the Grail. Sir Thomas Malory in particular heightened the link between the Grail and the Holy Blood, portraying the vessel as an intimate part of Christ's crucifixion and entwined with the Eucharist. '*Fair sweet Lord who art here within the holy vessel*' a sick knight prayed in his version of the legend, clearly associating the relic with Christ's sacrifice on the cross for the sins of the world, of which the Eucharist is a continual reminder."

"Interesting," Silas mumbled. The moment felt like a thousand puzzle pieces were dumped on a table, all scattered and confusing yet connected and useful for constructing the ultimate picture. He sighed and shook his head. They were no closer to figuring out what the heck was going on.

"Radcliffe," Celeste said, "I want to circle back to something you said earlier, or rather a reaction you had earlier to the mention of the Winter Solstice before we got off on Joseph of Arimathea. You seemed to wonder about its connection to the Grail."

"Ahh, yes!" Radcliffe said, sitting up and shaking his finger. "Thank you for helping gather my wits again. One of the particularly strong and resonate aspects in the Grail legend is the role Glastonbury plays."

"Glastonbury?" she exclaimed, face twisting with surprise. "As in, the Glastonbury of England?"

"Indeed. Most notably it has traditionally been thought to be the place Joseph of Arimathea founded the first Christian church in Europe. Not only that, the Medieval grail romances have Joseph bringing the Grail through Western Europe, possibly stopping first in France, and then traveling on to Britain where he founded the first church at Glastonbury, depositing an inauspicious wooden cup for safekeeping."

"Presumably the Grail," Silas said.

"Presumably. Adding to all this, there is a strongly pagan

history surrounding the place, as well. They even have a yearly Winter Solstice festival at Chalice Well, an excavated site that strongly suggests pre-Christian worship. Big affair with celebrants pilgrimaging to the site for the renewal of the earth and all. And when it comes to the Grail, over the years, it has become unmoored from its Christian connotations, with some attempting to connect it with occult matters—beginning with Glastonbury."

"So the MET, Genoa, and Valencia," Silas mumbled. He shook his head, and said, "If Glastonbury doesn't scream the next Nous target, then I don't know what does."

Celeste stood, and said. "That settles it. Tonight we leave for England."

Gapinski stretched out on the couch and sighed. "I've got a bad feeling about this."

DAY III

DECEMBER 19

CHAPTER 9

GLASTONBURY, ENGLAND.

The Gulfstream hit a pocket of air, sending a shudder rippling through the aircraft. Silas clutched his armrests tight, closed his eyes and took in slow, deep breaths to calm his nerves. He had never been one to fly. That's why he joined the Army instead of the Air Force. Or the Navy and Marines, for that matter. Hated the water as much as the air, anything that took his feet from God's green earth. As far as he was concerned, Dad was right: if God meant for man to fly he'd have given him wings; had he meant for him to float across the water, he'd have given him gills. Dad definitely had a point.

The plane dipped again and shuddered, sending Silas back for the armrests. It lasted for only a few seconds before the plane resumed its smooth-sailing course, the soft purr of the jet engines lulling him back into a state of comfort and trust. He took a sip of his water, then exchanged it for an even longer sip of his Scotch. Between the private air travel and the on-board libation, the Order sure had its perks.

Silas settled back into his seat and reached into his bag for a tablet Zoe had given him filled with research she had compiled on Glastonbury. Might as well get to it before landfall. He retrieved the device and turned it on, and then he waited for it to boot up. As it did, he looked over at Celeste who was sound asleep under a thin red blanket in the seat across the aisle. Her dark-brown hair was braided and resting over her shoulder, a long lock falling over her left eye. Her right hand was curled up underneath her cheek, with her head turned toward Silas and mouth slightly agape.

He couldn't help but smile at the woman. The one who had saved his life not once but twice, pulling him from the wreckage of Dahlgren Chapel and then saving him from getting shot. The one who came to him a few months later for help when the Order's back was up against the wall. The one who delighted his heart when they worked together, in tandem, side-by-side combing through research and putting clues together to find one of the most coveted lost religious relics of them all.

Silas chuckled softly to himself, remembering the first time they met. He didn't like her too well. Thought she was arrogant, high on herself, out to prove to him she could go toe-to-toe with anyone. And she could. Which is what he had grown to adore about her. And when she had gone down after the bullet to her leg, and then almost bled out...He closed his eyes at the memory, trying to shut away the feelings of helplessness and hopelessness that had consumed him while cradling her in his lap. Then when she came down that aisle of the National Cathedral's nave a month ago, he thought he was going to pass out from his heart stopping at the sight of her, limping but alive and healthy.

She sighed and adjusted her position. He wondered what she was dreaming, and he wondered what it would be like to be part of those dreams.

But then he frowned, wondering if he was the kind of man she would even want in her life, in that way. Wondering if he was the kind of man who even wanted a relationship to begin with—and all that came along with it. He was his own person who liked his freedom, doing things his way when he wanted to do them. Had always been that way; he was his own best friend. But no one had made him feel the way Celeste had made him feel. And if he was honest with himself, it scared him.

"I feel you staring at me."

Silas startled and shifted in his seat with embarrassment. He cleared his throat, and said, "Sorry."

Celeste smiled and opened her eyes. "Don't be. I quite enjoy being ogled from across the way."

"I was not ogling!" he protested, his face turning a shade redder.

She sat upright and stretched. "Whatever, creepster. But I'll tell you a little secret." She leaned across the aisle. Silas looked at her and hesitated, but then leaned over to meet her in the middle. "I quite enjoyed it." She giggled like the high-school flirt she probably was back in the day, and then she adjusted her red blanket, wrapping it tighter around herself.

The Gulfstream dipped and shuddered again, sending Silas gripping for the armrests once more.

She giggled again. He snapped his head to her and furrowed his brow. "You mocking me, Celeste Bourne?"

"Don't tell me a former Army Ranger is afraid of flying."

Another dip, another round of shuddering. "So not cool." Another minute and the aircraft evened out and returned back to its level flying pace.

"So, did you have a further think about the Grail and what we're getting ourselves into whilst I was dozing off?"

"I meant to go over Zoe's research, but then—"

"Were enraptured by Sleeping Beauty?"

A grin curled upward on one end of his mouth. She sure was something. "No...Well, yes, but I was also—" he stopped short and threw his hands up in the air. "Alright, you caught me!" He thought he might as well play along, see where it went.

She sure was. "What can I say, you're a thing of beauty, Celeste Bourne who was a Bourne before Jason Bourne was a Bourne."

She giggled again, this time blushing herself. She pulled the blanket up to her face to hide behind, then said, "Perhaps we should put our primary school antics in abeyance and get on with it before we land."

"As long as it's temporary," Silas said reaching for the tablet.

"Alright, you two lovebirds back there," bellowed Gapinski from the front, his voice gravelly and groggy. Silas and Celeste sat up straight, like two high schoolers getting caught passing notes during Algebra. "Pilot says fifteen minutes 'til touchdown. I'm going to try and get some more shut-eye before we land, so could you keep it down back there?" The sound of him turning over in his seat was heard over the din of the jet engines.

Celeste flashed Silas a grin at getting caught, then said, "So what did Zoe send us?"

He brought up the app Zoe had programmed specifically for SEPIO missions. It was like Evernote, but on steroids, integrating a complex Boolean search engine with the Order's vast libraries of digital resources for real-time dynamic content updates. He found the binder containing the information she had uploaded for Glastonbury and leaned over the aisle so Celeste could have a look.

The faint scent of lavender and vanilla filled Silas's senses, speeding up his heart rate. He swallowed hard and began to read what Zoe had prepared.

Apparently, all of the Grail romances were in agreement that the relic had subsequently come into the possession of Joseph of Arimathea. But it wasn't until the thirteenth century that Glastonbury and the abbey, the most famous of the Arthurian romance sites and storehouse of relics in the region, began to be connected with a legend surrounding the man. However, the basic contours of the legend, mainly that the

English church had been founded by him, was affirmed in the fifteenth century by the Council of Constance.

"So there is a legend of Glastonbury and Joseph of Arimathea, then," Celeste said pointing at a paragraph on the screen. "And affirmed by an ecumenical council, no less. I had no idea!" The two continued reading through the material in silence.

As the legend went, twelve missionary hermits under the leadership of Joseph of Arimathea arrived on the shores of the distant island during the first century, being greeted by a sympathetic pagan king who granted them land around modern Glastonbury Tor. There, they built the first Christian church in Britain, until it fell into disrepair and crumbled after the last hermit died. Another pagan king was said to have repaired the site and rebuilt the original church. During the fifth century, the famous Patrick, apostle to Ireland, became the first abbot of a proper monastery in the city. Subsequently, the legend surrounding Joseph was strengthened by a history of British Christianity by William of Malmesbury, who chronicled Joseph of Arimathea's founding of Christianity on the island and his custodianship of the Grail.

"Fascinating about Malmesbury," Silas added, "The only problem is that most of his material for his so-called history of Glastonbury and Joseph of Arimathea is taken from the Grail romances—which were fully fictional accounts."

"Sure, but it isn't like we don't know anything at all about Joseph of Arimathea. There's plenty of material from the Gospels themselves and early Apocrypha accounts. And then there is the possibility of an actual tradition sitting behind the legends."

Silas nodded. "Sure. And from them, we know that Joseph of Arimathea was a Jewish man who followed Jesus, obtained Christ's body after his death on the cross, buried him in his personal unused tomb, was miraculously sustained in prison, and subsequently carried the Christian message of the gospel westward into Europe."

"So then, this truthful foundation was expanded upon by the Grail romances, where he became associated with English Christianity generally and Glastonbury specifically."

"Right. And the research says here that this legend was particularly useful during the Reformation, where it provided the English Reformers with ancient roots of British Christianity. But where things take an interesting turn is how the Grail romances offered a foundation for pro-pagan and Celtic legends. Which perhaps gets us closer to why the city and the surrounding area may be important to our Grail quest."

"And to Nous," Celeste added.

As Zoe's research explained, during the late nineteenth century there was a revival of interest in the Arthurian legends combined with an interest in spiritual renewal, giving birth to a new esoteric and mystical view of Glastonbury as the successor to pagan Avalon that was featured in the Arthurian legends. This added layer transformed the birthplace of Christianity in England by one of Jesus' followers, the man who bore the chalice of his blood, no less, from a Christian-centric site to a center for the pagan sacred feminine. In 1909, the Glastonbury Abbey was taken over by a trust that ushered in a new era of mysticism—of which the Grail was an essential part. Although for some it was a Christian relic, for others the Holy Grail severed as a pagan talisman and occult force, symbolizing the power to transform our present reality into a future one of hope and promise.

Silas hummed audibly as he read, arousing Celeste's curiosity. "Do tell, Agent Grey."

He smiled and adjusted his position. "It's just that the Glastonbury of England and the Avalon of Arthurian legend are so well established and linked that many believe the site to be a pagan center of worship long before it was a Christian one."

"That's true."

"However, the archaeological evidence seems murky on the subject, neither confirming it was a stronghold of Druid origin nor a site of Celtic Christianity with nature-centric worship. But that hasn't stopped the idea of goddess worship being central to pagan worship and Celtic Christian sympathy with feminist paganism from influencing the modern spiritual movements of Glastonbury."

"Yes, but that's in no small thanks to the red spring of Chalice Well rising from the foot of Chalice Hills."

He leaned in closer to the tablet. "I guess I haven't gotten that far yet."

"What?" She exclaimed, feigning surprise. "Something the venerable Doctor Grey doesn't know. I am shocked. Positively shocked!"

Silas threw her a look and playfully punched her arm. "Well, school me then, Agent Bourne."

"As Zoe's research explains, with its high iron content, excavations of the site show Chalice Well to be a site used for pre-Christian worship, as there were uncovered buried yew stumps symbolized by the Celts for death and rebirth. The opening of the spring amongst the rocks would have been regarded as some sort of entrance to the Underworld by the pagan spiritualists, as well as a source for healing from the goddess Sulis who was worshipped in the surrounding area."

"Fascinating," he said. "So then the legend of Joseph of Arimathea and the Holy Grail, with its symbol of death and rebirth, as well as of healing and eternal life, coincides perfectly with the existing pagan, Celtic cults—especially the latter's belief in rebirth through reincarnation, a pagan mirror to the Christian belief in the resurrection through the power of Jesus' blood."

"Right. And combined with the ceremonial vessels Celts used to catch blood offerings, the site makes a promising match for Nous's apparent search for the supposed Grail of power."

Celeste was the first to lean back in her seat. Silas followed, resting the tablet on his lap and staring off toward the front of the cabin. They sat in silence, processing the revelations.

"Well, one thing is clear from Zoe's research," Silas said.

Celeste swiveled in her seat toward him. "And what's that, professor?"

Suddenly, the plane dipped and banked right. He looked out his window. Below was barren farmland dusted with snow, with clumps of naked trees and snaking streams. Bristol Airport was fast approaching in the distance. They would be landing soon.

He put his seat in its upright position and fastened his seatbelt. "We're definitely hot on the heels of Nous because it's the perfect next target for Holy Grail number four."

CHAPTER 10

After taxiing to yet another private hangar, the trio exited the airport in yet another Order-issued SUV. Driving south to Glastonbury, it took them just over forty minutes, mostly through frozen fields layered with a thin blanket of frost shimmering in the bright, rising sun. Knee-high stone walls dotted the landscape, as well as thatched-roof cottage-style homes and forests of naked trees. It was a picturesque drive through southwest England in the dead of winter.

Celeste was positively giddy being back in her homeland. She hadn't visited since a year ago Christmas, and it had been ages since she had been in that part of her country. Silas liked seeing her like that. Seemed like a different person, less hardened and serious, more carefree and childlike. He had taken her as more of a city girl, but the stories she told of childhoods past and her delight with their road trip through that part of England made him think she was more of a country girl at heart. Which he liked, a lot.

"So this part of the Motherland wasn't where you grew up in, was it?" Gapinski asked.

"Not at all. Daddy and Mummy both worked in the city.

Well, Mum actually in the city, for a London publisher. Daddy at home, taking care of me and tending to his writing."

"So was he, like, rocking the whole Baby Bjorn carrier thingamabob before it became an American suburban thing?" Gapinski asked.

"Totally, rocked the Baby Bjorn!"

"Right on. And just you? No siblings?"

She shook her head. "Mum wasn't supposed to have children. She was high risk for preeclampsia—"

"Hold the phone, sister. I'm not down with the whole pregnant woman lingo."

Celeste smirked, and said, "There was a high risk she would die during pregnancy."

"Got it."

"I didn't know that," Silas said with more of an edge of irritation than he intended.

She shrugged. "You haven't asked. Anyway, I was an oopsie, but Daddy and Mummy trusted the Lord to carry them through it. Near the end, she had to go on strict bedrest. But I was born at thirty-six weeks and four days and lived to tell about it. After that, Daddy got fixed."

"Goodness," Gapinski said. "Well, bravo for your parents for trusting God with the whole thing. That's gotta be a rare thing nowadays."

"Would you look at that," Silas said from the back pointing ahead.

Celeste and Gapinski broke off their conversation and looked at where Silas was pointing. Rising from the barren land and peeking above the quaint English cottages up ahead was a massive mound. It looked like a frosted rugby ball, and fixed on the top was a tower of some sort.

"Glastonbury, here we come," Gapinski said as he entered the roundabout toward town. Weaving through the village, the closer toward the center of town they got they could see the mound was terraced. The tower on top also seemed more like the remains of an ancient cathedral than something used for observation or protection. They reached High Street and hung a right, but it was slow going as crowds of people were milling about for the Winter Solstice celebrations.

Boutique shops beckoned shoppers to sample their wares. The smell of baked goods and frying meat drifted through the streets from open doorways of cafés and pubs, inviting patrons to take a load off with a tea and scone or a beer and shepherd's pie. Tents along the walkways also sold goods, local merchants hoping to score big during the festivities.

The street curved past a massive Christmas tree commanding a small plaza, brightly colored bulbous ornaments and lights weighing down its branches. Gapinski braked hard for a family trying to cross the street. The father scowled before waving thanks. Gapinski smiled and waved in reply. He looked to his left as they and another couple crossed, eyeing a green awning with the words *panini, baguette, and cappuccino* emblazoned in white.

"Panini..." he moaned as the pedestrians finished crossing. A chorus of horns from behind jerked him from visions of toasted meat and cheese sandwiches. "Yeah, right back atcha, mates. How about we park and find us some good English grub?" He pointed to the sign, and said, "Heaphys Café looks promising."

"I suppose it is that hour, isn't it?" Celeste mumbled.

"What hour?" he said pulling into a public car park down the road.

"The one when Gapinski needs to fill his grumbling-rumbling stomach," she said smiling. "That hour."

He twisted his face in confusion as he slid into a parking spot. "OK, I have no idea what you're talking about."

"Oh, come on, mate. Inevitably at some point in a mission, and usually at the most inopportune time, you need to go off and have yourself a steak sandwich or cheese log or something or other."

Silas covered his mouth and turned toward the window, snickering in the back.

He opened his door and scoffed. "Whatever."

"Gapinski, man, she's just messing with you," Silas said as he walked around the back of the car.

"How many times do I have to tell you two. I'm big boned, alright?"

Celeste saddled up alongside the man as he sauntered up Magdalene Street back toward the restaurant. She slipped her arm around his, trying to make up to him for the slight ribbing in the car. "Sorry, mate. Just having a laugh back there."

"Yeah, buddy," Silas said coming along the other side. "And besides, without your clockwork-precision stomach, I'm not sure we would ever be as well-fed as we are on these missions. One of the reasons I agreed to join SEPIO in the first place. We never miss a meal. And often have two or three extras."

"Ha, ha, ha," Gapinski said. "And for that, you're buying."

"I right believe Radcliffe is buying, actually," Celeste said.

"Even better."

The trio came up to a set of shops that clearly spelled out the occult reputation the city had garnered. A shop named *Man, Myth, Magik* stood before the crosswalk near the café, followed by *Elestial* and *Cat & Cauldron*. Each store featured healing stones, dream catchers, ceremonial masks, and books on spells and other magical incantations. By the looks of it, they were doing brisk business with the Winter Solstice crowd.

They crossed the street and came to a chalkboard sign promising "Whole food and soul food" with "Savory home-made lunches." Sounded just what the trio needed for the brisk late-morning. A man with long silver hair dressed in a white robe holding a long wooden staff with vine carvings up the side thrust a pamphlet into Gapinski's hand.

"Here you go, stargazer." The man smiled widely then let go of the piece of paper before Gapinski could refuse.

"Gapinski!" Silas called to him. He looked up, seeing him and Celeste enter the café.

"Thanks, stargazer man. Or, whatever." He nodded and ran to meet his companions.

After the trio ordered and retrieved their food, they commandeered a table near the window that had just been vacated by a small family. They immediately dived into their food: Celeste a bowl of soup, Silas a panini, Gapinski two of the same.

"So, this whole Grail thing," Gapinski said, crunching into his second panini. "Is this just a bunch of bulldookie or what?"

Silas smirked. "If you were to ask me, and I'm not one to second guess my commanding officers or anything..." He smiled wryly at Celeste as she grinned before taking a spoonful of soup. "But if it mattered, I'd say it is a royal bucket of bulldookie since there is nothing to the supposed Grails and the Church hasn't considered them a relic. But that's just me."

"How about you, Celeste? What's your take on all of this?"

She wiped her mouth with her napkin, choosing her words carefully. "I think if Nous has an interest in the so-called Holy Grail, and they are certainly making plays on all the ones that claim to be such. If they're interested, then the Order is interested. End of story."

"But I guess that's the missing ingredient in all of this," Gapinski said, finishing one of his sandwiches.

"Oh, yeah?" Silas said turning to him as he finished his first and only sandwich. "And what's that."

"Why the heck are they going after them if there's nothing to the legends? Especially if it's no concern to the Church?"

Silas said nothing. Celeste sat finishing her soup. Gapinski looked out the window, considering his own question as much as the other two considered it. After depositing their waste in the garbage, they were back out into the crowded streets.

"So where to, chief?" Silas asked as they snaked through the crowded sidewalks.

Celeste shook her head. "Not sure. I say we have ourselves a look around and pray we run into something that rings true to our case."

They ambled past the Christmas tree they had driven by earlier, its ornaments twinkling in the emerging high-noon sun, then turned back toward where they had parked a few blocks south. The Winter Solstice celebrating crowds were thicker than before, and dressed for the part. Yes, there were plenty of people dressed in black—leggings and trousers, jackets and capes. But there was plenty of purple and white, green and orange, as well. Most of the people ambling along the street popping in and out of the shops were your run-of-the-mill, middle-classer, the kind of person one would expect cele-brating Christmas and showing up for Christmas Eve Mass. Not out and about anticipating and celebrating a pagan holiday.

"Listen to this," Gapinski said, looking over the pamphlet as they reached their car, then turned to follow a series of signs leading to the Glastonbury Abbey and Chapel ruins. "According to the Smithsonian Magazine, '*At 51 degrees north latitude, Glastonbury Tor is a man-made mound in southern England that historians believe was built to celebrate the Sun and the path it takes through the sky. On the Winter Solstice, a person standing on the nearby Windmill Hill can watch as the rising Sun appears to roll along the slope of the mound from base to top, where the ruins of St. Michael's Church still stand.*'"

Silas could see the remains of the church commanding the center of the massive mound of dirt in the distance. Joining it was a slew of tents covering the face of the Tor—tents of all shapes, sizes, and colors.

Gapinski continued, "Apparently, Glastonbury is one of the top ten places to celebrate the Winter Solstice. Right up there with Chichen Itza in Mexico, the Karnak Temple of Egypt, and—"

"Let me guess," Silas interrupted, "Stonehenge?"

"You got it."

"Then we're in the right place for all things pagan and occult."

Celeste added, "But what the bloody hell does any of it have to do with the Grail, and what is Nous planning?"

The two men shrugged, continuing to wade through the crowd of celebrants and into the main compound containing the ruins of Glastonbury Christianity. The Chapel was what you would expect of a sacred religious building from the Middle Ages: a two-story structure of pale cut stone dirtied by time with arched windows at the top for light, brown grass growing where a roof once stood and crumbling at one end, ironically where the high altar once stood. They bypassed the structure, heading for the grassy place where the abbey once stood, now looking like sets of broken teeth jutting up out of the sod.

As they neared, they could hear a woman calling out to the crowds standing in the middle of the ruins. She was saying something that sounded vaguely familiar.

"Hast thou seen the Holy Cup that Joseph brought of old to Glastonbury?" she said.

"Hold up," Silas told Celeste and Gapinski. "I recognize that line. Pretty sure it's Tennyson."

"Tenny-who?" Gapinski said.

Celeste threw him a look.

"What?" He shrugged defensively.

She said, "As in Lord Tennyson, the Poet Laureate of Great Britain and Ireland during much of Queen Victoria's reign and architect of one of the more beloved Grail romances."

Gapinski rolled his eyes, then approached the woman. "I'll handle this. Excuse me?" he said coming up behind her.

"Oy!" she exclaimed and spun around.

He threw his hands up and took a step back. "Sorry, ma'am! Didn't mean to alarm you."

"Dear me, you gave me a fright! How do you get off sneaking up behind a poor, defenseless old woman?"

"I, uhh, I..." Eyes wide and hands still raised, he looked to Celeste for help, as if needing someone to help him navigate a foreign culture or offer to translate.

"You'll have to forgive my friend here," Celeste said, stepping in to undo the damage. "He's a Yank."

The short, stout elderly lady with long gray hair wearing a purple cape chuckled and nodded, as if in on the joke. Silas and Gapinski looked at each other, brows furrowed, clearly not in on the joke.

"Dear me, well what brings you all the way to these parts, then?"

Silas nodded toward the Tor, and said, "Winter Solstice, same as everybody else." She smiled and nodded. He continued, "We were touring the abbey grounds before heading toward the Tor when we heard you quoting Tennyson."

"Ahh, yes. The legend of the Grail." She leaned in close, looking up into Silas's face and whispered, "Are you a believer?"

He smiled and shrugged. "Haven't given it much thought. And frankly, much stock, but that's probably born more out of ignorance than knowledge."

She leaned back and smiled, as if pleased by the answer. "A man of wisdom, you are. Never one to dismiss a tale without having all the facts?"

"I like to think so. But all I know of the Grail is what the movies have said."

"Ba!" she replied, making a sputtering sound with her mouth and grimacing. "Stuff and nonsense, they are."

"But you know the truth? The mystery that lies behind the legend?"

She straightened slightly, placing one hand on the other in front of her. "That I do." She said no more.

Gapinski said, "Well don't hold back now, sister. We're... stargazers. Seekers of the truth."

She eyed him suspiciously, then glanced at Celeste before turning back to Silas and leaning in again. "It's quite the colorful legend, love, filled with monks escaping no uncertain danger, secrets and intrigue, tunnels and passageways, and even a crusader."

"Do tell," he said stepping closer. She eyed him again, then grinned slightly. Then she looked into Silas's eyes, as if she were ready to divulge a well-kept secret that went generations deep.

"Well, as the legend goes, a cartful of monks—seven, I believe—escaped from the Glastonbury Abbey with a sacred object just as King Henry's bloody henchmen stole into the night and descended upon the place to plunder its sacred relics and treasures. After a perilous flight into the night across the Welsh mountains, these seven monks arrived at a certain abbey in Dyfed, they did. Well, it wasn't called Dyfed at the time. Ceredigion, if I remember it right. Anyway, there they were sheltered by a kindhearted family. When the last of the seven monks passed, the sacred relic, the Grail in case it wasn't clear by now, the cup was passed along to the family for safe keeping, being entrusted to their care and protection. It is said that through the years, they allowed any and all to come drink from the chalice to cure what ailed them. And they did. Men, women, and children were healed by its power, they were. Over the years, the poor thing fell into disrepair until it came into the possession of a Mrs. Margaret Powell, who has kept it at her Nanteos estate."

"And you've seen this cup, this...Holy Grail?" Silas asked.

"Aye, I have. A wooden thing that's mostly a piece of the original. But a mighty fascinating beacon of divine power, it is."

"Sounds like it."

"You could always see it for yourself if you'd like."

Silas looked at Celeste, eyes widening.

"What do you mean by that?" Celeste asked. "That we can see for ourselves?"

The woman pointed to the imposing hill crowned with the centuries-old brick tower, flanked by tents with a queue of people snaking down its back.

"They've brought the Grail for a public viewing, they have. First time in 140 years it's been on display. Brought it out special for the Winter Solstice, they did. Crowds have been lining up for days to bask in its divine power, they have."

Silas smiled and looked to Gapinski before looking to Celeste. "Thank you, friend."

Now they were getting somewhere.

CHAPTER 11

G rass crunched underneath the trio as they walked over the remaining thin layer of frost still sparkling in the noon sunlight, the day now warming from the frigid late-December. They worked their way through the tents commanding the base of the Tor and onward toward the queue near the base of the hill.

A path snaked up the spine of the ancient mound toward the ancient tower standing tall and proud after surviving war and weather. The Tor was steep and narrow, with a series of flagstone steps leading the way and packed gravel from years of pilgrims making the trek to the sacred spot venerated by Christians and pagans alike. The line moved slowly, a few steps then stop, a few more steps then stop.

"Man, I could really use another—"

"Gapinski!" Celeste and Silas said in unison.

He startled and tossed his hands in the air. "What'd I do?"

"Enough of the food talk already," Silas said.

"And that's a direct order," Celeste added.

Gapinski huffed and folded his arms, then mumbled something under his breath as the line inched forward again. It was like that for half an hour until they finally reached the still-standing ancient church tower.

Silas turned around and took in the sight: the people snaking behind him down below and the tents scattered about; the quaint town of English cottages and High Street shops; to the south, acres upon acres of frozen, barren earth and clumps of naked trees. It was quite the sight.

He turned around as the line continued forward, and said, "Well, we have one thing going our way."

"And what's that?" Celeste said.

"So far, no sign of Nous. Just a bunch of Winter Solstice revelers."

"Which you know can change on a dime," Gapinski said.

"Then what's the plan? Do we lie in wait, hoping they don't show but prepared if they do? Commandeer the cup ourselves in anticipation they will surely come for it?"

Celeste shook her head and looked around the area. "Not sure. Let's play it by ear." She nodded ahead as the line moved forward and they reached the threshold of the tower.

He caught sight of a clear case up ahead at the center of the tall sacred remains, flanked by two Rent-a-Cop security guards sitting on two benches. No doubt there to ensure the safety of the precious relic. Inside, he could see the remains of what looked like a cup, slightly curved and worn, as if the thing had cracked in half. He scoffed to himself and shook his head in disbelief. Every fiber of his academic, relicologist being wanted to scream at the idea that it was somehow the Holy Grail, the holy chalice from Medieval myths bearing the wonder-working-power of Jesus' blood.

"What a bunch of malarkey..." he mumbled as they edged to the entrance to the small tower, standing a few feet behind the chalice as a woman observed it.

She jolted upright and turned toward him, twisting her face in disgust and offering an equally disgusted huff. Then she bent back down and hugged the entire case, as if trying to soak up its power for herself. One of the guards quickly stood and intervened, gently pulling her back while the other one stepped forward to inspect the case.

"Eww," Gapinski said. "Doesn't she know how many people have touched that thing? Gotta be a germ cesspool after all these years!"

The woman sauntered out of the tower, and the trio stepped inside the ancient church ruins and up to the case for their own viewing. The space was cramped, no more than twenty-five or thirty feet wide and long. Two benches of the same flagstone as the path outside sat on either side, along with two narrow glass-less windows above. The tower rose high, with its roof long gone, exposing the inside to the elements. In the middle of the tower sat a circular stone pillar. On top was a modest case, made of thick glass or high-density polycarbonate, about ten inches wide, long, and deep. Inside sat a red velvet pillow, and on top lay the Nanteos Cup.

It was nothing more than a curved piece of wood at that point, visibly scarred by time and curiously stained by a dark brown substance. Could be anything, wine or broth.

Or blood...

Silas nodded toward one of the seated guards and stepped up to the ancient object, crouching down to come to it at eye level. He smirked, and said, "That's it? This is what people have been venerating for centuries?"

"I guess so," Gapinski said crouching on the opposite side. He eyed it, then said, "What a piece of crap!"

Someone behind him cleared their throat. Silas stood and turned. A scowling burly, bearded man dressed in black nodded his head toward the exit, as if both chastising him for his slander and chasing him along.

He bent down again and shook his head, considering the vessel that some had insisted was the Holy Grail, brought to

England by Joseph of Arimathea bearing the remnants of Christ's blood.

"I'll tell you one thing," Gapinski continued, "George Lucas sure got it right. I mean, look at the thing. The cup of a carpenter, if I ever saw one. Something a bunch of poor fishermen would have used around the dinner table during Passover. Not that silver eyesore from—"

A scream sliced through the frigid afternoon air, cutting him off.

Silas bolted to his feet and pivoted toward the sound, behind them. It was coming from down the path. The guards stirred and moved toward the entrance. They looked at each other, faces stricken with panic, as if neither of them had expected anything remotely like what was going down on their watch.

A spattering of *pop-pop-pop* gunfire sent up a wicked chorus of screams, sending a group of tourists running inside the cramped church tower for cover.

This seemed to kick the guards into a sort of heroic resolve, for they both withdrew their weapons and pushed through the crowd out onto the Tor path.

"Can we just get one mission where we aren't interrupted by terrorists!" Gapinski complained as he brought out his own SIG Sauer from behind his waist.

"Where'd you get that?" Silas asked.

He looked at his gun and furrowed his brow. "From the Order armory. Before we left. What, you're not packing heat?"

Silas frowned and crouched behind the stone pedestal. He looked to Celeste, who was bearing her own SIG Sauer.

Gapinski said, "Can I give you a word of advice, bro, for Day One of your new job? Never leave home without cold, hard steel."

Celeste nodded, facing the tower entrance. "I concur, mate. But don't worry, we've got your back." She winked as another round of firepower outside the tower sent another wave of bodies cresting toward them.

"Gee, thanks."

Another set of *pop-pop-pop* gunfire sounded, then another. Different tone, different timbre. Apparently, the Rent-a-Cops wanted in on the action after all.

Then, almost in slow motion, the heads of both security guards jerked backward, and they crumpled to the ground.

"There goes the cavalry," Gapinski complained, chambering a round. "Guess it's up to us now."

"Nous wants this cup that badly, do they?" Celeste said. "Well, they best be ready for a fight. Because I'll be damned if they get it on my watch."

Three small black heads coming up the path were visible as the crowd of desperate men, women, and children thinned. They were continuing to fire widely, as if sweeping them forward with a hose.

"Follow me," Gapinski finally said. He got up from his position and hustled backward through the east gate of the tower. Celeste and Silas followed.

He led them around the south side of the ancient structure, weapon outstretched and ready for business, startling a scared family crying and huddled against the tower.

As he passed them, he said, "Don't worry, folks. We're the good guys."

He came up short at the edge, then eased himself around for a look. Celeste was close to his side. Silas was behind her, feeling completely helpless and exposed. He cursed himself for leaving on mission without his Beretta. *Never leave home without cold, hard steel* was going to be his new mantra, that's for sure.

The three hostiles were getting closer as the crowds left the grounds. Silas caught sight of a few bodies lying along the path. He clenched his jaw in anger and disgust at the loss.

Then Gapinski raised his weapon and popped off five

rounds; Celeste followed with the same—both finding success. One of the men was sent to the ground, clutching a leg. The other two crouched and sent an angry reply.

The two SEPIO agents twisted away just as stone and masonry exploded in angry fits, the bullets from the Nousati chewing the tower of Saint Michael's Church to pieces. The rage was relentless.

And getting closer.

"Come on!" Gapinski yelled, hustling back east along the side of the tower, then around to the north side, the other two close behind.

He twisted his head around the entrance to the central portion. Seeing a target, he took aim and leveled covering fire, instructing Celeste and Silas to run across toward the north side of the tower.

They did, and he hit his target. Square in the chest. The man staggered backward and tumbled to the ground.

Gapinski grinned. "Yes!"

But a few seconds later, the downed man propped himself on his elbows and shook his head, then sat up and slowly stood. He extended his automatic rifle and sent an angry, relentless barrage of bullets back at Gapinski.

He ducked back behind the wall. "Why you lily-livered, chicken-hearted lickspittles! Body armor. So not a fair fight!"

He twisted back toward the entrance, then took the risk and rushed across to join the other two.

"I see our lucky friends are wearing body armor," Celeste said leaning her back against the stone wall as Gapinski came behind out of breath.

"Definitely adds a layer to the fun," he replied. "At least we know it's only chest coverage, since the other man we managed to hit is still squirming on the ground from a bum leg."

"At least you can do something about it," Silas complained.

Suddenly, the gunfire died down. They looked at each

other. Celeste eased around the edge, SIG Sauer poised for a response. She popped her head around for a look. Other than the one man down who was crawling down the slope of the Tor, the other two were missing.

She nodded to Gapinski to check behind them when he heard voices, low and guttural and menacing. He quickly retreated. "We've got more company. Inside the tower. And they've got us flanked now."

Celeste gripped the butt of her SIG tighter and sucked in a lungful of air. Their options had dwindled down to a singular one.

"Follow me. But be at the ready."

She backed up to the edge of the Tor, weapon extended and pointing toward the west entrance. Gapinski did the same, pointing his own gun toward the east. Silas hustled along with them, seriously regretting his decision not to pack his heat.

They peered over the edge of the man-made hill, the tents flapping violently as the frigid December wind picked up pace. The area was completely empty, the crowds having taken cover. In the distance, the whine of angry sirens drifted along the wind, but it would be a while until they reached them. By then it would all be over. One way or another.

Celeste said, "Over the edge, mates. Watch yourself and be quick about it." She knelt and began shuffling backward down the side of the hill, one hand steadying herself, the other steadying her aim.

Gapinski crossed himself, even though he was a Southern Baptist. Figured it was good insurance. "Sweet Jesus take the wheel," he said joining her on all fours.

The trio edged down the side of the Tor, its walls rocky and slick now, the morning frost having melted from the high-noon sun. They were taking a big risk edging down the steep hill, with being exposed like they were. But a path snaked around to the east side of the church tower that would give them a perfect vantage point to finish what they started.

That is if they survived.

Silas made quick work down the side given his hands were free. He slid quickly to the path. Celeste followed close behind, using the slick grass and loose dirt to her advantage by similarly sliding in one motion.

Gapinski was another story. He hated heights as it was, and the gravel and slick grass made the descent that much more difficult. He edged farther down, then some more. Halfway down the Tor his knee gave way on a slick patch, sending his two-hundred-and-forty-pound body sliding.

"Crapola," he said, losing his weapon in the wild descent. It skittered down the side and bounced hard on the thin path. Silas reached and grabbed for it. It nearly slipped through his fingers, but he caught it by the barrel. Apparently, four years as a wide receiver for the Falls Church Jaguars wasn't for naught. Finally, something went their way!

Gapinski tried stopping himself, but he kept plummeting. Down, down, down. He hit the level trail hard, sending him flat on his butt. His back slapped backward. Celeste and Silas grabbed his shoulders before he continued plunging farther.

"Jeez Louise, sister," he said breathless and dirty and slick from his descent. "Next time, choose an easier plan of escape!" He turned to Silas, and said, "You got my weapon?"

He grinned and shoved it against his chest. "Can I give you some friendly advice, bro? Never slide down a Tor without securing your cold, hard steel."

Gapinski smirked and grabbed his SIG Sauer from him. Silas offered the man a wry grin as his partner chambered a round before shoving the weapon into the front of his pants.

"Come on!" Celeste said. "No time for dilly-dallying." She hurried east along the path, holding her arm outstretched with weapon at the ready. They rounded the north side of the hill which came to a point on the east side. Farther down, a new path started that snaked down the rest of the Tor. Directly above, the hill rose high back toward the tower. Celeste started climbing.

"You've gotta be kiddin' me," Gapinski moaned.

Silas said nothing and quickly started ascending close behind Celeste.

"Can't we just take the path around to the other side?"

Silas turned around and told him to quiet down and get his butt up the slope. The man scoffed and started scrambling along with them, the gravel more compact and grass less slick. Within minutes, they had reached the top, crouching behind a wide stone disc just over the hill.

They had a perfect vantage point of the tower and the hostiles. Which had doubled in number.

"Where the heck did the new muscle come from?" Silas asked.

"They must have come up the second path along the south side of the Tor!" Celeste said.

"Always something," Gapinski growled.

Two of them were on the north side, peering over the edge. Probably wondering where the visitors with firepower had run off to.

Three others were inside the tower surrounding the encased Grail, a taller man in the middle having picked up the case. He turned and walked out into the open, cradling it in his arms, his face masked with a black hood like the rest of the hostiles.

Celeste looked to Gapinski, then to Silas. She nodded. They nodded back.

Now or never.

The two stood and opened fire while Silas crouched behind the stone disc. Celeste took the three coming out of the tower.

Gapinski took the original two on the right—sending one to the ground, blood spraying from his neck.

He mumbled a curse. "Sorry, bro. Only meant to maim. My bad."

Amidst the sudden barrage, the tall man with the case stuffed it under his arm like a football and took off running around to the south side of the tower, then disappeared down the edge.

Silas gritted his teeth and steeled his resolve.

Not on my watch, partner!

CHAPTER 12

Silas took off toward the tower, staying low and veering left along the southern front of the Tor toward the secondary pathway that wound its way down the south face of the hill and back east again to freedom.

Using the stone disc as cover, Celeste and Gapinski kept at it from behind, the Nousati agents answering back up ahead with equal measure from inside the tower.

He could see the tall man ahead running down the steps made of the same flagstone from the other path. He was fast and making quick work getting down the face of the Tor.

Dirt sprayed near Silas to the right as he made his way forward, catching him off guard and sending him stumbling. He lost his footing and went tumbling down the side, landing his head hard on one of the stone steps.

He lay there as stars and dimming blackness entered his vision. He took a deep breath as the world returned, then sat upright. He shook his head, pain radiating from the back. He winced as he eased himself forward, feeling the back of his head for blood. It wasn't slick, so that was good. But a goose egg was already forming. No matter. He stood and took off toward the man, who now had a several-yards head start.

Silas barreled down the steps, leap-frogging several of them and sprinting on the narrow stretches of the beaten stone path. The man ahead was fast, real fast. But Silas was faster, gaining on him as the path curved north.

Suddenly, his foot caught on a large stone, and he fell forward, scraping skin off his hands on the gravel and nearly tipping over the lip of the path. That was going to leave another mark.

He cursed himself for being so stupid, but picked himself back up and tore after the man. He had reached the final descent, pivoting right and winding down another set of steps to the bottom before it gave way to trees and then to barren fields—and to freedom.

Not if I have anything to say about it!

Within several seconds, he himself pivoted right and was gaining on the man down the path. In the distance, he heard a sound. A thwapping, like one of those high-powered kitchen stove vents. A sound he had memorized over the years in the desert sands of the Middle East through two tours for Uncle Sam.

Helicopter. And a heavy-duty one, at that. The kind he and his men flew in on during combat.

Must be coming to retrieve his guy. Silas looked up and around as he willed his legs to move faster. He saw a black oval in the distance up ahead northeast of their position, growing ever so larger and banking south toward the east side of the Tor. Beyond the trees, there were plenty of barren fields, frozen solid—making it the perfect landing zone for an easy extraction.

Not if I can help it!

They both continued down the stairs, then wound left before pivoting right for the final descent.

Come on, just a few more yards...

The man sloshed through muddy water that had spilled

over onto the path from a recent late-December rain, having melted during the afternoon. Silas was close behind, taking long strides through the chilly, chocolate water to catch up.

The man glanced backward briefly, before pumping his arms and legs faster.

Too bad, pal. Almost...

The man reached the last of the stairs, then made a sharp right toward another path through a grouping of naked trees. But he lost his footing. He nearly lost the casing had he not been gripping it like a football. The man landed on his free hand, but he was able to recover and push off the path.

He regained his footing and continued running, but that momentary slip gave Silas the chance to make up precious lost ground.

He was within striking distance as they cleared the trees and banked left toward an open field. The thwapping was getting louder, and Silas could see the bird high above closing in toward their position.

Now or never.

Silas jumped for the man, grabbing his waist and leaning his full weight against him in a tackle. They both fell forward onto the cold, hard grassy ground.

In the fall, the man lost the Grail case. It tumbled a few feet away and landed near a clump of bushes still clinging to its leaves. The man stood to grab it, but was weighted down by Silas who had managed to hold the man in the fall. He was reaching for the top of the man's jacket, trying to climb on top and finish the job.

But the man wouldn't let him.

He twisted himself on his back, so that they were facing each other. Silas's face was a mix of exhaustion and adrenaline-fueled rage; the man's was still masked but breathing heavy from the pursuit. He instantly brought both of his hands together as fists and slammed them against Silas's head.

Silas groaned and recoiled in pain, allowing the man to inch himself backward out from under Silas and land a kick to his face, sending him to the ground in even more pain.

Blood gushed from Silas's nose. The man scrambled across the wet grass to retrieve the glass case. Above, the helicopter came in fast and pulled up to hover in wait, the wind from its deafening blades swirling the world below and creating confusion.

Silas wiped his nose on his sleeve, blood smearing thick and crimson. He screamed with rage at the assault as much as from an adrenaline-rush to get back in the ring. And he did. He lunged for the man a second round.

The man connected with the glass case, but he lost it when Silas climbed on his back. Silas grabbed his head and smashed it into the ground. Not as impactful as the man's foot to Silas's face, but it worked the same magic, stunning him as blood came bubbling up out of the man's own nose.

He struggled to work free of Silas, but his grip was tight. He arched his back and pushed off with both arms, then got to all fours.

Silas was now riding him like a bucking bronco, holding firm to the man's head and reaching around for a chokehold.

But the man arched even more, so that he was on both knees and Silas was hanging on his head. Then he fell backward.

Silas lost his chokehold grip, but he continued clawing at his head. The only purchase he found was the black wool mask. They struggled on the ground, but then the man turned to break free. He succeeded, leaving Silas behind, as well as his mask.

The man spun around and scrambled to stand, his nostrils flaring and blood dribbling down his chin, mouth grinning almost with satisfaction at being found out.

Silas was panting, as well, but quickly stood, meeting the man face to face.

When he did, his face fell, and he instantly recoiled, stumbling backward amidst the flattening grass and swirl of the chopper blades above as if he had seen a ghost. In many ways, he had.

His own.

"Seba?" he said in disbelief. "Sebastian?!" he said again, his voice angry and straining with emotion above the noise of the hovering, thwapping chopper.

Standing before him was a near-perfect replica of the image Silas had seen in the mirror his whole life, except for blond hair and blue eyes.

There he was. Sebastian Grey. His twin brother.

"You..." he roared, his face twisting in a vortex of anger and hurt and confusion and fear. He lunged for his brother, head first into the man's gut.

Seeming to anticipate this, Sebastian stepped to the side and used Silas's momentum against him, grabbing him by his back and shoving him forward.

Silas collapsed to the ground. Sebastian cackled with glee as the thwapping of the descending chopper grew louder, the wind more fierce.

Sebastian grabbed a gun from the back of his waist, cocked its barrel, and leveled it at Silas's head as he recovered, a mixture of defeat and agony splaying across his face.

"I figured it would be you, riding in on your white horse to save the day. Always the way it was with you, brother."

"You stupid, stupid person!" Silas roared, throat thick with emotion and spittle flying from his mouth. "What the hell is wrong with you? Why are you in bed with these, these people? With *Nous*?"

Sebastian laughed at his brother's pathetic attempts to reason.

"Oh, Silas. You really are so thick, aren't you? You wouldn't understand. But you will, soon enough. These Germans know a thing or two about the Zeitgeist and what it will take to advance humanity into the next realm of enlightenment and progress and possibility."

Silas shook his head in disbelief, his face twisting with anger. "What the hell are you talking about? You of all people, an educated man of science who prides himself on standing above the sheeple, as you say," he sneered. "Chasing after a mythical Holy Grail?"

"It's not as mythical as you may think," he sneered back, waving the gun in the air toward Silas. "And any so-called relicologist worth his salt would know what was nearly discovered..." He trailed off as if stopping himself for saying anything more.

A black rope snaked down to the ground from above. Sebastian saw it, flashed Silas another grin, and waved. "Au revoir mon frère."

He grabbed the Nanteos Cup case, shoved it back under one arm, then leapt for the rope, grabbing on with his other hand and twisting his legs around the rest of it for support.

Within seconds, the chopper above started slowly lifting, along with Sebastian and the Grail relic.

Like hell you're getting away!

Silas scrambled to his knees, then lunged forward for the tail of the rope as it ascended. Success!

He grabbed it with both hands, but just barely. As it continued rising, he was swinging wildly eight or ten feet from the ground. Then the chopper stopped, hovering above the barren field as if waiting for the fight to play itself out.

"Sy!" a voice screamed at him from above. "You were always a dogged asshole, weren't you? Always nipping at my heels."

Silas screamed and thrust one hand over the other, then again—hand over fist, hand over fist until he had gained a few feet on the rope and was nearly at Sebastian's feet.

"I don't think so, brother."

In one motion, Sebastian inched his body down the rope, then brought one foot down on Silas's hand. Then again and again, ripping the skin off his brother's fingers.

Silas had to let go from the force of the blow. "What the hell are you doing?!" He was swaying, holding on with one hand, now fifteen feet from the ground.

His brother didn't answer. Instead, he grinned wildly, his eyes reflecting the same maddened satisfaction. He inched himself lower and stomped on Silas's remaining hand. Once, then twice, bloodying and bruising his knuckles. That's all it took.

Silas let go, falling to the ground feet first, arms raised. Immediately, his Ranger training kicked in. He relaxed his body, bent his knees, then brought his arms down and leaned to the right.

The impact was instant, but he was able to absorb it through his legs and fall to the side, bringing his arms on the sides of his head with elbows facing forward and fingers laced behind. He bounced once, then landed hard. He was sore, and his legs hurt like hell, but he had survived.

He scrambled to stand as the chopper lifted higher, Sebastian now climbing into the side door.

"Sebastian!" he screamed as the steel bird retreated farther into the sky.

As it disappeared in the distance, the sky felt as though it were spinning, the earth as though it were wobbling on its axis from a minor earthquake. Silas heaved heavy breaths as if his life depended on it. And it did.

He fell to his knees and clutched his chest, then doubled-over and pushed against his knees.

He was having a panic attack.

CHAPTER 13

Get a grip, Grey!

Instinctively, he reached a trembling hand toward a front pocket in his jacket searching for a little blue pill that would take it all away. In the moment, he had forgotten he had dumped the pills a week back before his trip to Punta Cana. He had been getting along without them just fine for the past few months. Figured he had kicked the demons that had plagued him since his tours in the Middle East. Plus, only a weak man needed a little blue pill to get him through life. And he was sick of being weak.

Except now his twitching fingers were inching their way into his pocket—and coming up dry.

He eased his head down in disbelief at the hand inside his jacket, then slowly inserted his other hand into the other pocket. Same result: nothing.

He closed his eyes and tried to recall the coping mechanism he had developed after coming back home a wrecked man, but it was no use. His brain wouldn't work, reverting back to the same state of mush that had lit the fuse to his post-traumatic disorder in the first place.

It was a day not unlike that day, except about a hundred

degrees warmer. The sun was riding high in the same kind of cloudless sky, though he and his men were driving through the desert sands of Iraq toward a village to play nice with the locals. Community relations, the chiefs up the ladder called it. Didn't matter what they called it, so long as it was a thousand miles from seeing any combat he was fine with it.

Until it wasn't.

Their convoy had been set to deliver truckloads of goods, practical things like water and canned food. They were also set to play a rematch game of football, or soccer, or whatever they called it in those parts with the local kids. Silas was particularly looking forward to a rematch against the scrappy Iraqi who bested him at the goal not once but twice. But some other locals had other plans, which involved a staged breakdown in the middle of a desert road two klicks from hell and a series of IEDs carefully placed and ready to explode by remote detonation.

One moment, Silas and his buddy Colton were shooting the breeze, dreaming about what they would do when they got out of the military and got back to the life waiting for them back home. The next moment, their Humvee was an overturned beast missing half its legs with a gaping wound in its side. The same for his buddy. Half of Colton had been blown to bits, and the parts that were intact and barely alive had landed in Silas's lap.

It was in moments of anxiety-inducing chaos, the kind Silas was experiencing in a barren, nearly-frozen field in the middle of Glastonbury, England—it was moments like that one when the memories of those smells of burnt flesh and singed hair, that twisted face of disbelief and the realization of a life cut short, the eyes that slowly drained like sand through an hourglass until it reached the end and the pupils dilated to nothingness—it was then that those foul, possessed memories came rushing to the surface, anxiety and fear submerging his consciousness and drowning out any hope and life.

Sebastian. Nous. Sebastian and Nous. It made no sense...

And without his little blue pill or someone to bring him back to reality, he was dead in the water of that confusion.

Celeste reached him first. He was still doubled-over, his body rocking back and forth, his face still twisted with brow crinkled and mouth wrenched open with that pained expression of grief and confusion and anger at the sight of his brother.

"Silas, Silas!" she said coming up in front of him "Oh, dear God, what happened to you?"

He said nothing, the betrayal and the realization that his very own flesh-and-blood was actively working against him and actively plotting to destroy his faith positively paralyzing him. He thought the gig during the election was a one-off. Now he knew the truth.

"Silas!" she said again, this time louder. She took his shoulders by both hands and shook them.

No recognition, no movement, no nothing.

Gapinski huffed over and plopped down next to Celeste. "Good Lord, what's wrong with him?"

"Don't know entirely, but he's positively catatonic."

Gapinski looked toward the horizon as the black helicopter receded into the distance, its thwapping no longer audible. "Do you think Nous did something to him? Maybe shot him up with some drug to make him go all One Flew Over the Cuckoo's Nest?"

"Haven't a clue. But it looks like some dissociative state brought on by acute stress or trauma. He's apparently suffered from bouts of PTSD since returning from military service. Kept it at bay with medication. I've seen him enter milder states, but nothing like this."

"Nous be damned!" he growled.

Silas slouched against Celeste's hold, still non-responsive.

She huffed in frustration, but also concern for her comrade, her mate. "Agent Grey!" she said more commandingly than before. He stirred, his head bobbing with recognition. Then she said, "Soldier, wake the bloody hell up!"

That seemed to do the trick. He snapped his head to attention, eyes wide with fright and mouth still agape as if permanently in shock.

She locked eyes with him, forcing him to meet her gaze and follow her eyes. "Listen to me, soldier. Don't take your eyes off of me, do you understand?"

His eyes flickered with recognition.

Celeste's stomach flittered with hope; her mouth curled upward slightly in response.

"I'm going to count down from a thousand, and you're going to count with me. Do you understand, agent?"

His head lolled forward.

"Soldier Grey!"

His head snapped back to attention, jaw clenched and eyes more lively. Celeste was smart to take him back to the scene of the original onset of PTSD as a soldier when he would have responded instantly to such a command.

She nodded, then started counting backward from a thousand.

1000...999...998...997.

She was parroting back to Silas the ritual that he himself had developed through therapy to get him out of such states when his pills weren't around. However, those episodes were far milder than the one Celeste was helping him climb out of. They didn't involve ultimate betrayal from his brother. And for the third time!

949...948...947...946.

He was mumbling along with her now, joining in the countdown. His eyes blinked with recognition as his mouth moved in sync with Celeste's, and his breathing became more natural, less labored.

918...917...916...915.

Suddenly, Silas broke off the count and looked at Gapinski, as if coming out of a hypnotic trance. He turned toward Celeste again, his face twisting with confusion until falling with recognition.

He took a deep breath and sat down with a heavy plop, head between his legs and saying nothing.

Celeste looked to Gapinski for answers. He shrugged, then came alongside Silas.

"Buddy, it's alright. Celeste and me, Gapinski, we're right here, man." He knelt down and grabbed Silas's shoulder, but the man jolted. He kept his arm there, squeezing Silas with reassurance until he popped his head up and took another deep breath.

Celeste took a deep breath, as well, not knowing how to proceed. She looked to Gapinski again, then started to say something before Silas interrupted her.

"There's something I have to tell you both," he said slowly, breathy.

She looked at Gapinski again, relieved that Silas seemed to be back to his regular self, but also concerned with what was going on.

Gapinski said, "Spill it, brother. We're here for you."

Silas glanced at the man and smiled weakly, then shook his head. "I don't think you're going to like what I have to say." He paused and took another deep breath, then said, "It's my brother."

"Sebastian?" Celeste said, brow furrowed and head cocked to one side.

Silas swallowed hard and nodded.

"I don't under..." Then she took a deep breath, swallowed hard herself, and sat back on the ground.

"What's your brother got to do with anything?" Gapinski said.

Silas looked up, the pained expression on his face telling him all he needed to know.

"Wait, was that Sebastian you chased? The one who nabbed the Grail and shimmied up into the chopper? He's with Nous?"

Silas looked away and back to the ground, saying nothing.

"Blimey, Silas," Celeste said. "But this makes no sense? Out of the ocean blue the man joins the Church's archenemy and shows up here, in Glastonbury, England, of all places to steal a purported Holy Grail relic? Utter rubbish! I can't make sense of it."

He continued staring at the ground, a mixture of disgust at the truth of the matter and regret at hiding it twisting in his gut. He took another deep breath knowing what he needed to do. He said, "It's not out of the blue."

"Excuse me. I can't understand you?"

He lifted his head and cleared his throat. "I said, it wasn't out of the blue, him being here and working for Nous. He was involved with them months ago. And I knew about the connection."

The two fell silent, the weight of the revelation settling in.

"What do you mean you knew months ago?"

Silas lifted his head. "I found out he was working for Nous during our last mission, when I met Amos Young at the Lincoln Memorial. He showed up with the guy. Apparently, he had been helping Nous get Young elected."

She sat forward, her face growing hard. "And you said nothing? Your brother, working to undermine the Church and destroy the Christian faith—you kept that to yourself?"

Silas said nothing.

Gapinski moved next to Celeste, and said, "Jeez Louise, Silas. That's some heavy ball of wax you just tossed us."

He looked up at Celeste, her face registering clear displeasure at him hiding the truth from them, from her. "I know," he said softly. "And I'm sorry I didn't say anything before. I guess I was ashamed of the truth. Embarrassed, scared even, that my own brother was Nousati. Didn't want to acknowledge it. Thought, if I just left it unsaid, maybe it would become un-true again." He paused, then said, "But I understand I probably put us and the Order and the mission in jeopardy by not saying anything. I take full responsibility for that."

She held his gaze. Then she took a breath and softened her face. She closed her eyes and nodded her head. "I understand. You did what any of us would do, I reckon. But let's have no more secrets, alright? Full disclosure next time, especially something of this magnitude."

He nodded. "Understood, boss." A smile curled on one side of his face.

She reflected him with a wry grin of her own. She stood and offered her hand to help him up off the ground. He looked at it, then took it.

She led them back toward the gravel path, and said, "Let's go have ourselves a chat with Radcliffe. He's going to need a full debrief, including the revelation about your brother. I'll warn you, saying he's going to be displeased is an understatement."

"I understand," Silas said, limping from the beating his brother had given him and the truth of his identity.

Gapinski said, "Don't worry, pal. We all step in it. Some more than others. Don't let me forget to tell you what I stepped in on my first day on the job! But it's all good. Because, you see, we're family. And family sticks together, through thick and thin, right?"

Silas smiled weakly and nodded. He understood in theory what he meant. But in practice...that was a whole world he was entirely unaccustomed to.

Which the last hour had proven in spades.

CHAPTER 14

Sebastian Grey eased his nose into the wide-mouthed Baccarat crystal wine glass and breathed in the Malbec's juicy, spicy aroma. This one was French, and so it was heavily laden with the scent of tobacco and coffee with a strong backbone of blackberry. He opened his mouth and eased the crimson liquid inside as the plush Bombardier Challenger glided through the clear blue skies toward his next destination. He closed his eyes and held the heavy liquid in his mouth, its savory, tart, firm tannins tingling his taste buds with pleasure and putting every fiber of his body at ease.

After what he just went through, he needed it.

He swallowed the wine and settled back into the creamy leather seat, adjusting the flamingo-pink pillow at his lower back for comfort during the rest of the journey. He rested both arms on the chair rests, holding the crystal glass by its stem with one hand and cupping the soft leather armrest with the other. He breathed in deeply, held the breath, then exhaled, taking in the sight of privilege around him, with the Persian-rug runner of intricate weave paving the way through an aisle of cream carpet, housed in a cylinder of pure white with polished mahogany trim and chrome nobs and buttons summoning whatever its pampered passengers wished.

Sebastian was certainly accustomed to the finer things in life, having meticulously crafted his own world using his private tuition salary combined with penny-pinching know how. A life of expensive sweaters and wine, vacations in Europe and South America, and a row house in the urban up-and-comer Adam's Morgan district in DC complete with suede recliners, oak cabinetry, and baby grand piano was the life he lived. His father hadn't been good for much growing up, being mostly absent and emotionally distant saving the world from terrorists—that is, before a pair of them took him out at the Pentagon. But the one thing he did well was instill in his boys the art of financial responsibility combined with elbow grease and stick-to-itiveness. Sebastian's affinity for luxe was his own doing, but it was made possible thanks to Dad's fatherly advice. And now, flush with cash from his recent freelance gig with the organization calling themselves Nous, let's just say his luxe life was now set for life.

Sebastian used one of those chrome buttons to recline his seat back. He took another sip of his wine, then another and purred with contentment. He could get used to this.

He smiled at the thought, at how preposterous it all was that he of all people was running around like some special-ops lunatic doing the bidding of a spiritual entity stretching back millennia. That was his brother, not him. And yet it felt right, felt proper. Felt good, even, that he had a real chance to make a difference in a world gripped by sectarianism and the nonsense being peddled as religion nowadays.

Oddly, it felt evangelistic...

He shuddered at the notion and looked out his window. Sebastian Grey, an evangelist! He scoffed at the thought and drained his glass. He looked up toward the front of the aircraft, held up his glass, and nodded at a young man for a refill. He promptly walked over with a bottle wrapped by a linen napkin to prevent spillage. He poured another half glass of the divine red nectar, then turned the bottle with the flick of his wrist and withdrew it like a professional sommelier.

Sebastian thanked the man and promptly took a mouthful, then he fixed his gaze on the horizon once more, contemplating the turn of events in his life that brought him to sitting on a private jet as an agent of the archenemy of the Church. He frowned at the thought, and a curious sadness began welling up inside, chased by a feeling of regret, remorse even.

It wasn't supposed to be this way...

The Grey family was a committed Catholic family. Dad fell down at many parental responsibilities trying his damnedest to raise the two boys himself after their mother died giving birth. But the other thing he got right was taking his boys to Sunday Mass, week in and week out. Never missed a Sunday, no matter where they were stationed during his military career. Oh, the Grey twins protested, Silas more than he. But Dad brought them up right in the Church, having baptized them into the faith at birth and later enrolling them in Catechism and shepherding them until First Communion.

Between the boys, he was the more religious of the two, having been drawn towards spiritual things at an early age. While Silas had always been more interested in earthly pursuits—sports, girls, his hair—Sebastian gravitated toward the spiritual, pestering Dad with questions he didn't know the answers to and then pestering a string of priests who offered answers that only partly satisfied his curious religious heart. He hadn't so much doubted faith, like famous Thomas from the Christian Gospels, but questioned it and poked it and prodded it, even at a young age. He was like the father of the young possessed boy who asked Jesus to heal him. When Christ responded, "If you can believe, all things are possible to him who believes," the father offered a retort that rang true to Sebastian: "Lord, I believe; help my unbelief!"

That's the way it always was with him, a tenuous walk straddling belief and unbelief. But, he persisted, becoming an altar boy and serving Father Rafferty during Mass, holding the liturgical books, preparing the gifts, ringing the bell shortly before consecration. His joy of joys, though, was serving at the parish soup kitchen, ladling soup and joking with the folks in line.

His mouth curled into a stiff smile at the thought. *Oh, how far I have fallen.*

And he knew the exact reason why it all began to unravel. Time, location, and moment.

Moments...

Sebastian clenched his jaw at the thought, then took another mouthful of the wine, letting the tobacco and coffee and blackberry carry away his lingering pain and humiliation and shame.

Since then he had been on a quest to dismantle the lie he had been fed from birth. The lie that God loves us and has a plan for us, that the Church is his vessel of love, the hope of the world that stewards and shares that plan. The very institution that ravaged his soul and then left him holding the shattered pieces.

"Was that your damn plan, you damn Spaghetti Monster?" he whispered, gripping his armrest and his wine glass even tighter.

Suddenly, his thumb shattered through the rim of the delicate crystal from his vice-like grip. He dropped his mouth in surprise and almost dropped the glass. A quarter-size piece of jagged crystal sank to the bottom of the chalice, his blood running down into the nectar from the underside of his thumb and mingling with the crimson liquid.

He winced at the pain as the same flight attendant came up

to take the glass from him. The man offered him a cold, damp linen to staunch the bleeding.

"Thanks," Sebastian said, taking the offering. The blood was running down his hand now, so he mopped it up with the towel before firmly pressing it against the cut. He took a deep breath, then settled back against his seat.

"Can I get you anything else, sir? A bandage or arrange for a doctor at the landing site?"

Sebastian waved the man off. "I'm fine, really. More embarrassed than in pain."

"Are you sure?"

He took a sharp breath and scrunched up his face, almost laying into the poor soul. Instead, he thanked him for his concern and asked for a Band-Aid.

The man nodded and trotted off in search of the first aid kit.

He exhaled and stared back out toward the horizon. A few minutes later, he winced again as he removed the linen to check the damage. It was a goodly cut, that was for sure, stretching the width of his large thumb just beneath the knuckle. But not too deep. The knuckle must have done most of the heavy lifting breaking the thin crystal. But the white fabric had been transformed into a set of red and pink watercolors.

The bleeding had lessened, thank—

He almost thought "thank God." Funny how childhood and childish spiritual habits tended to linger deep in the recesses of the brain, how they are tapped into on impulse during moments of trial and tribulation. Whether thanking the Spaghetti Monster for saving one's thumb or whimpering to sweet Jesus to come and take them to their sweet by and by from the belly of a foxhole.

Same stupid habits, same stupid results. Nothing!

Because God knows—he chuckled to himself, he had done it again. Anyway, *Spaghetti Monster* knows he sure cried out for relief those twenty-some years ago from the clutches of evil, praying that the fires of hell would consume the Satanic forces consuming him!

He breathed a heavy breath as he continued applying pressure to his thumb, trying to damper his rising blood pressure at the memory pushing its way to the surface.

I know what I need...

He closed his eyes and shook his head. *No! It's been too long. I vowed never again.*

But his tongue tingled with anticipation. Then his forearms itched from the memory of a hundred moments of relief born from that skin, that blood.

His blood.

Sebastian looked up to see the flight attendant walking his way. He stiffened in his seat, straightening himself and looking as not-guilty as he could, as if he was blameworthy simply for the impulse to carry out the deed from his past. He smiled as the man handed him something.

"Here you go. Just what the doctor ordered. I also got you another towel to wrap your thumb, along with a plastic bag for discarding the used one. Is it doing OK?"

He took the Band-Aid and damp linen and nodded. "Thanks. And, yes, I believe I'll live."

The man nodded back. "Good to hear. Would you like a refill?"

He thought about it but passed. "I imagine I should leave the bubbly well enough alone for now. Probably the reason for my clumsiness to begin with."

They shared a chuckle at the accident. The man told Sebastian to let him know if he needed anything, then went back to the front of the aircraft.

Sebastian winced as he removed the blood-soaked towel and deposited it in the plastic bag. Blood seeped from the wound, triggering within him a hunger. His mouth watered and gut seized with pleasure at the thought of ingesting the coppery liquid, his drug of choice that had gotten him through those teenage afternoons.

He looked up at the front and around behind him. No one was looking. He was free to imbibe.

And he did. He quickly brought the side of his thumb up to his mouth and sucked at the point of laceration. It ached from being reopened, but he didn't care. His head was swimming with delight at drinking from the coppery fount of pleasure.

That's enough. Just a taste.

He removed his thumb from his mouth and glanced up to make sure no one was looking. He was still good. He quickly applied the new towel to the wound with pressure to staunch the bleeding once more. He would apply the bandage once they landed.

Sinking in his seat and riding high, he considered the next series of moves that would offer the world a taste of a different kind of blood. The kind that was spilled into that chalice, whichever one it was that had been floating around in the world for nearly two millennia. The kind bearing the remnant of the enlightened One he had once served that would be used to offer a new and better kind of salvation to the world.

"Sir," a different man said interrupting his thoughts, having come up behind him from the rear of the plane. One of the hired help Rudolf Borg had sent along.

Sebastian startled and transfixed him with a glare of irritation. "Yes, what is it?"

"Rudolf Borg rang and said the excavations Nous is undergoing are proceeding as planned."

"Good. So they have resurrected the Holy Grail, then?"

The man shook his head. "Not yet, but our men on the ground did reach a breakthrough."

Sebastian stared at the man, waiting for him to continue. "Go on!" he snapped.

"Ground penetrating radar discovered a hidden passage that lay undiscovered."

Sebastian sat up straighter. "That is a breakthrough."

"They'll continue the excavation through the day and into the night. The hope is that by daybreak some sort of chamber will be unearthed, just in time for your arrival. But we shall see."

"Excellent news." He went to turn back toward the window for a bit of rest. The man cleared his throat, interrupting him instead. "Is there more?"

"We're ready to broadcast, sir."

Sebastian sat up again and looked at the man with confusion. "What, here? Now?"

"Borg wanted to get the message out as soon as possible now that we've secured the Glastonbury Grail and made our descent for the final chalice."

Another man came down the aisle and set up a camera. The one man held up a small clip mic, then held it out as if offering to attach it to Sebastian.

He sighed and nodded. "Alright. I suppose now is as good a time as any. "

Time to evangelize to the masses the good news of the new era of salvation.

CHAPTER 15

LONDON, ENGLAND.

The revelation of Sebastian continued to twist Silas's stomach into a bundle of knots as the car dipped underneath Westminster Abbey, the London extension of the Order of Thaddeus and secondary European operation center of SEPIO. He tried willing away the truth of it all over the course of the three-hour drive into London, his brain working its best to rationalize it into a dream. But the nightmare was reality, the undeniable fact of his brother had sunk its teeth deep into his consciousness. And it wasn't letting go.

My brother is an operative of Nous. My brother hates the Church. He wants to kill Christianity.

After Silas had recovered from his episode in Glastonbury, the trio left the Tor and carefully made their way back to their parked car. The authorities had begun arriving in force, and the SEPIO agents were barely able to slip out of the city unnoticed. The last thing they had wanted was to get wrapped up with the ensuing investigation given what they were up against. Along the way, Celeste dialed Radcliffe, who apparently was already halfway across the Atlantic. He thought it best to be closer to the action given the gravity and mystery of the ongoing mission. As they drove and he flew, she brought him up to speed on the developments in Glastonbury—what they learned about the region, with its connection to paganism; the viewing of the Nanteos Cup, and ensuing terrorist attack on the civilians; the theft of the fourth purported Grail relic, and the explosive identity of the main Nous agent responsible: Sebastian Grey.

Radcliffe was positively gobsmacked at the revelation, couldn't believe it given how the man had helped them earlier in the year at the Church of the Holy Sepulcher. She agreed, saying how confusing it all was. It was then that Silas had to come clean and tell him what he had known, that his brother had been working with Nous at least since the American presidential election—and maybe longer.

The Order Master was gentler than Silas probably would have been with someone keeping to himself a key piece of intel. However, he said he understood the dynamic, but instructed Silas never to let something like that happen again, especially now that he was an official agent with SEPIO and member of the Order. Silas apologized and agreed. Radcliffe instructed the team to rendezvous at the Order's London extension and satellite operation center. They would consider next steps and try to coordinate the pieces of the puzzle together that still obscured the meaning of the mystery surrounding the Holy Grail and Nous's interest in it.

LED lights embedded in the wall flashed by as it guided the trio downward toward their destination, reminding Silas of the trip he first took earlier in the year when he was brought to the Washington National Cathedral. The layout was similar, with an east-side entrance off Abingdon Street servicing their spiraling descent into a well-lit cement parking structure. Gapinski pulled into an open spot between a Land Rover and Jaguar, both black and both sporting tinted windows.

They exited the vehicle, and Celeste led the way through the entrance, its frosted-glass doors swooshing open automati-

cally. The familiar sanitized air from the Washington headquarters, smelling of a thunderstorm and static, seemed to ease
the tension that had built up inside Silas, as if it helped remind
him why he was in England in the first place as an agent of
SEPIO—to contend for the once-for-all faith entrusted to God's
holy people, the Church of Christ. His brother might be
involved in helping to undermine that faith and destroy the
Church, but he would be damned if he went without fighting
him tooth-and-nail along the way.

She continued guiding them through the slate-gray corri-
dors arrayed with doors and entry keypads. It was as if the
extension site was an exact replica of the facility in Washington,
only on a smaller scale. They arrived at a set of dark oak double
doors that reminded Silas of Radcliffe's study. Celeste pressed
her palm against the entry pad. It pulsed blue before pulsing
green and unlocking the doors. The inside had a similar vibe as
DC, with its wood-paneled walls and floor-to-ceiling bookcases, the fireplace with popping fire and lingering smoke, the
red-and-blue-patterned Persian rug on top of hardwood floors
with a set of overstuffed leather couches and chairs—but,
again, on a smaller scale.

"Nice digs," Gapinski said. He continued walking toward an
alcove at the other end of the room opposite the fireplace. "If
it's anything like Radcliffe's joint, there should be....Oh, yeah!
Plenty of libation to grease our planning pow-wow. You two
care for some Scotch?"

"Yes, please," the two said in unison.

"Coming right up!"

Silas flopped down on one of the couches and brought his
feet up onto its leathery surface. He nursed a headache with his
forefinger that had begun needling the back of his eyes an hour
ago. Celeste came up behind him at the head of the couch,
knelt down, and began rubbing his shoulders. He startled, not
expecting the show of affection.

"Just you relax," she said. "I reckon you've earned it, given the beating you went through. Actually and metaphorically speaking."

He almost protested, but he relented. He smiled and nodded instead. "Thanks. I guess I do."

"Now, don't you go feeling all lucky because the pretty Brit is giving you a back rub," Gapinski said, walking over with their drinks. "She's given me the same treatment after I've gotten my butt kicked a time or two." He winked at Silas as he handed him his Scotch, neat. He set Celeste's Scotch-on-the-rocks down on a wooden coffee table commanding the center of the meeting space.

"Thanks, mate." She stopped rubbing, grabbed the drink, and took a sip. Then she patted Silas on the shoulders and withdrew to her own overstuffed chair.

The door to the study clicked unlocked and in sauntered Rowan Radcliffe, his black cassock with golden buttons and thin red piping swishing with each step.

Celeste said, "Rowan, dear, you don't look your best."

"Caught a terrible cold crossing the Atlantic. And I've forgotten what travel does to this old sack of bones."

She got out of her seat and gave him a gentle hug. "Care for some tea?"

He smiled and sighed. "That would be lovely."

"Coming right up!" She walked over to the alcove, retrieved a teacup from a cupboard, plucked a sachet of English breakfast from a tin, and prepared his cup.

"How are you getting along, my boy?" Radcliffe asked Silas as he sauntered to the couch.

Silas swung his feet down to the carpet, winced, and stood. "Took a beating, but I'll live."

The old man offered a smile of compassion, then put his hands on Silas's shoulders. "I mean the bit about your brother. Couldn't have been easy standing your ground against your enemy, face to face, only to realize that he was your own flesh and blood, unmasked before your very eyes."

Silas's eyes fell to the floor, and he swallowed back a sudden rise of emotion. Then he looked up and offered a weak smile. "No, it wasn't. But Sebastian made his bed. And I guess he's ready and willing to lie in it." He shrugged, then said, "Not much I can do about that."

Radcliffe nodded and withdrew his arms. "Unfortunately, there isn't. When it comes to matters of faith, we all make our beds, and we all lie down in them—in one bed or another."

He wandered over to the other overstuffed chair opposite of Celeste's and settled in, blowing his nose with a handkerchief he withdrew from his cassock.

Celeste walked over with his cup of tea. "Two lumps of sugar and a spot of milk. Just as you like it if I remember correctly."

"Ahh, blessed child, you have. Thank you, my dear." Radcliffe took a sip, and then he sighed with pleasure. "Only a fellow Brit can appreciate the finer luxuries of a good tea with a solid backbone." He took another sip and smacked his lips, then set it down on an end table next to him.

He went to say something, but the phone buzzed, interrupting him. He huffed and punched the line. "Yes, what is it?"

"Another broadcast, chief," Zoe said through the speaker.

"Not again," he sighed.

"Afraid so. Similar to before, all over the internet. Facebook, Twitter, YouTube, you name it."

Radcliffe was already out of his seat and making his way toward the television hanging above the fireplace. He used the remote to turn it on, and then he changed the channel to the BBC. When he did, there was a gasp behind him.

He turned around, his brow wrinkled with confusion. Celeste was holding her hand over her mouth. Silas was looking at the floor, arms crossed and shaking his head.

Gapinski stood with his hands on his hips, face twisted with disgust.

He walked back over to the group, and said, "What the bloody hell is it? You look like you've seen a ghost."

Celeste said nothing. Gapinski put a hand on Silas's shoulder as the blond-hair man with similar features as him began his broadcast.

"Hello, fellow humans. My name is Doctor Sebastian Grey, a scientist at George Washington University. And I am here with a message of enlightenment and liberation."

"Dear me..." Radcliffe said slumping into his chair.

As Sebastian spoke, his eyes gleamed with delight and he wore an inviting smile that encouraged the listener to engage him. "Like many of you around the world, I was born and raised on religion. In my case, the Christian variety, though only by happenstance since I was born into a Catholic family in the middle of Christian America. Some of you listening will have been born into a different kind of faith tradition. Again, purely by happenstance, the circumstances of your birth and upbringing, the religious dynamics of your country or region of the world entirely outside of your control."

"What are you playing at, young fool," Radcliffe whispered. He caught himself and glanced at Silas, frowning. "Sorry, my boy."

"It's fine," Silas huffed, then took a mouthful of Scotch. "The man truly is a damn fool."

"For years," Sebastian continued, "I was thoroughly captivated by my religion, with its rituals and rhythms, its teachings and tenor of the faith. But..." he trailed off, then added, "things changed. I grew up. Escaped the bubble of my cloistered Christian life and ventured out into the real world, where I discovered a whole host of ideas and ideals that were far more compatible with reality than the sort officially sanctioned by the Church. I followed my heart's fascination with the universe and became a scientist. And yet, with all of my study of physics and material properties and quarks, I never lost sight of the ground of our being embedded in the cosmos. Oh, there was a time, to be sure, when I fancied pure atheism in graduate school. But the more I explored the fullness of what the universe has to offer, the more I discovered that there is an eternal, immutable, all-pervading principle that binds our existence—manifesting in the polarities of spirit and matter, life and form. All matter is ensouled by life, you see. Of which the collective religious consciousness testifies."

The man chuckled, licking his lips and smiling and moving slightly closer in toward the viewing public. "Now, you may be asking yourself, why on earth is a scientist so interested in the collective religious consciousness? Because there is a divine wisdom embedded within the universe itself that links all living things. Life is everywhere throughout the cosmos because all originates from the same unknowable divine source. Everything from the subatomic to vegetation, slithering and four-legged creatures and fowl to humans, the planets orbiting the sun and the stars at the center of countless more planetary systems—all of it is alive and humming, evolving and progressing to greater possibilities. And at the root of it all is a divinity, in which every facet of the cosmos lives and moves and has its being, expressing itself through spiritual, intellectual, psychological, ethereal, and material ranges of consciousness and substance."

He was waving his hands and working up a visible sweat now. Silas had never seen him act like this before, so spiritually passionate, so religiously preachy. So, dare he say, *evangelistic*. It was unnerving to see the transformation, from atheist to proselyte of New Ageism. He didn't even recognize the man. Although, that wasn't entirely true. There was a spark of the teenager who had been a passionate, preachy Catholic before he jettisoned the faith.

Now look at him...

Sebastian continued, "To be sure, there has been an ungodly level of antagonism between science and religion, especially for the past two hundred years with the dawn of the Enlightenment. But this didn't have to be. In fact, the Christian Church itself could have moderated the conflict." He sighed and shook his head, letting out a short *tsk-tsk*. "But, alas, the early teachings of the Church concerning such matters were lost. Nay, destroyed and suppressed by those in power who sought to subject the Roman world to a life of ignorance. And they succeeded, for a dreadfully long time. We call that season the Dark Ages for a reason. Anyway, the forebears of *gnosis,* of pure, unadulterated knowledge who were the intellectual heart of the early Church, possessed a divine knowledge of nature so true that it could not possibly have come into collision with the scientific inquiries and insights of the recent generations. Unfortunately, they lost the fight, outnumbered and outmatched and outflanked by the Church, and so the conflict between the informed and the ignorant, between the scientifically enlightened and the religiously committed has raged."

Sebastian took a break from his sermonizing and settled back into his seat, gripping the plush, creamy armrests as he stared into the camera, his eyes bright and mouth smiling with delight. Then he continued.

"However, a few days ago my colleague spoke of a new dawn, leveraging one of the greatest assets humanity has enjoyed for the past two millennia. The person of the Christ. Now, perhaps I am biased, given my Catholic predilections with its commitments to the man Jesus of Nazareth," he smiled and chuckled softly again. "But the Christ is bigger than a mere mortal. The other world religions give testimony to that. After all, the word *Christ* is simply the Anglicized *Christos* from the Greek, which simply means *Messiah. Savior. Liberator.* And isn't that what the world needs now? Liberation from the systems of chaos, from the ignorance that blinds and binds humanity?"

He leaned in again, bringing his hands together in front of him and drawing his face into a series pose. "No doubt there was a power that flowed through that man's veins, a power that could command legions of followers to deny themselves and take up their cross and follow him—both metaphorically and literally! There was something in that man Jesus' very blood that has the power to form a nucleus of the universal brotherhood of humanity, without the distinction of race or color, creed or caste, sex or sexuality that we ourselves can tap into in order to push the human race forward into a new realm of enlightenment and divine salvation."

"Geez Louise, this guy is mental," Gapinski said.

Silas glanced at him but said nothing, his face set as flint, his mind reeling in a bundle of confusing and contradictory thoughts. He had no way to explain what was going on.

"And we aim, myself and the fellow you met earlier, Rudolf Borg, we aim to leverage the full power of that blood in order to offer the world a new path for saving our lives, for *liberating* ourselves. One that follows in his goodly example of love and insight in order to offer the noble ideal dream of a brotherhood of all faiths, influenced by his teaching and way of love emanating from the universal divine essence and human ideal. In two days' time, at the dawn of the Winter Solstice, a new humanity will be birthed, guided by the blood of the Christ. Until then, remember: there is no religion higher than truth. And as the man Jesus said, the truth will set you free. It will be your liberation."

Sebastian smiled and waved. The screen went black and then to color bars.

Radcliffe turned off the television, his face downturned.

The four said nothing. The only sound was the crackle and pop of the fire as they contemplated the meaning of it all.

CHAPTER 16

So, it's come to this. Me on one side, Sebastian on the other.

Perhaps it was poetic that their roles would be reversed from childhood: the altar boy turned pagan, the heathen turned Church operative. It took every ounce of mental energy, as well as the strengthening hand of the Holy Spirit, not to crumble under the weight of what had become of their relationship, what was left of his family.

He had to giggle at how preposterous it all was. At first, it was a small slip through the nose. Another followed, this time from the belly. Then he couldn't control himself, his mind and body letting loose in a cascade of guffaws that triggered a stream of tears from the peals of laughter emanating from deep within himself. Right there, outstretched on the couch, his head whipped back with uncontrolled hysterics. His arms clenched his stomach because it hurt so bad. He couldn't stop himself. He didn't want to stop himself. It was the only thing he could think to do without spiraling down the rabbit hole of anxiety-induced pain and panic once again.

He knew the other three had to be thinking he had seriously flipped his lid. Perhaps he had.

And then it stopped. With one final hurrah and one big sigh

of relief from having expelled his body of the pent-up emotions that wouldn't translate into tears of sorrow. He hadn't been able to plumb the depths of that part of himself since his tours in the Middle East, still wounded from what he had experienced. Laughing about it was the closest he could come to an emotional expression, as inappropriate as it seemed given the circumstances and stakes.

Gapinski was the first to respond. "Uhh, you alright, dude?"

Silas turned toward him, smiling. "Yes. I do believe I am."

"You jolly well didn't sound like it, my boy," Radcliffe added.

"Well, what the heck am I supposed to do, Radcliffe?" he said sitting up. He shook his head. "Sorry, didn't mean to sound so aggressive. Anyway, laughing about it all is about the best response I can come up with at this point. Especially in response to that New Age mumbo-jumbo we heard, straight from my brother's mouth, the scientist-turned-terrorist."

Celeste said nothing. Instead, she reached over and squeezed his knee, offering a smile of support. He smiled back.

Gapinski drained his Scotch, and said, "All I have to say is, what the heck is that man smoking? Because I want in. That was some heavy sh—"

"Gapinski," Celeste interrupted.

"What? It was."

"Theosophic stuff and nonsense is what that was!" Radcliffe scoffed.

"Theo-whatchamacallit?" Gapinski asked.

"Theosophy," Silas said. "Literally, *divine wisdom*. It was a pseudo-spiritual movement that formed in the late nineteenth century that's stuck around for some time now in the West. Equal parts religious, philosophic, and scientific."

"A pantheistic form of ancient Gnosticism is what it is," Radcliffe added. "And, oddly, highly influential in the National Socialist German Workers' Party."

"The Nazis?" the three said in unison.

"Like, the goose-steppers from mid-twentieth-century Germany?" Gapinski said.

Silas turned to him with raised brow, and said, "Do you know of any other Nazis?"

He shrugged. "Some skinheads on my grandpappy's side of the family, actually."

Celeste cleared her throat, as if to get the discussion back on track. "Tell us more about that connection, Rowan."

He adjusted his posture, as if settling in for the long haul. "Theosophy was largely the invention of a one Helena Blavatsky, a Russo-German aristocrat. It was arguably the most influential occult doctrine of the late nineteenth century after its first society dedicated to the neo-spiritualism was founded in New York City in 1875. Apparently, Blavatsky was inspired by her travels to India and Tibet and drew heavily from Hinduism and Buddhism, as well as from Darwinism and Egyptian religion in forming her alternative spiritual sect. But the real innovation was its genuine attempt to combine natural science and supernaturalism, rationalism and mysticism into a coherent set of teachings."

"So Oprah before Oprah was Oprah," Gapinski said, "Got it."

Celeste threw him a grin at the notion, and said, "And what's the connection with Nazi Germany?"

"Well, one of the more obscene and, frankly, contradictory notions within the upstart pseudo-religion was its racialist undercurrent. It may have publicly advocated for the progressive, cosmopolitan belief in forming a universal brotherhood of all races, creeds, castes, and colors, but they also aimed at bringing a so-called sixth root race into existence that was thoroughly Indo-European."

"Hence, the Nazi fascination with theosophy," Silas said.

"Indeed. Blavatsky's movement quickly found purchase throughout Germany and Austria, which incorporated more overtly racialist and imperialist elements into the fold. A few prominent fellows within Germany founded the German chapter, and one, in particular, found favor with members of the Third Reich. Rudolph Steiner was his name. He had come to the movement through occult circles in Vienna after seeking a path that unified scientific materialism and religious supernaturalism. He said he joined the society because it embraced the reality that a truth stood above the world religions and sought answers to unexplained natural laws and powers within humanity. Spiritualism, clairvoyance, telepathy, and parapsychology were mainstays of the movement."

He adjusted his posture and took a sip of tea. He hummed at the taste of the warm liquid. He cradled the cup in his lap, then continued, "The man dedicated himself to bridging the gap between natural science with a spiritual awakening that befit the modern, industrial age, synthesizing knowledge and belief into an End Times vision of humanity's history and future—which was entirely co-opted by the Nazis in their völkisch, Ario-Germanic ideology. His teachings and articles published in occult journals were a pre-cursor to the Nazis' interest in Asian religions, Gnosticism, and the fringe occultist belief in Luciferianism."

"Luciferianism?" Gapinski said. "As in devil worship?"

Radcliffe took another sip of tea and nodded. "Basically. And the Middle Ages saw a merging of the ancient Ario-Germanic pagan witchcraft with the more Eastern heresy of Luciferianism in Germany, which reverses Lucifer from being the devil to being a liberator, a guardian or guiding spirit toward true *gnosis*. Even considers him to be the true god as opposed to Jehovah of the Old Testament, a belief which is thoroughly Gnostic and obviously utterly opposed to Christianity."

"Obviously."

"Yes, indeed. Now, let me be clear. Theosophy isn't to be

equated with Nazism, or even devil worship itself. But there is a strong connection with the new-spiritualism and the occultism of Germany that was strong during the decades at the close of the nineteenth and early twentieth centuries."

"Interesting…" Silas said leaning back and staring off toward the fireplace, the dancing flames bringing a memory to the surface.

Celeste glanced at him. "Are you having a think about something?"

He shook his head and leaned forward, then said, "Just that it reminds me of something Sebastian said back at Glastonbury."

"And what was that?" Radcliffe asked.

"Something about Germans knowing a thing or two about the Zeitgeist, the so-called Spirit of the Age, and what it will take to offer human progress and enlightenment. And then he said that any relicologist worth his salt would know what was nearly discovered."

"Nearly discovered?" she said. "What was nearly discovered? When, where?"

"He didn't say. He trailed off, as if stopping himself from revealing something. Some important clue. But I thought it was a throwaway comment. Until now."

Radcliffe groaned and smacked himself on the forehead. "How could I have been so daft!" He mumbled something to himself, as if he was having a moment of self-flagellation.

Celeste asked, "What is it?"

"A piece of the puzzle. Perhaps an important piece, in light of our conversation."

"I know!" Gapinski exclaimed. "The Nazis really did find the Grail and hid it away at Castle Brunwald."

Silas and Celeste both threw him a look. Gapinski grinned and settled into his chair.

"He's right, actually," Radcliffe said.

"Huh?" Silas said.

Gapinski sat up straight. "I am?"

Radcliffe grinned. "Well, not entirely. But about the Nazi connection, yes. With the support of Himmler himself, the theologians of the New German faith who had resurrected the ancient Germanic paganism led expeditions in search of the mythical Holy Grail, in addition to excavating a whole host of pagan holy sites. And a fellow by the name of Otto Rahn, whom many have called the real Indiana Jones, was deputized by Himmler's chief esotericist to conduct research into the Holy Grail, among other misadventures."

"That George Lucas..." Gapinski said.

Radcliffe cleared his throat and continued. "The object was one of a number of pursuits through various archaeological endeavors seeking to leverage the relics of various religions for their magical, pagan interests. But Hitler himself had spoken of an apparent 'brotherhood of Templars around the Grail of pure blood,' invoking the myth of Aryan racial purity and conjoining it with the traditional Christian motif of faith. Of course, this fascination with the Grail wasn't unique to Nazism, but it did gain new life among the late nineteenth-century pagans, völkisch-esotericists, and German Christians. And the Grail was invoked during those dark days leading up to and through the Third Reich's reign. Of particular interest was an idealistic nationalism in Germany exploited by Richard Wagner in his grand opera *Parsifal,* which peddled the notion that the elite would seize upon the bejeweled chalice symbolizing a pure form of religion that rose above the religions of the masses—and especially above historic Christianity—which he insisted came between man and the divine."

"Fascinating history of the Grail and the Germans and Nazis and all," Silas interrupted, "but how does this help us?"

Radcliffe went to respond but was intercepted by another

buzz of his phone. He huffed and jabbed the line again. "Yes, my dear?"

"Good news, chief," Zoe said.

"Well, it bloody well be after what we witnessed."

"We were able to backtrace the live steam feed using a reverse algorithm to bypass their multi-layered encryption and—"

"Zoe, my dear," he said interrupting her, "I'm an old man with nary a technical bone in my body, and I'm withering away to dust over here. Do cut the technical theatrics and get on with it, please."

There was an audible sigh, then she said, "We know where he is."

"Praise the Lord! And where is that?"

"Over southern France in the Languedoc region, south of Toulouse and descending toward the border with Spain."

"Good work, Zoe! We'll take it from here." He ended the call and clasped his hands together. "Now we've got them!" He sprang from his chair with new vim and vigor, as if the Holy Spirit himself had descended upon the man.

Celeste called after him as he strolled to one of his bookshelves. "Rowan, what are you playing at?"

Gapinski said, "Forget what Sebastian is toking on, I want whatever's gotten into him!"

Silas laughed, and shouted, "It's the Cathars, isn't it?"

Gapinski leaned over to Silas, and said, "What are the Cathars?"

Silas went to answer when Celeste said, "Not a what, a who. They're a heretical sect of the Church from southern France."

Silas smiled and raised a brow. "Impressive, *Doctor* Bourne!"

"Once in a while," she winked.

Radcliffe returned with a hardback book bound in fraying crimson cloth. He tossed it to Silas. He caught it and opened it to the title page. "Crusade Against the Grail," he read. Then the subtitle: "The Struggle Between the Cathars, the Templars, and the Church of Rome. By Otto Rahn."

"Celeste is right. There was a cult of Luciferians in southern France known as the Cathars. They were quite the headache for the Church during the twelfth and thirteenth centuries, propagating Gnostic theology that taught an intrinsic connection between the material and spiritual, between good and evil, even between God and Lucifer himself. This belief in the connectedness of all things within the universe was rooted in a doctrine of two divine principles—one a perfect and eternal god who created all things spiritual, and the other a demonic lesser god who created the material world.

"Now, Rahn argued in his book there, Silas, that the Cathar heresy, Buddhist religion, and Holy Grail were somehow interconnected by an Indo-European Gnostic tradition. He insisted that Catharism was brought to the German people, which is why he cared so much about it. And, according to Rahn, the Grail itself was bequeathed to the Cathars from the Indian mani spiritual leader after the divine, magical relic fell out of the sky. He further speculated that the fabled chalice of Christ's blood was indeed genuine and sat at the center of the group of medieval heretics and cult of Luciferians. He believed that Wolfram von Eschenbach's particular grail romance among all others, known as *Parzival,* held the keys to the mysteries of the Cathars and the secret location of the Holy Grail."

Celeste's face perked up, having immediately recognized that name. "Wolfram von Eschenbach? We leveraged him during our research into the Ark of the Covenant affair a few months ago."

"Indeed," he said nodding.

"But we determined that von Eschenbach's epic wasn't about the Holy Grail at all, but the Ark," she said, having recalled the crucial text from a previous SEPIO mission that fall.

"Right you are. But Mr. Otto Rahn felt different. He saw *Parzival* not as a work of fiction, and certainly not one pointing to the other fabled relic of biblical proportions, the Ark of the Covenant. Instead, he believed it was a historical account of the Cathars and the Knights Templar and their guardianship of the Grail, a 'stone from the stars,' as it was called. According to him, the Crusade against the Cathars became a war pitting Roma against Amor, Rome against Love, in which the Church triumphed with flame and sword over the pure faith of the Cathars."

Silas sat forward at the edge of the couch. "And where exactly in southern France were these Cathars located, and this purported Grail that they guarded?"

Radcliffe grinned. "In the Languedoc region, south of Toulouse. A town called Montségur."

"I guess it's back to France we go," Silas said.

Gapinski sighed and stood. "Man, I'm growing to hate that place."

DAY IV

DECEMBER 20

CHAPTER 17

MONTSÉGUR, FRANCE.

s the Gulfstream hummed through the stratosphere south toward Montségur, Silas devoured Rahn's missive on the Cathars and the Grail while Celeste and Gapinski slept during the two-hour flight before the next leg of their mission. They had already cleared the English Channel and Paris, and had just cleared the airspace of Toulouse. Reading helped take his mind off the fact he was flying again, and he wanted to finish before they landed.

Rahn's *Crusade Against the Grail* was an examination of the heretical sect and the purported relic, and it drew upon Rahn's account of his explorations of the Pyrenean caves where the heretical Cathar sect sought refuge during the thirteenth century. Even though he thought it was entirely laughable, the Grail itself and also the Nazis' pursuit of it, he thought the account might hold some clues to Nous's plans for the legendary chalice and its location.

He paused to take a sip of coffee he had gotten from the galley earlier. It had cooled to an unacceptable lukewarm black brew. But caffeine was caffeine no matter the temperature, and he needed it to calm his nerves and focus his mind at figuring out what the heck Nous was up to. He took another sip and grimaced, then set down the Styrofoam cup and continued reading.

Like many others before him, Rahn was convinced that those who founded the Church leveraged the pagan symbol of the Grail for its own dogmatic purposes, Christianizing it and utilizing it for its own teachings concerning the power of Christ's blood to save sinners from their sins, death, and the fires of hell. It was clear that Rahn had his own ideas about what the Grail symbolized, developing it into an icon for the survival of the human soul outside of Christian orthodoxy.

Apparently, it was during his youth that Rahn became attracted to studying Wolfram von Eschenbach's grail romance and the history of the Cathars. He was fixated on the mention of the Holy Grail being concealed in the holy mountain of Montsalvat, which he took as the Cathar stronghold of Montségur that boasted a nearby cave system known as Montsalvat. Curiously, *Parzifal* was first written down between 1200 and 1210, at least thirty-three years before the siege of Montségur during the Crusade that wiped out the Cathars— providing an interesting connection to the historical Medieval grail romances and this heretical Christian sect.

Of particular interest to Silas, was a chapter on the Cathar doctrines a third of the way into the book. Several sections intrigued him. He dog-eared them and then highlighted specific sections with pencil along the way. Oddly, they mirrored classic post-Enlightenment perspectives on Jesus and his relationship to Christianity—that what mattered about him was his exemplary life of love, not his bloody death for sins— showing that there really wasn't anything new under the sun, as King Solomon had quipped.

He shook his head as he read, coming across a passage with a familiar ring, an interpretation of Jesus that was common among the crowd of academics that congregated at conferences espousing alternative theories to the founding of Christianity:

The Christian religion came into being only after Christ's passage, and based its existence as a universal religion on the conceptualization of him as the Savior of mankind—an idea that he never espoused while he was traveling back and forth across Palestine, preaching. The Christian religion created within itself a means that permitted its believers to participate in salvation. As the gospel was originally conceived, it should have collapsed by itself, and the ignominious end of the man on the cross should have marked the end of his doctrine.

He looked up and out of the aircraft window, considering a maxim he had memorized concerning the prevailing attitude of the day about the Jewish Messiah: 'A dead Messiah was a failed Messiah.'

In many ways, it was true that the Christian religion came into existence because of the cross. Had Jesus not died—or, rather, had he not been sacrificed for the sins of the world in such a ghastly manner, as Christians believed—he would have been thought of like any other upstart prophet of the day, a sort of Gandhi on steroids who offered nice fortune-cookie ditties and an exemplary life of love.

But Rahn was wrong that the gospel should have collapsed with his 'ignominious end' on the cross, as he wrote. Because his death on the cross was the very center of his good news: he was the Lamb of God, as the apostle John testified in his Gospel, who was led away like a lamb to the slaughterhouse, as the Jewish prophet Isaiah foretold, to shed his blood in order to pay our price and take away the sins of the world. Jesus himself predicted as much. Silas recalled those words of prediction from Mark's Gospel, chapter ten:

"See, we are going up to Jerusalem, and the Son of Man will be handed over to the chief priests and the scribes, and they will condemn him to death; then they will hand him over to the Gentiles; they will mock him, and spit upon him, and flog him, and kill him; and after three days he will rise again."

Of course, the first time Jesus mentioned his demise he got an earful from his follower Peter, who basically told him to shut up about any such talk of dying at the hands of Rome. Because, as the maxim went, for Jewish Peter a dead Messiah was a failed Messiah. He and his people had been waiting for a great and powerful Deliverer to come riding in on a white horse to vanquish their Roman oppressors, free them from exile and reestablish the fabled Kingdom of David, and reinstitute the temple to its proper glory and function.

Little did they know that the real power of Jesus wasn't in wielding a sword against Roman soldiers, but in laying down his life and spilling his blood upon those Roman boards of execution.

Silas picked the book back up and continued reading, coming to a fascinating section about the early Europeans:

For the Druids, a Christ emerging from the house of the adulterous and murderous king David appeared as a contradiction. The Christ who died on the cross could never be the divinity of light. A god cannot die, they said, nor would he allow others to kill those who think differently in his name.

Sounds about right, he thought. The cross has always

sounded like a bunch of crazy talk. Who would have ever thought in their right mind that God would have come to Earth as a helpless baby, setting aside his glory and humiliating himself with such needs as eating and sleeping and going to the bathroom, and then willingly dying for humanity in the most brutal way ever devised? Nonsense!

The Druid opinion that a god could not die and a man dying on the cross could never be true divinity was a popular opinion, even in the earliest days of the Church. Again, a passage from the Bible came to Silas's mind, from the apostle Paul's first letter to the Church of Corinth, chapter one:

> *For the message about the cross is foolishness to those*
> *who are perishing, but to us who are being saved*
> *it is the power of God. For it is written,*

> *"I will destroy the wisdom of the wise,*
> *and the discernment of the discerning I will thwart."*

As crazy as the idea of the Holy Grail was to Silas, he did appreciate the legend and its connection to the ritual of the Eucharist, for it made the blood of Jesus the center of the Grail's power, symbolically and literally able to heal the penitent. The weakness of a sacrifice triumphing over the power of evil and death was indeed foolish. Equally so for Jews and Greeks, because both couldn't stomach a god being borne a man and then dying on the cross. The notion did not compute! But as Paul continued: "For God's foolishness is wiser than human wisdom, and God's weakness is stronger than human strength."

Silas returned to Rahn's book, reading about how the Cathars did not recognize the reality of the miracles of Jesus, disbelieving he could cure physical illnesses because the body was considered an obstacle to the redemption of the soul. Pure Gnostic heresy that denied the goodness of creation! He read how the Cathars spiritualized everything that Jesus did, so that "when he cured the blind, he was curing men who were blinded by sin and allowing them to see reality. The bread that he divided among the five thousand was his Word, the bread of the soul that gave real life. The storm that he calmed was the storm of passions unleashed by Lucifer."

Silas knew different. Because the beauty of the Church's good news is that God is entirely interested in putting our human selves and the rest of the created order back together again—from cancer-ridden bodies to failed marriages, our groaning creation to our societal injustices. And the Church believes the power of Christ's shed blood on the cross makes all that possible.

Of course, the Cathars even dismissed that death as a pseudo-death, echoing the mistakes of past heresies that denied Christ's physical incarnation as a real, live human being. He read:

Because the body of Christ was not of Earthly nature, his crucifixion was only an apparition; this was the only way possible that he could rise to Heaven. A heavenly ascension with a body of flesh and blood appeared absurd to the Cathars. A human body cannot go to heaven; an Eon cannot die.

The problem is that if God in Christ did not become a real person, experiencing everything that broken, busted creation has to offer, and if he only *appeared* as a human, then his death did nothing. Another passage from the Bible bubbled to the surface, from Hebrews chapter two:

Since, therefore, the children share flesh and blood, he

himself likewise shared the same things, so that
through death he might destroy the one who has
the power of death, that is, the devil, and free
those who all their lives were held in slavery by
the fear of death.

But that's not how the Cathars saw it. Which oddly mirrored the way many contemporary people see the power of Christ, as well. As Rahn explained, "For the Occitan heretics, the passion of Christ represents nothing other than the grandiose myth of the 'sacrifice of love' that renders divine."

There it is. The power of Christ's blood is that he was just a Gandhi on steroids. His power was in showing us a way of love—not in ransoming us from death, freeing us from the power of sin, and forgiving our guilt and shame.

It was clear that for the alternative Christian sect, like many modern interpreters, Christ was merely a symbol of the universal human ideal of love, which can be perfected in humanity as it ascends, all on its own, to greater heights of enlightened love. Nothing about the power of his blood or his death. Again, he read:

Despite everything, the Occitan heretics never stopped insisting that they were Christians. And they were, because they followed the supreme commandment of Christ: "I am giving you these commands so that you may love one another. By this everyone will know that you are my disciples, if you have love for one another."

Silas immediately recognized the verses from the Gospel of John in the New Testament of the Bible, John 15:17 and 13:35. For them, the power of Jesus was his life of love, climaxing in his example of love as a martyr on the cross. But such a death isn't martyrdom; it's suicide! Which isn't at all worthy of emulation —and not at all powerful.

He shook his head and flipped forward, scanning for anything else that was interesting and could give him insight into Nous and the Cathars. Halfway through, a chapter on the Crusade against the Cathars caught his eye:

The Cathars saw in the veneration of the cross an insult to the divine nature of Christ. The repudiation of this symbol was such that—as an example—we can cite the cry of one of the Sons of Belissena: "I would never want to be redeemed by such a sign!"

"Sorry, pals," Silas mumbled. "Deny the cross, you deny Christ's blood. Deny Christ's blood, you deny his true power for salvation—dooming and damning yourself to eternal death."

He sighed and closed the book with a thud, then tossed it next to him. He marveled at how nothing had changed in eight hundred years. People were still venerating Jesus for his life and completely ignoring the meaning of his death—at their peril. The one meant nothing without the other. There was no hope for humanity without the cross. For without the shedding of blood there is no forgiveness of sins. And that's where the power of Christ truly lay.

He turned to a tablet filled with research Zoe had arranged for him that explained more of the journey Rahn took to search for the legendary Grail. As he scrolled through it, records apparently showed that Himmler himself agreed to finance Otto Rahn's trip to the Languedoc region in 1931, sending him there on a special mission to find the Grail and bring it back to Nazi Germany. He stayed in the village of Lavelanet and became certain that Montségur was indeed the Montsalvat of the *Parzifal* legend. This trip led to his book *Crusade Against the Grail,* in which he traced the story of what he had achieved. The book found a ready-made audience in leading Nazi figureheads, including Himmler and the Führer himself. Over the next few years, the historian and philologer became involved with the hierarchy of the Nazi party, later returning to the area of Montségur for a short while to ensure that the Grail and other rumored treasures had remained undiscovered. However, the supposed Grail that was stashed away in the Montségur stronghold was never recovered.

Zoe made reference to a passage in the *Crusade Against the Grail* that might hold a clue to where to start looking for the fabled relic. Silas reached for the book, but the plane dipped and began to bank left. He caught his breath, then set the tablet on his lap and looked outside the window. They had come out of the clouds and were fast descending toward the land below, the barren pastoral landscape of Glastonbury replaced by one of rugged snow-capped mountains. A wave of turbulence shuddered through the plane, sending Silas for his armrests, and waking Celeste next to him.

She yawned and stretched, then brought her seat into its upright position.

"Hello, sleepyhead," Silas said, grabbing the tablet again.

She adjusted her blanket and looked over at him, then down at his tablet and over to the book sitting next to him. "Have you been researching all this time?"

He shrugged. "It's what I do."

She smiled and leaned over the aisle to have a look, the familiar scent of lavender and vanilla making him tingle with delight. "Find anything interesting?"

"Plenty. The Cathars were the perfect modern interpreters of Jesus Christ."

She furrowed her brow. "What do you mean?"

"They pretty much rejected Jesus' shed blood on the cross in favor of his life example of love. Many within the Church since the Enlightenment have been making the same mistaken interpretation. That the power of his blood wasn't in his sacrifice for sins, but in his example of love."

"That is interesting."

"Zoe sent along some research, as well, and I was going to check out something from the book." Silas retrieved Rahn's book from the seat next to him and turned to the page Zoe had flagged. "Here, listen to this." He read:

Esclarmonde, the "Light of the World," kept the oriflamme of the Cathar faith in Montségur. At the most critical moment of the siege, four audacious knights took that emblem, "the treasure of the heretics" (as the Inquisitors called the Cathar relic), to the caves of Ornolac in a mountain journey filled with adventures. If we find a reference to the Grail in the "treasure of the heretics," we will have found several points to support our hypothesis.

Celeste said, "If that doesn't sound like a clear clue, then I don't know what does."

He closed the book and smiled, pleased they finally had some clear direction for this wild goose chase.

CHAPTER 18

The Gulfstream landed without a hitch on the quaint airport landing strip of Aérodrome de Pamiers resting among the frosted barren fields near the base of the Pyrenees Mountains—for which Silas was grateful. With barely any air travel occupying the airport, the private aircraft taxied quickly into a hangar.

Silas's breath frosted the air as he exited the private aircraft, a deep freeze having settled over southern France two days before the Winter Solstice. He zipped up his windbreaker jacket tighter against his neck, wishing he had brought a heavier coat. Celeste came up behind him and gave an audible shiver. Gapinski finally thanked the pilot after talking shop with the guy about the nuances of the aircraft, then bounded down the stairs. Waiting for them was a black G-Class Mercedes 4x4 SUV, an all-terrain vehicle that would prove useful for where the trio was heading.

"Pimp. My. Ride," Gapinski said and whistled at the automotive hardware. "I'll take those." He grabbed the keys from a SEPIO agent who had driven the vehicle down from the Order's Paris operation center at the old Port-Royal des Champs Abbey. He slid into the driver's seat, beaming like a kid on Christmas.

"Remember, mate," Celeste said. "This ride is the Order's ride. So handle with care."

He scoffed. "When have I ever not handled the Order's prized automotive possessions with anything but kid gloves?"

She tilted her head and hummed. "Let me see. I seem to recall us pretty much destroying a similar G-Class Mercedes earlier in the year. Except that one was silver."

He turned around to face her in the back. "So not fair. Because I also seem to recall a Beamer hosing us down with lead for a mile stretch east of Paris. And, little missy, you having something to do with that, too."

She smirked. "Just get us there in one piece, flyboy."

"Man, sounds like I've been missing out," Silas said as he shut the door to the passenger's side.

"You have no idea," Gapinski said, throwing the vehicle into gear and speeding out into the evening that was quickly slipping away to dusk.

A full moon began emerging as the clear blue sky gave way to amber and then to deep purple and an emerging indigo as the sun slipped beneath the horizon. As Gapinski navigated the drive down the main thoroughfare toward the small resort town of Ornolac-Ussat-les-Bains, Silas returned to Zoe's research to read up on the so-called Cathar Cathedral of Bethlehem, the most important of the Cave Churches of Ornolac. Which seemed ironic, given the season.

In order to reach the ritualistic chapel, one must climb a steep path through a dense forest up a cliff, the Path of Initiation as it was called. The Cave of Bethlehem may well have been the spiritual center of the Cathars, for it was there that the 'Pure' underwent an initiation ceremony that culminated in what was known as the *Consolamentum*. Apparently, four aspects of the cave were utilized in the ceremony: a granite altar upon which the Gospel of John lay, a pentagram hewn into the wall, telluric currents emanating from the rock walls and floor, and a square niche in the wall in which stood the veiled Holy Grail.

Sounds like the perfect starting place for our little investigation.

Within thirty-five minutes, the trio had arrived at the quaint mountain villa nestled within the Pyrenees. A long, low-slung building built of logs with a large bright sign advertising the local tourist bureau sat off the side of the thoroughfare. Silas pointed to it, and said, "Gapinski, pull off into there, would you? Looks like the best first stop as any. Maybe someone can help us find a guide or something."

As he eased the SUV off the road and into the parking lot, he said, "You really think it's a good idea to go marching off into the woods at this hour? Bad things happen when the sun goes down, man."

Silas shrugged. "You've got a better idea? We're out of time, and this is our only lead. And besides," he said getting out of the car, "we're in France."

"My point exactly!"

He smirked and told them to stay in the car and keep it warm. A wreath dotted by holly berries with a large golden bow anchoring the bottom greeted him at the door. He opened it and walked inside, the warmth from a crackling fire a welcomed relief from the chilly outdoors.

The inside looked like a ski lodge, with the roughhewn logs, a stone fireplace, and overstuffed couches and chairs off to the side. A small Charlie-Brown Christmas tree sat on top a wooden table in the seating area. Next to it was an urn of hot water with little packets of hot cocoa. The scent of pine and lingering scent of chocolate from the crowds that had been through earlier delighted his senses.

A small counter commanded the center of the building. Behind it was a door, closed. Silas walked up to the counter and spread his arms, looking around for any signs of life. He noticed a tiny copper bell. He rang it and waited for a response.

After several seconds when he received none, he called out, "Hello? Anybody here?"

As he waited for a response, he picked up a travel brochure off a pile on the counter. It was in French. He flipped through it, trying to tap into what little he learned from his graduate days at Harvard for reading the original historical theological Church writings, but he was rusty. He frowned and went to turn it around to read the English side when a tall, husky man with a dark green jacket and a black beret perched on top a shaved head emerged from the back. Looked like a ranger of some sort.

"Puis-je vous aider, Monsieur?"

Silas set down the brochure and tried his best to respond. "Parlez vous anglais?"

"Oui, Monsieur. I speak English," the man said in a thick accent. He spat something brown to the side before adding, "Although, we are about to close for the evening..."

Silas furrowed his brow briefly at the move, both in disgust and curiosity. Was the man chewing tobacco?

"Then I'll be brief," he looked down at a name tag attached to the man's jacket, "Louis. You see, I..." he gestured outside, "and my colleagues out in the Mercedes, we need some help getting to a certain popular tourist spot that I understand is a bit of a hike from here."

"Alright," the man said warily, glancing outside and then back to Silas, eyeing him with squinted eyes. "And how can I be of service to you and your...colleagues."

"We need access to the grotte de Bethlehem."

The man's eyes widened slightly, then he licked his lips and gave a chuckle. "Lagrotte De Bethléem? No, no, no. The sun is setting. It is nearly nighttime."

Silas eased closer against the counter. "I understand this is an unusual request. And we would just hike the damn thing ourselves, but we don't have time to figure out how to get there. We need a guide. In fact, it's for the Church."

"The...Church?" he asked with reservation, then spat to the side again. "How so?"

He cleared his throat, coming up with the best explanation on the fly, hoping that wielding the power of Christianity would buy him goodwill and a guide up to the cave. "You see, we are agents of the Vatican on an important mission with grave consequences for the faith. And we believe there is an important clue inside that cave."

The man leaned back and scrunched up his face, as if he wasn't buying what Silas was selling. Silas lowered his voice. "Please, we need your help. We'll pay you for the trouble. But we need to get to that cave, and we haven't got much time."

Louis folded his arms, and said, "How much?"

"Name your price."

He did, and they agreed. Silas brought out a wad of cash, American one hundred dollar bills. He paid the man and motioned out the window for Gapinski and Celeste to come inside. "We'll need these," Louis said, setting four heavy-duty flashlights on the counter, "and you do exactly as I say. No questions asked."

Silas nodded. "No problem."

"The temperature is supposed to drop in the next few hours and snow is on the way. So we need to move it, and we can't linger once there. Should take half an hour to reach the site. And we stay for no more than an hour."

"Perfect."

"I need to make a phone call, and then we leave."

"A phone call?" Silas said as his two partners came into the building.

The man hesitated, then said, "My superiors. They need to know about my trip. Especially given the dangers with traveling at night. You understand."

Silas looked to Celeste, who raised a brow in caution.

"Well, we would like to keep this off the books, just between us. For security reasons, given the nature of the Vatican and all. You understand, right?"

The man huffed and held up his mobile. "No call, no hike. Es-ce bien?"

Silas gave a short sigh, but relented. "Bien. We'll meet you outside."

THE SEPIO OPERATIVES were fortunate to have been able to secure Louis as a guide, for the path was wholly uninviting and lacked the proper signage one would expect directing the way. They would have spent hours searching for the fabled Cathar cathedral had Providence not shined as brightly on them that evening as the nearly-full moon was lighting their path forward. Their flashlights joined in, swaying and glistening off the packed snow.

The crunch of boots and shoes on the frozen ground echoed softly through the forest as the four hiked the trail. A soft metal clang rang with each step up ahead from a kerosene lantern Louis brought along for the cave. He spat into the woods as an owl hooted in the distance, and something farther ahead scampered away with force through the trees.

"I've got a bad feeling about this," Gapinski said, eyeing the treetops and startling every so often as if something was about to pop out at him from behind a trunk or boulder.

"Boo!" Celeste yelled from behind him, grabbing him by the shoulders. He screamed like a school girl and whipped around so fast Silas thought he was going to deck her.

"Oy, mate!" she exclaimed, holding her hands up in defense.

"Jeez Louise, sister! You almost gave me a heart attack."

Silas laughed. Celeste joined in. Even Louis could be heard snickering under his breath up ahead.

She said, "Just having a bit of fun, is all. No harm."

"Easy for you to say. You didn't grow up with the ghost stories of dead slaves haunting the hills of Georgia. I can still hear those clanging chains in my sleep—What was that?" He spun around toward a large bush off to the side of the path.

"Probably a rabbit, scaredy cat," Silas said.

"That's what they all say until—"

"Regardez!" Louis said, interrupting the fun and games. He pointed ahead with his flashlight, swaying its beam across a steep incline that rose for two hundred yards.

Silas joined him up ahead, Celeste and Gapinski followed close behind. They ascended the path alongside the cliff, struggling across the frozen ground. Gapinski slipped not once, but three times. Celeste nearly fell herself in the slick snow had it not been for Gapinski's quick arms keeping her upright. Soon they reached the top, where they were greeted by a wall of brick that had been constructed into the side of the original cave mouth. A small entrance shorter than a man opened up to the inside, the wind whistling through it and echoing off the interior walls with ungodly calls.

"Here we are," Louis announced, shining a light inside and motioning with his arm for the trio to enter the small chamber.

Silas nodded and ducked inside, Gapinski and Celeste followed close behind. A rickety set of wooden stairs, pockmarked with age and wear, led down into the grotto. A large flat stone, the size of a small couch, propped up on three rounded boulders the size of basketballs, commanded the space. Probably weighed a ton or two, and looked to be some sort of ceremonial table. Must have been where the Gospel of John lay during the Cathar initiation ceremony.

The three carefully descended into the cavern. Behind them, Louis stood at the top and lit the lamp, its amber light glowing softly throughout the space. He handed it to Gapinski, who set it on the stone table.

"This place is giving me the creeps," he complained.

Silas ignored him, scanning the interior of the small chamber. He caught sight of the pentagram etched onto a wall off to the side. Underneath was an unmistakable image painted in white.

A chalice. The Holy Grail!

He shuffled over to the wall. Celeste followed, Gapinski did not. Silas crouched beside it and touched the eight-hundred-year-old pictogram with his fingers, tracing it and wondering what it meant. Had the Cathars indeed held in their possession the cup that bore Christ's blood? In that very chamber? Was it still there?

"What do you make of it?" Celeste said crouching down next to him.

Silas shook his head. "Not sure. I mean, it sure looks like a Grail."

"But what does it mean? Clearly, there's nothing here. Just an empty chamber."

He stood and sighed, then put his hands on his hips and scanned the place again. "Otto Rahn said that the Cathars believed the death of Christ represented nothing more than the 'grandiose myth of the sacrifice of love that renders divine.' It is thought that in this chamber an initiation ritual known as the *Consolamentum* was performed."

"What was that?"

"Apparently, a ceremony in which the Cathar was purified, the Perfecti he was called, both at initiation and at death so that their souls could return to Christ. For the Cathars, Christ was an emissary of the Light sent into this world to lead humanity back to God, for each individual contained within them a shard of the Divine Light, the Angelic Soul which was trapped in a garment of flesh, the body, by Lucifer. Which is a classic Gnostic idea about human nature. While confined in this garment of matter, the Soul forgets its origin with the Divine and instead finds itself captivated by the pleasures of this world. Cathars held to a Doctrine of Reincarnation, believing that the Soul was doomed to return back to this world over and over again until it went through a process of spiritual growth and purification. Only then was it able to return to God through Christ and the Holy Spirit."

He sighed and leaned against the cavern wall. "But what that has anything to do with the Grail is beyond me."

She turned to him, and said, "Well, maybe it was a symbol for what it contained."

"What do you mean?"

"The very light of Christ, the example the Cathar Perfecti needed for their soul to return to its divine source. As you said yourself, they didn't care for the orthodox belief of the power of Christ's shed blood being able to save sinners from sin and death. Instead, the power was in his example."

"So they never had the Grail then? Just this pictogram painted on the side of a cavern wall?"

She shook her head. "Maybe they had something, a chalice of some sort. But they idealized the power that it contained into some powerful talisman for good works. Psychology of religion has shown such physical symbols can be powerful motivators for behavior. It's why we have rituals in the first place, even tangible ones like the Eucharist."

"And for the Cathars, the Eucharist didn't mean what it did for the Catholic Church, the wine transforming into the actual blood of Christ with the power to provoke and nourish the faith of Christ's followers. In fact, they refused to participate in the ritual, believing that the symbol of his sacrifice was all that mattered, his loving example."

"But where is it then?" Gapinski interrupted. The two turned toward him and waited for him to continue. "Nous is clearly after a boatload of purported Grails, but nothing's here but us three. And so far everywhere we've chased such fables, there's been the blokes with the bird tattoos. So what gives?"

Silas shrugged. "Good question."

"Because from where I stand this is a big fat nothinburger. And I don't know about you, but I'm shivering in my skivvies over here and would love to get my heinie back down this mountain and into our cozy pimped-out ride."

A buzzing in Silas's pocket interrupted his reply. He reached inside and withdrew his phone. "Hold on. It's Radcliffe." Putting it on speaker, he answered, "Hey, chief. We're at the caves of Ornolac in Monstégur, but this looks like a dead end."

"That's because it is," said Zoe from the other end.

Celeste shivered and brought her arms up to her chest. She breathed out a chilly breath and looked around, then said, "I agree. I think we've gotten all we're going to get from this place. I'll be interested in your intel, Zoe."

Silas nodded. "Alright, hold on. We've been in some sort of ritualistic cave. We're going to get out of here."

"I don't think so," Louis said, spitting to the side. He was holding a pistol, black and menacing.

"Always something," Gapinski huffed.

CHAPTER 19

Mysteriously, the thick French accent of their supposed helpful tourist representative of the great nation of France had been replaced by an even thicker Southern twang.

"Hey, how'd you do that?" Gapinski asked the man.

"Hands up, partner," Louis ordered.

Gapinski did as he was told, and mumbled from the side of his mouth, "Have I told you how much I hate France?"

The man waved his weapon at Celeste. "You, too, little missy. And turn off the phone, Jack Bauer. Don't even think of trying anything."

Gapinski to Silas and snickered. "Jack Bauer. That's funny."

Celeste and Silas both looked at him, not amused.

He shrugged. "Well, you do kinda look like him. A little taller, though."

"I mean it!" the man yelled.

Silas ended the call and went to slide the phone into his pants pocket.

Louis took an angry step down the stairs. "Do you think I'm stupid? Turn it off."

Silas glanced at Celeste and frowned. He obliged, making a

show of shutting it down in front of the newly hostile Louis, then he slid it into his pocket. He said, "What the heck is going on here? Who are you?"

"Who do you think, Silas?"

He stiffened at the mention of his name. Then his eyes narrowed, and he dipped his head slightly, drilling the man with his eyes.

"My brother..." Silas growled.

Louis spat again, then smirked. "Righto, partner."

"You work for him, or something?"

"Or something. Now, let's go."

Celeste protested, "Wait? Where are you taking us?"

"Where do you think? The master himself."

"Sebastian?" Silas said, his stomach tightening with a mixture of apprehension and disgust at the thought of this brother's involvement.

The man nodded. He slowly continued his descent down the wooden stairs with the gun fixed on the trio, then he pivoted away and motioned with his weapon for them to walk toward the exit above.

Gapinski hesitated and looked to Celeste. She nodded forward, so he walked toward the stairs and started ascending. Celeste followed, then Silas. He glared at Louis, his jaw clenched with fury not so much at the fake Frenchman, but at the depths to which his brother had sunk.

"Wait outside the grotto opening and don't try anything stupid. I have orders to kill on the spot," Louis said, his accent grating to the senses. "And I will. With glee. Including you, Bauer." The man grinned as Silas passed, rancid breath of chewed tobacco steaming into his face.

Silas said nothing, his footfalls up the wooden stairs echoing loudly in the heathen chapel.

After Louis met the SEPIO operatives outside the grotto

entrance, the four began a slow descent through the darkened forest, the only relief from the frigid air a full moon continuing to shine bright and strong through a cloudless sky. Louis had the ease of it, having prepared for the journey with thick-soled boots. Each of the three others had slipped at various points, Gapinski more than the other two. Within twenty minutes they had reached the bottom at the trailhead leading out into the dead-asleep village.

They crunched along a road that wound back to the tourist agency post. The lights were still on, and the Mercedes was still parked.

"Who's got the keys to this beaut?" Louis asked, motioning toward the SUV.

The three said nothing.

"Come on!" he yelled. "Who's the chauffeur, as they say in these parts?"

Gapinski finally raised a hand. Louis said, "Then take the wheel and let's giddy-up."

"Hold a second," Celeste said, putting up a hand and step-ping forward. "We're not going anywhere with you."

The man took a step forward himself, smiled, and licked his lips. "Yes, you are, sweet thing."

Silas took a protective step directly in between the two, causing Louis to recoil and outstretch his weapon. "Whoa, there, partner. I almost blew yer head off!"

"Back off," Silas growled, head lowered and eyes narrowed with fury.

Louis laughed. "Well, how 'bout that. Ol' Sebastian didn't tell me his big bro had a sweetheart."

Silas stepped forward slightly, clenching both fists. He growled, "I said, back off."

The man chambered a round and pointed the gun at Silas's head. "One way or another, y'all are coming with me. Bodybag or not, makes no difference to me."

Celeste lightly touched Silas's shoulder. He flinched and glanced over at it. She said softly, "Let it go."

"Celeste..." he began to protest.

"That's an order. Let's get on with it."

Louis smiled widely, a ring of chewing tobacco nestled in his lower gum showing through for the first time. He turned his head to the side and spat.

"Eww," Gapinski grimaced.

"You heard the missus. Best get a move on. You," Louis said motioning with his gun toward Gapinski, "take the wheel. Silas, you get up front. I'll take the backseat with the Brit. Something says I need to keep my eye on you the most, sweet thing." He grinned and winked.

All three said nothing and cooperated, climbing into the SUV. Louis sent his used chaw out of his mouth all over the snowy lot with one flick of his finger. He wiped it on his pants, and then he settled in the back.

Gapinski brought the vehicle to life, and asked, "Where are we heading, chief?"

"Monstégur, to the original Cathar fortress on a cliff there. Sebastian should be waiting. He wanted you brought straight away after you showed yer faces. Figured you'd come rootin' around for the final Grail. Stationed me as a lookout at that there tourist post after we took out the poor soul who had been working late. Guess he was right."

"Bastard," Gapinski mumbled under his breath as he eased the Mercedes out of the parking lot and back onto the throughway.

He backtracked toward the small private landing strip and crested around the base of the Pyrenees toward Monstégur. Silas remained quiet up in front, trying not to let the latest slap in the face with his brother send him into an anxiety-induced state, but finding it hard to focus as the darkened, frosted world flashed by.

What were they going to do? Sebastian had thought of everything. Was far more resourceful than he had given him credit. More wicked than he thought possible. He closed his eyes and rubbed his temple with his forefinger, trying to massage away another headache that was threatening his concentration.

Think, Grey!

It was getting hard to breathe, as if a wool cap had been shoved down his throat. His chest was tightening. His head pounded harder, with searing pain lancing across his forehead. His stomach tensed, then his mouth started watering, as if making way for a geyser from within his belly.

No. Not now!

Silas quickened his breath and started swallowing, trying his damnedest to stave off the magma reaching for the surface. His head was spinning, and his stomach was nearly there, the sensation in his mouth like a never-ending waterfall preparing the way for his stomach to jettison the contents within. He was hot, stifling from the sensation. He swallowed again, then again as his stomach nearly lurched forward.

Hold it together, Grey...

Then all at once, the feeling subsided. His mouth stopped watering, his stomach settled somewhat, his entire body melted with relief from the tension. It was as if a switch had been flipped. But then along with the relief came a wave of perspiration. From top to bottom, his entire body soaked through with sweat, and he felt clammy from the release. He sighed audibly.

Celeste reached over to him.

"Whoa, sweet thing," Louis said, reaching one hand to stop her and the other hand forward with his weapon.

"I'm just checking on my partner," she snapped, with an equally snappy look.

Louis eased back but kept his weapon trained on her.

She leaned forward some more, and whispered, "Are you alright?"

"I'm fine," Silas said quickly.

"Are you su—"

"I said, I'm fine," he snapped, then sighed and leaned against the window. He needed out of the car, and fast.

"Alright," she simply said, leaning back into her seat.

They continued driving in silence along the frozen, abandoned mountain road under the cover of the full moon. Soon, they were coming up to a stretch of road that looked remarkably different from the rest.

"Slow down, partner," Louis said.

On either side sat marked parking spaces, and up ahead were bright lights set high on twenty-foot poles, the kind you would find at a Friday night football game. They were pointed away from the road and toward a path that disappeared through tall naked trees. There was also a rumbling noise coming from the other side of the lights, and the faint sound of voices echoing through the deadened night. Shining from above were several more similar lights, all arrayed at the top of a massive cliff with a structure jutting up, looking like the jawbone of a jackal with cracked, jagged teeth.

Château de Montségur. The castle-fortress of the Cathars. It was there that the heretics made their last stand in 1243 against the Crusader siege. It was also there that Otto Rahn thought they had secreted the purported Holy Grail from von Eschenbach's Medieval grail romance.

Louis pointed toward the right. "Bring the SUV over there, take up all the spaces and put it in park."

"Why's that?" Gapinski asked.

"Because we're going to wait right here."

"For what?" Celeste asked.

Before he could answer, a caravan of four darkened SUVs came up from behind and braked hard just past them in front of the lighted path. A man got out of the lead vehicle and saun-tered over to them.

"Roll down your window," Louis commanded Gapinski. He obliged.

The man, wearing black and white military fatigues, the kind made for arctic operations, peeked his head into the idling vehicle. With a thick German accent, he said, "Where's the Grey brother?"

Silas sat up straight and looked over at him. Louis waved his weapon toward him, and said, "This one, Lars. Can't you tell?"

The operative brought an automatic rifle around to the front that had been slung around his shoulder toward the back, then motioned with his hand and said, "You, out."

There was no use protesting. Silas glanced at Gapinski and looked at Celeste. Her face remained steely, but she nodded.

He got out of the vehicle and slammed the door. He rapped on the window of the rear passenger's side door and pointed toward the ground. Louis put down the window.

"Can I help you?" Louis said.

"What's going to happen with them?"

"Don't you worry yer pretty little head about them, partner." He grinned widely and lobbed a large ball of slimy spittle out the window, the thick sludge sailed past Silas and landed some-where in the snow. "I'll take good care of them."

Silas leaned toward him, and said, "You better."

Smiling, Louis put the window back up and waved just as it cleared his face.

Silas stood still, glaring at the man through the tinted window, then walked around the front of the Mercedes to the awaiting operative, presumably with Nous.

Lars grabbed him by the upper arm, rough and in-control like. Silas tightened his arm and yanked it back, then stepped back. "That's not necessary. I'll go."

"Fine," the man said. "Second vehicle from the front. Your brother is seated in the back."

Silas walked forward and stopped at the door, then looked back at his fellow operatives, his friends, his family.

Lord Jesus Christ, Son of God, you better protect them!

CHAPTER 20

S ilas opened the door and slid inside. It was stuffy, sweltering like a sauna and threatening another wave of nausea. He took a deep breath of the crisp, cold air outside and closed his eyes. Then he closed the door.

Keep it together, Grey!

"Ahh, nice of you to join us, big brother," Sebastian said. "After all, our little jaunt into the forest is much more up your alley than mine, anyway."

The caravan lurched forward between the lights. Silas's stomach went with it. He swallowed hard and faced his brother as the SUV rumbled along a path through the forest.

His brother continued, "Reminds me of our little jaunt to Jerusalem earlier in the year when we raided the Church of the Holy Sepulcher. I have to admit, 'tis one of my fondest family memories, the two of us working side-by-side to prove, or in my case disprove, the Christian faith. Sort of a metaphor for our lives, don't you think—even our relationship?"

Silas said nothing, his mind still trying to process the fact he was sitting in the back of a darkened SUV before the base of the fortress compound for a heretical sect of Christianity, presumably in search of a purported Holy Grail. And with his brother, who, by all accounts, was leading the charge.

Did not compute.

He glanced out the windshield as they rumbled forward, then jolted with a memory from that fateful trip to the Holy Land.

"The Edicule..." he said turning toward his brother. "When you were shot and left to die. Or, I guess, supposedly shot and left to die. That was all a fake-out, wasn't it? Shot by Jacob Crowley to throw me off my game?"

Sebastian glanced at him and said nothing, the corner of his mouth curling slightly instead.

Silas let a chuckle slip as he sat mouth agape at the notion. He said, as if only to himself, "The bullet did miss all the major stuff, if I recall. Perfectly placed. And when you were almost killed by those Nous operatives lurking outside your home... that was all a set-up, too? A ruse to scare me away from pursuing the scientific authentication of Jesus' resurrection?"

Again, nothing. And, again, that same grin Silas wanted to slap off his brother to kingdom come.

He narrowed his eyes and clenched his fist instead, then sighed and said, "What the *hell* are you doing, Seba?"

"Now, now. No need to curse, Sy."

"I'm serious," Silas roared, causing the driver to glance behind. "What the hell are you doing, here and at Glastonbury, with Nous and this Rudolf Borg character?"

"Making magic," Sebastian whispered.

Suddenly, the SUV ascended upward along a narrow ridge that had served as a footpath for traffic getting to the ancient fortress ruins. The noises Silas had heard in the distance were growing louder now, and the lights were growing brighter against the night sky as they made their way upward.

"What the heck does that mean?" Silas asked.

"Ahh, what a little scientific ingenuity and archaeological

gumption can accomplish when brought together in marital bliss! You should try it sometime."

Silas clenched his jaw and looked away. Sebastian was always mockingly accusing him of being anti-science because of his Christian faith and relics pursuits. But instead of offering a clever retort or getting angry, as was often the case, he said nothing, choosing to let his brother flap his gums. Maybe he would learn something useful.

"The promises of therapeutic gene editing..." Sebastian continued before trailing off. "Well, anyway. We shall see what the boys have discovered up ahead. With any luck, we will have ourselves our fifth Holy Grail, and the promise of a new Savior!"

The SUV eased to a stop and the caravan along with it. "We're here!" he announced, his face beaming with pride and anticipation. The man in the fatigues from before opened Silas's door and grabbed him by the arm, forcing him to exit. His brother was close behind.

"There she is," Sebastian said, bringing the collar of his coat tight against his neck, hands stuffed in his pockets.

A hundred yards farther up the narrowing path, a once-mighty fortress stood proud, bathed in white light. Plumes of dust and debris rose into the darkened sky from behind thick walls still standing after eight-hundred years, presumably from the noisy mechanical earthen equipment that echoed down below.

"And you think you're going to discover what Otto Rahn couldn't for the Nazis?"

Sebastian chuckled. "Oh, brother, from what I understand we have most definitely discovered what Otto Rahn couldn't for the Nazis. A chamber was unearthed deep beneath the main tower keep. Must have been a bear to excavate back in the Dark Ages. At any rate, should be any hour now before we've extracted what has been lying in wait to be resurrected and leveraged for the benefit of all humanity."

The rest of the way forward toward the lighted ruins was a slow, rocky ascent made worse by the worsening weather conditions. They crunched along the frozen path in silence, a bitter, biting wind picking up pace the farther up they walked, chased by the emerging snow Louis or whatever-the-hell-his-name-was had mentioned. They were completely exposed to the late-December elements, and Silas only had a windbreaker built for Punta Cana.

The promises of therapeutic gene editing...

What the heck was Sebastian getting at? It had to mean something important. Silas prayed for wisdom, for some sort of guidance from the Holy Spirit, anything to help him make sense of it all. He tripped on a rock jutting up from the middle of the path, sending him stumbling hard onto the ground. His phone slipped out of his pocket and nearly skittered over the side before he grabbed it and shoved it under his body.

"Oh, Sy...Always the clumsy one," Sebastian laughed.

He stayed on the ground another few seconds, feigning his recovery as he quickly turned his phone on. With any luck, it might catch a signal and be of some use to SEPIO command.

Silas slid the phone back inside his pants pocket, stood, and brushed himself off. A shiver walked up his spine in response to a gust of wind. He grabbed his shoulders and rubbed his arms as they continued forward.

Therapeutic gene editing. Therapeutic gene editing.

A thought was worming its way to the surface, a remnant of a memory from an episode of Silas's favorite NPR show, Fresh Air. A writer with The New Yorker discussed emerging biotechnologies that was increasingly making it possible to remove disease and change the characteristics of life by rewriting cellular genes or something. But what the heck did that have anything to do with the Grail?

As they neared the complex, Silas wondered what it was they would find. He recalled from the research Zoe sent over that some of the Cathar heretics had escaped the Crusader siege, adding to speculation that they took the Grail with them. Others speculated it might have been hidden away inside the fortress complex itself. Apparently, Nous and Sebastian was of the latter camp. Did they really discover a chamber containing some sort of chalice, a Holy Grail even? And if so, what did it matter? It's not like the damn thing contained—

Unless...

The idea was preposterous. That there was blood inside a purported Grail buried in some hidden chamber deep beneath a pile of rubble on a cliff in southern France, or in one of the other stolen Grails. Even more preposterous was that one of them contained the blood of *Jesus*, spilt from his wounded side while he hung on the cross paying for the sins of the world!

Silas knew it was technically possible, that an archaeological artifact could bear the remains of human blood. He recalled a journal article from a few years ago about some Italian and German scientists who had found the world's oldest known human blood from the bones of a 5,300-year-old mummy nicknamed Oetzi, discovered in 1991. They used cutting-edge nanotechnology to verify the shape and molecular composition of the ancient blood.

But what if it was true, that a Grail had been hidden away inside that castle containing blood—the blood of Christ?

The party reached a set of rickety wooden stairs leading to a wooden platform standing in front of the ancient entrance to the stone ruins. The pieces were starting to gravitationally pull together in Silas's mind eye.

Nous didn't want the Grail cups for what they *represented*. They wanted the chalices for what they *contained*.

Blood. DNA.

But for what end?

Sebastian led the way up the wooden stairs. Silas hesitated, not wanting to confront the possibility of what lay inside.

The guard from earlier shoved the butt of his automatic rifle into his back. Silas fell forward, his knee jamming into one of the wooden stairs. He gave a moan.

Sebastian turned around and shook his head, then continued onward.

They reached the entrance, the earlier racket heard down below having ceased. The space inside was of a courtyard bathed in bright light, of frozen dirt and grass with stonework leftover from the previous life of the castle. Jackhammers and generators and other tools were scattered about, as well as clumps of men bundled in better gear than he. Some held the same kind of rifles as his pal from earlier, a few others held tablet computers checking something or other and moved in and out of the keep.

"Sebastian!" someone yelled from the distance.

Silas looked up to see a tall, trim woman with long blond hair come running toward them. Sebastian stepped forward, gleaming.

"Helen, my bright and shining love!" his brother exclaimed, arms open wide. She ran and jumped into them. The two kissed, and passionately so, then twirled like two teenagers high on adolescent infatuation.

My love?!

Silas's mouth fell open at the sight. He had no idea his brother had been seeing someone.

"Good news," Helen said, a thick German accent evident. "We've found the Grail!"

"Zip-a-dee-doo-dah!" Sebastian said. "Take me there."

Sebastian ran off with Helen. The guard shoved Silas forward, and they walked to the tower keep still standing among the ruins. The two lovebirds entered into an orange glow emanating from a small doorway. Outside stood piles of stone and dirt, with cables snaking inside. As Silas grew closer, he could see a hole the size of a kitchen table dug into the floor.

He walked inside to see Sebastian inspecting a silvery chalice, his face gleaming with pride and a power-lust that twisted his face into a Joker-like smile of glee. His brother turned his head and tossed Silas the cup.

"Take a gander, my relicologist brother!"

Silas caught it with one hand. It was a modest vessel covered in grime with an emerald-like base, made of jasper, perhaps. He turned the cup in his palm, inspecting it and noticing three gold plaques inscribed with cuneiform script in an ancient language. Hebrew, Greek, and Aramaic. He noted those were the languages of Jesus' day, as well as the languages of the three plaques at the head of his cross announcing that he was the King of the Jews.

Sebastian snatched the cup back from Silas and handed it to Helen.

"My darling, here," Sebastian said, grasping his love's hand, "is an expert in genetics, having graduated from the top of her class at the University of Heidelberg. Now that we've retrieved the chalice, next stop is testing it for—"

An explosion of gunfire interrupted him. It came from the entrance to the castle fortress. The guard from earlier, who had extracted him from the car below and shoved him into the stairs, immediately pulled Silas into the tower and told the rest of the excavation personnel to back away from the entrance. He started speaking rapid German into a comm unit as the melee continued outside.

The cavalry had arrived! Had to be SEPIO. Or the French military. Or both!

Silas tried to make out what Lars was saying, but he was more accustomed to reading German than listening to it. He caught his brother's name, as well as his apparent lover's. He caught *Monstégure* and *SEPIO*. And then *Externsteine*. Whatever that was. As the gun battle continued to rage, he couldn't help but throw Sebastian a grin of satisfaction. His brother carried a look that was a mixture of fear and frustration, unease and indignation. From inside the keep, he could see three bodies lying on the courtyard ground just inside the fortress entrance, and the ones that were still firing had retreated farther inside the compound. Looked like Nous was losing.

And bad!

Another two dropped, leaving three left. They gave up their ground, running for the safety of the tower. When they arrived, the guard, their commander perhaps, spoke with anger and urgency. Presumably chewing them out for abandoning the fight.

All at once, the gunfire stopped. In its place was a distant guttural sound he had grown accustomed to hearing. The low thwapping of a chopper coming in fast.

"Step outside, Sy!" Sebastian yelled, the barrel of a gun pressed into his back.

When he did, two familiar faces edged around the corner of the compound entrance, weapons outstretched and ready for action. Four others followed them dressed in the same black-and-white fatigues as the Nous operative.

"Celeste!" Silas roared. "They're—"

A hand reached around his face and covered his mouth. The barrel of the gun that had been at his back was shoved against his temple, sending a jolt of pain ricocheting back and forth across his head.

"Lay down your weapons!" Sebastian commanded. Following him was the commander and the three remaining Nousati operatives.

"Not on your life," she said, weapon outstretched and padding forward for a fight.

The thwapping grew louder. It would be overhead soon, presumably to extract his brother and crew. Maybe even himself as a hostage. Silas knew he didn't have much time. He had to act. But how? Between the roar of the incoming chopper and hand pressed against his face, his options were next to nil.

Then he had it. *Thank you, Sebastian!*

He only prayed she understood what he was doing.

"Let your brother go, Sebastian," Celeste yelled, her own SIG Sauer aiming straight between those blue eyes of his. "Lay down your weapons, and you'll be free to go."

The blond-haired man scoffed. "That's a good one, Ms. Bourne. But I don't think so."

She gripped the butt of her weapon tighter when she noticed Silas do something curious with his hands. He spread them out on both of his upper thighs, fingers flexed and outstretched. She furrowed her brow slightly.

What is he doing?

In the meantime, Gapinski had taken over the negotiation. He and Sebastian were engaged in a heated discussion she was entirely content to let play out. She prayed her partner continued holding the villainous man's attention while her other one was sending out a desperate signal of some sort.

Silas did it again, bringing both hands into fists and then laying them flat against his legs as if he was signaling her, readying her for something. But what?

He nodded ever so slightly. But in the gleam of the excavation lighting, she could see it. She nodded back, signaling she was ready for whatever he was planning.

His right hand moved to his side, but his left hand stayed open. His eyes drifted toward that hand, then he licked his lips, swallowed, and nodded.

Suddenly, his hand made a fist. Then he bobbed it off his leg and extended a single finger. It closed into a fist again before he extended the same finger again.

Then his palm went flat on his leg as before, as if pausing.

What the bloody hell, Silas?

He continued staring at her, then glanced down at his hand and continued motioning his message. *Finger, fist, finger.* Palm. Then *finger, finger.* Another palm.

It's a code!

She cursed herself for not paying closer attention to what he was doing from the start. But what kind of code was this?

She glanced down as he motioned *finger, finger, finger.* Then palm again.

It wasn't anything she had seen—

Blimey...it's Morse code!

It had been years since she had learned the simple coded language from her training as a recruit with MI6. She was rusty, but a remnant of her training surfaced from within her subconscious that connected with what he was motioning on his leg.

Finger, fist, fist, finger, Silas motioned. Then he flattened his palm before another set: *finger, fist, finger.*

He blinked twice and put his hand at his side.

By now the helicopter was hovering overhead, creating a vortex of windy, snowy confusion. Gapinski and Sebastian were shouting now, but it would soon be over. She glanced up to see a metal carriage dropping toward the courtyard ground for Nous's escape. With Silas held hostage, there was precious little they could do about it.

Dear Lord, please let that not be all!

She prayed the Lord would prod Silas to repeat the coded message, just one more time before Sebastian ended his speech and took him away.

She widened her eyes, then nodded toward his leg. He furrowed his brow, then glanced at Sebastian.

Come on, mate. One more time...

He nodded, then started the coded message once more. He flew through the letters, forcing Celeste to keep up and either translate on the fly or memorize. Within ten or twelve seconds he was through. And so was Sebastian.

The carriage settled onto the frozen ground with a thud. Sebastian shoved his brother inside. He quickly followed, as did a woman and a man wearing the same kind of arctic fatigues as the SEPIO operatives. The other three Nousati were out of luck, and they knew it. They started shouting in angry, rushed German as the carriage ascended toward the hovering chopper with a jerk. Outnumbered two to one, the men quickly laid down their weapons and put their hands in the air.

Gapinski and the other four SEPIO agents quickly surrounded them. Celeste stood planted where she was, pointing her weapon skyward as the metal carriage reached the chopper. She could see eight feet step off into the side of the metal bird. Then that was that.

She continued staring into the sky as the chopper rose and withdrew into the clear, moonlit sky, the wind whipping her hair and the snow, and stirring her emotions. She wiped away a tear as the bird flew off into the distance.

Taking away the only man she had ever cared about.

CHAPTER 21

What a disaster.

The snow was coming in more heavy now, a sheer of white magnified and accentuated by the bright white excavation lighting and beginning to blanket the interior of the castle fortress. A strong gust whirled through the courtyard, whipping up the white powder and sending Celeste for her collar.

She brought it tight against her neck, wishing she had brought a thicker coat. The welt on her cheek was smarting, too, against the bitter, biting wind. She brought her hand up to it and touched it. She winced, anger returning at what had happened below.

After Silas was seized from the SUV by the Nous agent down below the castle and carted away, she and Gapinski sat with the weasel Louis waiting for their own fate. She knew their options didn't look good, even without the look in the man's eyes and that sultry grin that made her skin crawl. Her years of training with MI6 and gut instinct told her the two of them were dispensable and would be dealt with soon. Their options were limited to nil with the man training a gun on them both without any leverage.

"So what's next?" she asked him.

"Excuse me, little missy?" Louis said grinning.

"Gapinski and me. Surely you don't need us anymore. It's clear Sebastian wanted his brother."

The man sat back and grinned.

She lowered her head and her voice, and said, "We can pay you, if that's what you'd like."

The man merely laughed, which made Celeste's ears burn.

She leaned back herself and grinned slightly. "Look, chap, I guarantee our cavalry are already marching to war after your stunt. So if I were you, I would be looking to cut a deal. And fast. Because if you don't..." She leaned forward and drilled the man with her dark eyes. "There will be hell to pay."

The man's grin faded. In an instant, he swept his weapon across her face, landing a blow to her cheek and sending her back against the window. She gave a muffled cry and jolted from the pain. Gapinski whipped around toward the back and yelled in protest.

"Shut up, little missy. Not another word. And you—" Louis swept the weapon toward the front and aimed it at Gapinski's head. "You keep the SUV running and the heat cranked. It will all be over soon enough."

Celeste clenched her jaw and narrowed her eyes, then sat straight in defiance. The back of her head throbbed, and her cheek was radiating with pain, but she refused to give the Nous operative the satisfaction by touching either.

Instead, she looked out of the windshield, considering their narrowing options—coming to grips with the possibility that the two of them would soon enough reach their demise at the hand of this man. She had stared down the face of death once before on a similar mission working for MI6 in the wake of the infamous 7/7 London bombings.

After four suicide bombers struck in central London killing fifty-two people and injuring more than seven hundred following coordinated attacks on the London Underground and on a double-decker bus during rush hour, she had led a small team of intelligence and military operatives deep inside Pakistan. The country had been in the grips of fear and terror following the attack, and the government worried more were on the way. They were sent to follow a scant trail of leads to ward off any future plots of further mayhem.

But then she made a calculated risk that put her team in danger and ended one of her teammates' lives.

She thought about Martin as the back of her head continued to throb, a memory chaser of the bullet that blew off the back of his head. She still recalled the sound it made, like a hollowed-out pumpkin thrown against a concrete sidewalk. And when she closed her eyes, she could see the image of his head lolled at that ungodly angle, and blood and brain matter spread across the wall of that dimly-lit room on the outskirts of Islamabad, like orange-seedy goop of that same pumpkin left behind.

Gapinski coughed, a deep, hacking cough that shook her back to the present. She tightened a hand into a fist and vowed that would not be their fate. But she was sure that they were both dead if they didn't act soon.

She ran through a number of scenarios through her head, none of them looked good. She settled on one; perhaps it would work. It did back in Islamabad.

"I have to go to the bathroom," Celeste said flatly.

Louis laughed. "Tough, little missy. You're gonna have to hold it until the chief and yer partner return."

She turned toward him. "I can't. I'm about to burst."

He shrugged. "Sorry, sweet thing. There ain't no way I'm letting you outside. Though I have to admit, I wouldn't mind catching a glimpse of you—"

"Hey, pal," Gapinski bellowed from the front, "show the

lady some respect. And let her use the little girl's room, would
ya? You can use me as leverage. Blow my brains out if she runs."

Celeste grimaced at the idea, the memory of Martin's head
rushing back to the surface.

"No way, no how. Hold it, or just let it go."

"Right here?" she scoffed.

"Makes no difference to me."

She went to protest when suddenly the SUV back door was
flung open.

A man with the same arctic fatigues appeared, his face
shrouded by a black mask and thick black goggles, and bearing
an automatic rifle slung around his chest.

"What the—"

Before Louis could turn and finish his sentence, the man
reached into the cabin and wrapped a thick arm around his
neck, then squeezed.

The cavalry really had arrived!

She lunged for Louis's weapon as he bucked up and down
straining against the stranglehold. She wrenched it from the
man as he flailed around in the cabin trying to find relief from
the vice grip.

Then she smacked him across the face with it like he
had her.

He immediately went limp.

"Nice move, director," the SEPIO operative said as he
dragged the body out of the SUV, his voice deep and Southern.

"Thanks, mate," she said climbing out into the frigid
midnight. "Is that Greer underneath that mask?"

"The one and only," he said as he pulled out a pair of black
zip ties, quickly immobilizing the man's hands and feet with
the plastic cuffs. He also gently inserted a syringe into the man's
neck to keep him out longer.

"Boy am I glad to see you! And the rest of your team." She
counted three more operatives, who had secured the perimeter

and were scoping out the surrounding area for any remaining hostiles.

Gapinski came around from the front and put his palm up in the air for a high-five. "Greer! Slap me some skin, my man."

The man chuckled and grabbed his meaty palm with his own, then the two embraced.

She thanked the men again and wondered out loud how they were able to track them to their location. Greer explained how Zoe was able to track the trio using Silas's phone. After her initial call into him while they were at the Cathar cave chapel, and she heard the threat before the line went dead, she immediately called for a small platoon of operatives stationed in Paris. Greer had been at the command post for a training exercise with new recruits, and so he had quickly mobilized them for the mission. Within thirty minutes, they were in the air and heading to the original location, which of course was dry. It wasn't until Silas turned the phone back on and they received another location ping that they were able to confirm the trio had gone to the fortress compound. Within minutes the chopper had lifted back off the ground and landed a klick west of the parked SUV.

The men had weapons for Celeste and Gapinski, and they awaited her orders. After a few minutes of planning, they set off toward the fortress compound on the hill, where they engaged in the successful firefight.

That is until they lost Silas.

Celeste shook her head, cursing herself for not being able to save him, for losing him to...She didn't want to think about what might be happening to him. What might have *happened* to him.

Again, Martin flashed through her mind's eye. She closed her eyes and took a breath, then shook her head.

No. He's with his brother. Surely, he wouldn't do anything rash...

Gapinski finished putting on the last of the black zip ties on the wrists of the Nous operatives, then walked over to Celeste. "We better get these guys down the side of this cliff before we find ourselves in a blizzard. This snow is really starting to pick up."

Celeste nodded. A buzzing drew her attention to her right pants pocket before she could respond. She brought out her mobile. *Zoe Corbino.*

Hope pinged her gut at the sight of SEPIO's operations technician.

"Hold on. It's Zoe." Celeste swiped the call to life. "I hope you're ringing with good news, love."

"The best news! We've located Silas."

Celeste's breath caught in her chest. She smiled widely, and a surge of emotion threatened to overcome her. She took a breath and cleared her throat. "Excellent work. Where?"

"A place called Externsteine."

"Come again?" Celeste said, pressing the phone against her ear as a gust of wind made hearing difficult.

"Externsteine," Zoe said more loudly.

"Externsteine? Sounds German, but where is that, or what is that? And why the bloody hell would they be there?"

"It is in Germany. The Externsteine is a distinctive sandstone rock formation located in the Teutoburg Forest, near the town of Horn-Bad Meinberg in the Lippe district of the German state of North Rhine-Westphalia. It's a sort of rock formation consisting of several tall, narrow columns of rock which rise abruptly from—"

"I don't need the Wikipedia entry, Zoe. Just tell me what the bloody hell it is." She regretted snapping at the woman, but Silas had been kidnapped, her emotions were frayed, and her head still throbbed.

Zoe paused, then said, "Apparently, it was a religious-cultural center for the German SS. But more than that, many of the high-ranking thinkers within the Nazi party and other völkish thinkers believed the site to be a pagan Germanic religious center and the so-called 'Irminsul,' a sacred sanctuary that played a role in the Germanic paganism of the Saxon people that was destroyed by Charlemagne. The Nazis held a number of excavations around the area proving it to be of cultic importance. It was literally built into a Neo-Germanic holy place that rivaled Christian ones."

"And this is where Sebastian has gone off to, taking Silas with him?"

"We're sure of it. Silas's phone is transmitting a clear and perf—"

Zoe stopped abruptly. Celeste looked at the face of her phone, thinking the call had dropped. It hadn't.

"Hello, Zoe?"

"I'm here. But we've got a problem."

Celeste closed her eyes and squeezed the bridge of her nose. "Spill it, love."

"Silas's phone was just deactivated. Could mean nothing, because we know he's at Externsteine. But…"

"It could also mean something entirely."

Zoe said nothing.

Celeste breathed deeply and sighed, then said, "Right. We best get moving if we're going to make it by dawn. It's four or five hours by helicopter from here with a refuel in Paris."

"Good luck," Zoe offered, and Celeste ended the call.

We're going to need more than luck for this mission.

DAY V

DECEMBER 21

CHAPTER 22

EXTERNSTEINE, GERMANY.

"Nice little parlor trick you played there, Sy," Sebastian said. He held the shattered remains of Silas's phone between his forefinger and thumb, like a stinking, deceased rodent.

Silas said nothing, but allowed one end of his mouth to curl upward in satisfaction. Apparently, his quick thinking had at least brought in the cavalry to free Celeste and Gapinski. He just hoped it was enough to bring them to wherever-the-heck they had gone.

Sebastian smirked and tossed the busted mobile to the floor of the resting chopper, what was left of the metal and plastic made a sickening crunch as it skipped across the metal.

After he and Sebastian had ascended into the Nous chopper, and it lifted up and away from the Cathar castle, they flew to a small airport in Lausanne, Switzerland to refuel before making their way north. After a few hours, they touched down on a frozen lawn beside a large house of brick and stone nestled in a forest that apparently was close to ground zero of the entire Holy Grail mystery—in Germany, if he was to guess. Before they disembarked from the helicopter, he was roughly searched by Lars.

That's when Silas's mobile device was discovered.

Sebastian had snatched it, cursed, and smashed it on the metal floor of the chopper. He stomped on it for good measure before holding it up as evidence that he was left to his mercy.

"I guess I should give you brownie points for trying. However, remind me to eliminate the incompetent fool who let you keep the damn thing! Now I suppose your Navy SEALs for Jesus will be on their way soon, swooping in to try and disrupt our carefully laid plans. No matter. It will all be over soon, anyhow."

"What will?" Silas shot back. "You still haven't told me what it is you've got cooking, brother. Which isn't like you. Usually, you're Johnny-on-the-spot with boasts of grandeur."

"All in due time, big brother. All in due time. But first, there's someone you need to meet." Sebastian motioned for his brother to get out of the chopper.

Silas stepped out into the frigid dawn and onto the frozen grass. A full moon shone bright above through a few scattered clouds. His brother disembarked, then gently, tenderly helped Helen out from the front cockpit of the bird. Silas was shoved in the back by a rifle carried by the muscle-head Lars. He glared at the man, then followed his brother and apparent girlfriend forward toward the house.

The night was still; not a sound could be heard except for the crunch of snow as they moved through the yard of a dimly-lit modest two-story brick mansion standing behind the chopper. Inside a bay of windows that wrapped around the back of the house, he could see a roaring fire beyond a grand piano. The smell of pine trees and burning wood filled his senses, the moonlight catching tendrils of smoke drifting out of the chimney in the middle of the stately structure. Beyond the home, Silas searched through naked trees for a glimpse of anything that might give him a clue of his whereabouts. Rising in the distance, he could see blocks of what looked to be cut stone, large and imposing. Reminded him of the Neolithic stones of Stonehenge that had been the focal point for pagan worship and seasonal celebrations—like the Winter Solstice.

As they reached the threshold of the house, Silas began to shake underneath his windbreaker, its nylon material doing little to keep out the near-zero temperatures. Sebastian opened the door, and the warmth laced with burnt wood and baking bread lured him forward. He gladly followed, but he set his senses on high alert for anything that might offer the final set of clues to lock the gears of the Grail mystery into place—as well as anything that might offer a means of escape.

The group thudded loudly through a narrow hallway across bare hardwood floors polished to an elegant sheen. The walls were accented by tasteful art from the Weimar period, if he placed it right. They navigated around a few Rococo-style tables lining the hallway until they reached an expansive, but cozy living room furnished with the black grand piano he saw earlier nestled in the bay of windows at the back of the room, a Steinway if Silas wasn't mistaken. Overstuffed leather couches and chairs were arrayed in front of the fire crackling and popping with purpose. A man was sitting in one of the chairs, black hair with a sheen greeting them above the chair's back. A cherry-wood Howard Miller floor clock rang next to Silas, startling him. Six chords chimed off, marking the six o'clock hour.

The man eased around to face the announcement. He brightened when he saw the company. "Right on time," he said, standing as the quartet entered the room.

He was tall, with wide shoulders. The angular face and bulging eyes made him immediately, unmistakably recognizable.

Rudolf Borg.

Walking toward Silas, he said, "You must be the illustrious Silas Grey."

The man looked larger than he had from the internet live

stream video. He was an imposing figure, and his greasy black hair shoved behind his ears and those eyes, along with his slight hunch and wide grin, set Silas on edge.

So this is the man my brother has been working with to undermine the Church and destroy the Christian faith...

His gut seized with anxiety, but he quickly turned it around into steely resolve. There was no way in hell he was going to let his brother and this man Borg get away with this. Whatever *this* was, exactly.

"Come, let us sit and have a drink."

The man motioned for Silas to accept one of the chairs near the fireplace. He hesitated, but shuffled over and took a seat. Sebastian sat in the middle of the couch opposite the fire. The other two left through a door behind Silas.

"Care for a brandy?" Borg asked as he walked to a bar across the room near the grand piano.

"Fine," Silas grunted as he leaned in toward the fire, its warmth a welcomed relief.

"Are you good with that, Sebastian?"

"Yes, thank you, Rudolf," Sebastian replied.

Silas turned to his brother, revolted by the fact he was on a first-name basis with the apparent leader of the Church's archenemy.

A minute later the man came bearing a silver tray with three crystal snifters filled with amber liquid.

"Here you go, Seba."

Silas blanched at the nickname Sebastian had only ever accepted from Silas. Clearly, the two were close. Probably closer than they were at that point. He was saddened by that realization.

Borg lowered the tray for Silas. "And for you, Sy."

Silas recoiled his hand at the mention of Sebastian's own nickname for him. He grimaced at the man, and growled, "Don't call me that. Ever."

Borg put a hand to his chest and offered an apologetic smile. "Vergib mir, Silas. Forgive me."

He clenched his jaw and swiped the glass from the tray, then took a mouthful of the German drink of choice. He swallowed hard, the sweet, thick liquid of intense dark fruits hitting his empty stomach hard and instantly working its magic. He would have to be careful if he was to keep his wits about him.

Borg set the silver tray on an end table, withdrew his glass, and took a seat in the chair across from Silas. He raised his snifter, the firelight dancing off the crystal and causing the brandy to glow. "An Asbach Freiheitsbrand," he announced. "Distilled in 1989 and bottled in 2014 to mark twenty-five years since the fall of the Berlin—"

"Can we get on with it?" Silas interrupted.

Borg sat with mouth open, still holding his drink. He smiled, and said, "A man of action. I like that." He raised his glass slightly higher, then took a large mouthful and swallowed. He closed his eyes and sank into his chair. "We've got lots to talk about, you and I."

"Do we?"

"For one thing, you killed my lover."

Silas shook his head. Had he heard him right? "I what?"

"You head me. Don't deny it. Earlier this year, at the Church of the Holy Sepulcher."

He searched his memory for the events of the harrowing mission from earlier in the year. But he didn't kill—

It dawned on him. Jacob Crowley...He hadn't been the one to pull the trigger, though. It was Celeste. But he wasn't about to throw her to this dog.

Silas took another mouthful of his amber alcohol. He let it linger in his mouth, staring down the man before swallowing it. Borg's face was firm and hateful.

"Yep. I did," he said. "But it was either him or me. And I chose to bat for the home team."

Borg's face morphed into a wicked crimson that bespoke a terror beneath the surface that Silas didn't want to tap. He was clenching his jaw, the muscles on the side of his head and neck bulging with fury. It looked like the man was going to pounce on him and smash his skull in with the crystal goblet. But then all at once, the hate behind the man's bulging eyes left, and his face softened into a knowing smile and Caucasian glow.

"No matter," he simply said. "Today, I will exact my vengeance."

The door behind Silas opened, and in walked Helen. She had removed her dark overcoat and was wearing a long, white coat instead. The kind a lab technician or doctor would wear. She was bearing a syringe with a long needle. Pink liquid glowed inside as she walked toward Borg.

"It's time, Rudolf," she said.

His face brightened, and he set to rolling up a sleeve. He held his arm out for the doctor, clearly eager to receive from her the vial of mystery liquid.

"What is that?" Silas asked as she stepped close, checking the vein faintly protruding as it ran across Borg's elbow and down his forearm.

"A serum to prepare for the transformation," Borg said as the woman inserted the needle in his vein. He winced slightly as she pushed the pink liquid into his arm.

"But you haven't even explained what the heck you plan to do here."

"Isn't it obvious, Sy?" Sebastian said from the couch.

Silas looked at his brother and shook his head, brow furrowed and searching for answers.

"It's simple," Borg said as Helen finished.

The man paused, his face registering nothing, as if goading Silas on, clearly relishing the reveal.

Silas sat back in his chair, irritated but curious.

Then Borg said, "I'm becoming Jesus."

CHAPTER 23

Borg said it so matter-of-factly that it barely registered in Silas's brain.

Helen withdrew the needle then whispered something to the man in German before leaving through the way she came. Borg promptly rolled his sleeve back into place.

"Becoming Jesus?" Silas said, his face recoiling with confusion.

Borg nodded, his face regular and relaxed, as if he had said he was becoming an American or growing a beard. "Well, a resurrected, modern incarnation of the Christian Savior. But, yes."

"Are you kidding me?" Silas said flatly. He turned to Sebastian, and said, "Is this some kind of joke?"

"On the contrary, big brother," answered Sebastian. "It's far more real than the fairy tale of that zombie Savior of yours."

Silas's face flashed with anger at Sebastian's comment, then twisted in a mixture of dumbfoundedness and horror at the words that Borg had uttered.

What in the world were they—

Then it hit him.

The Holy Grail, supposedly bearing the DNA-rich blood of

Jesus. The gene-editing technique Sebastian had referenced, which could only mean the CRISPR technology he had heard about on NPR.

Nous was going to edit the DNA of Rudolf Borg, rewiring him genetically with the DNA of Jesus of Nazareth!

And his brother was helping them do it.

"Impossible..." Silas whispered, his stomach sick with the horrific thought of what Nous was planning to do.

"Not," Borg said, cradling his brandy snifter in one hand and wearing a smug grin of satisfaction. "The maturing field of biogenetics has already paved the way through CRISPR technology. For instance, the day will soon come when we will cure someone of Alzheimer's by literally cutting out the gene variant ApoE4 that causes it, then using an alternative gene replacement to save one's faculties. And, of course, the other option is to mine alternative genetic material from other sources and introduce it into cells, transforming existing ones into new variants using new genetic code."

Sebastian added, "Some scientists have already mixed genetic information from two separate species, creating modern Chimeras by introducing the genetic information from one species into another. Recently, pig embryos that had been injected with human stem cells when they were only a few days old began to grow organs containing human cells. Then there's what that Chinese fellow just did with those twins—creating the first CRISPR-edited babies with the CCR5 gene used by HIV as a doorway for infiltrating human cells completely deactivated. The future truly is now!"

He paused and smiled proudly, then added, "My lovely Helen is going to release a Cas9 nuclease complex with a synthetic guide RNA into Borg's cells. The process will allow his cells' genome to be cut and existing genes to be removed, replaced with new ones."

Borg nodded. "We have already mined the alternative genetic material from Jesus' blood—"

"Wait a minute," Silas interrupted shaking his head, not sure he heard Borg right. "Genetic material from Jesus' blood, found in the Grail? One of the chalices you stole actually held blood?"

The man with bulging eyeballs grinned with satisfaction and nodded. "Oh, yes. Alas, my ancestor, Otto Rahn, was incorrect with his assessment. It appears the tradition at Glastonbury was correct, and the Arimathean tradition has been proven true."

"There was blood in the Nanteos Cup fragment?"

"Trace amounts, but it was there. Which probably shouldn't be a surprise, given the revelations embedded in the grail romances themselves. We will use the DNA we recovered to transform my existing cells into new ones using the genetic code found in the Holy Grail."

"A new prophet for our new day, Sy," Sebastian said. "A new Savior, even. Can you imagine that, big brother? And one cut from the cloth of your own religious figure."

"Literally," Borg laughed, taking another sip of his brandy. Sebastian echoed him and took his own sip.

"But that's assuming it was Jesus' blood in the first—"

"It is the blood of the peasant prophet!" Borg roared, his eyes wide with passion. "And thanks to the Grail of power, the Winter Solstice will rise to replace Christmas as the celebrated holy day when the divine became one of us—born of science, not faith!"

Silas recoiled at the eruption, sinking into his chair and dropping his head in contemplation. A shiver of fright wound its way up his spine. His head was swimming. Both from the brandy and from the sheer preposterousness of the science fiction. Fodder for technothrillers, maybe, but not religious reality!

Unless...

What if it wasn't fiction? What if they really had discovered the true Grail, the one leveraged by a string of writers that followed a tradition stretching back to the early days of Christianity surrounding Joseph of Arimathea—a true chalice containing the blood of Jesus and his genetic material? And what if it could be mined and mixed with the blood of another, replace the host DNA with the DNA found in that chalice? In essence, creating a genetic replica of Jesus of Nazareth, whom the Church has staked its claim as the Savior of the world?

What would the religious implications be for such an accomplishment? For the faith-lives of people around the globe —to have a new genetically-replicated Jesus walking around on the earth? In essence, an incarnation of genetics, not of divinity; an immaculate conception not of God, but of man?

Silas sank deeper at the dark thoughts, his stomach churning with the dreaded possibilities.

"So, Doctor Grey," Borg said, snapping Silas from the vortex of questions and implications engulfing his mind. "What say you?"

Silas said nothing, still too stunned by it all to offer a reply. He breathed deeply, wanting to retch, considering his next moves in order to stop the abomination.

"Cat got your tongue, brother?" Sebastian said laughing.

"Somehow that surprises me," Borg continued. "Can't imagine you've ever been one to hold back an opinion when—"

"It's horse shit, is what I think it is," Silas finally said.

The two chuckled. "Always love a good Silas cursing," Sebastian offered. "Sounds so earnest and sincere, yet awkward all at once."

Silas chuckled, as well. "Oh, I have never been more sincere in all of my life at the dumbass idea that you two have just concocted. Do you honestly think that anyone in their right mind would believe what you two are selling? That the Holy

Grail is real, that some...some chalice survived through the ages bearing blood—the blood of Jesus?!" He threw back the rest of his brandy and chortled with laughter.

"Think what you want," Borg said, spinning his brandy snifter with delight. "But the German people have always understood the true power of the Grail, and the blood that it contains. Wolfram von Eschenbach saw to that, as well as countless theologians revealing the true power of Jesus symbolized in that holy relic."

"And what is that?" Silas asked, coming off from his belly laugh.

"Why, the power of Jesus' teachings and example of love—his very life essence offered for all to receive as their own!" Borg roared with excitement as he stood. He walked back over to the bar, then filled his snifter nearly to the brim with more brandy.

He settled back into his chair, took a mouthful of the amber libation, and said, "One of the greatest theologians to have ever lived was a German. Did you know that?"

Silas said nothing.

"Friedrich Schleiermacher was his name."

Silas scoffed loudly. "Are you kidding me?"

"You scoff, but the man was brilliant. He said that Christianity is the most developed form of religion because of the person who exhibited the highest human ideal: Jesus of Nazareth."

"The highest human ideal?"

Borg nodded and sat forward, his eyes earnest to impart his revelation. "As Schleiermacher plainly put it, Jesus is the One in whom the human creation is perfected. The man was truly tapped into the sublime, the ground of our being that undergirds the entire universe. His life was determined by the universal human ideal that revealed itself in human existence because he possessed the God-consciousness in all of its fullness. This doesn't mean any of that silly nonsense the Church goes on about Jesus being in his very nature God. No, no, no! Instead, Jesus somehow grasped, in word and deed, the highest human ideal. And it is this spirit that Jesus sought to impart to his followers through his earthly life."

Silas smirked. "You know, I always love it when people outside the faith try to tell us who Jesus was and what he came to do. The Church has never taught this was Jesus' significance! Because, you know, there's a little thing called the Nicene Creed that spells it out in plain English and—"

"Greek, actually," Sebastian corrected.

Silas ignored him and took a sip of his brandy. Then he sat forward and said to Borg, *"For us and for our salvation,'* it says, *'Jesus came down from heaven, and by the Holy Spirit was incarnate of the Virgin Mary, and became man. For our sake he was crucified under Pontius Pilate, he suffered death and was buried, and rose again on the third day in accordance with the Scriptures.'"*

Borg went to interject, but Silas wouldn't let him.

"Did you hear that?" he said grinning. "Jesus didn't come to give us an example but to save us. He bled, died, was buried, and rose again. That's why Jesus matters! Schleiermacher and a string of others have denied this, redefining even his death as a modeling death of love, not an atoning death—one that paid the price of our rebellion against God in our place with his blood."

"Exactly!" Borg exclaimed, eyes wide with passion. "Jesus' life was far more significant than his death. The ideal life of love flowing through his blood is what matters! His death is simply the culmination of that life, showing us what it looks like to live the universal human ideal to its fullness!"

Silas sat back and shook his head. "Look, I don't deny that Jesus' life of love is a good thing. Of course it was! His teachings about human dignity and justice and neighbor love have been the bedrock of Western civilization stretching back centuries. But his life doesn't save us. His death does! Even those English and French grail romance writers knew that, using the Grail as a symbol of the Eucharist—which was itself meant to remember Christ's death, his shed blood for sins. "

"No, no, no!" Borg protested, waving a hand in the air. "His loving life is what saves, don't you see? The man Jesus, and the love that flowed through his veins, is important because of his revolutionary movement and model of a loving life."

Silas shook his head. "According to that logic, Jesus is the moral not the metaphysical Son of God. He merely acted like God, rather than actually *being* God."

Borg cocked his head to consider the argument. "I guess that's right." He turned to Sebastian, and said, "Hey, he's good."

Sebastian rolled his eyes. "Don't encourage him."

"But what good does that do anyone if he was just another Gandhi on steroids?" Silas exclaimed. "A dead Gandhi is still a dead Gandhi, no matter how you dress it up."

Borg filled his mouth with brandy, then swallowed and leaned forward and waved a dismissive hand. He continued, high on his pseudo-spirituality. "You don't get it. What you see in Jesus is the best view afforded to humans of the character of divine living. It flowed through his veins. You can see it in how he lived and what he taught. Jesus' mastery over life through his higher, more brilliant way of living and alternative message provides the solution to our problem. Fundamentally, the solution Jesus offers all of humanity came through his blessed Kingdom work. Or, as I like to put it, the Republic of Heaven."

Silas smirked. "Yeah, I caught that innovation in your live feed earlier in the week."

"Don't you just love it!" Borg said, brightening with passion again. "Jesus didn't come to start a new religion but to announce a new way of life. He was the founder of a new countermovement to all other human regimes. You see, the human problem is dysfunctional systems and destructive stories. Thus, we need a new system and a new story to repair and heal us.

Jesus provides humanity the solution through his teachings on the Republic of Heaven and example of higher living that transcends this chaotic one."

"No," Silas protested, "that has never been how historic Christianity has framed our problem. We're rebels in desperate need of rescue. Full stop. We're bent and broken from the inside, not—"

"No, no, no!" Borg interrupted, waving his hand dismissively again. "That's where the Church has gotten it wrong all these ages. Jesus' invitation into the Republic of Heaven was an invitation into the Übermensch, humanity emerging beyond itself as envisioned by the prophet Nietzsche. The entire human experience has been one of constantly emerging from what we were and are into what we can become. Jesus understood this better than anyone during his day, and anyone since —except, perhaps, Master Nietzsche. And I aim to speed that process up. In fact, this is only the beginning."

"What are you talking about?"

"If this little experiment of ours succeeds, the re-wiring of my own genetic code with that of Jesus', then why not open up the gates to any and all who would seek to become the universal human ideal found in the man's genetic essence? Why not mass produce the CRISPR-ready serum to edit the genes of humanity itself using the evolved genetic material of the Holy Grail—pushing our species into a truly post-human future led by the Grail of power bearing the power of the blood of Jesus?"

"You are deluded!" Silas exclaimed, throwing back his head in amazement. "The two of you...I can't even."

The pair chuckled at his retort.

"No, I'm serious," he continued, "You have no idea what the power of Jesus means for the world. This power you speak about isn't in his blood, in the genetic information that made Jesus the man of love he was and the way of love he taught. The power of Jesus is in his *shed* blood, in what he did on the cross by willingly offering himself as a sacrifice to pay the price of our sins in our place! Fulfilling all of the terms of the old covenant with its sacrificial requirements. For as the Bible says, 'without the shedding of blood there is no forgiveness of sins.'"

"There he goes," Sebastian sighed, "quoting that damn book of his."

"Shut up!" Silas shot back.

Borg went to protest, but Silas plowed forward. "Hold on! The Gospel stories of the New Testament show that his entire life was oriented toward the cross. Paul makes this clear in the first chapter of his letter to Christians living in Ephesus: 'In him we have redemption through his blood,' he writes, 'the forgiveness of our trespasses, according to the riches of his grace.' Not his life, not his teachings and example of love—but through his shed blood do we find the rescue from dysfunction, as you put it, that we're all so desperate for!"

Sebastian said, "Sy, are you seriously—"

"Shut up!" Silas snapped again. He closed his eyes and sighed. "I'm sorry, but let me finish. Later, in his letter to the Church of Rome, Paul wrote that God presented Jesus as a sacrifice of atonement, and freely declared people 'not guilty' through the shedding of his blood. A clear connection to the Jewish sacrificial system outlined in the Torah, where in Leviticus the Lord said blood makes atonement for our sins— which is exactly what we need! Atonement, someone or something taking the blame for the ways in which we have failed to love God and love people."

"Jesus' death doesn't do anything for us!" Borg roared. "It's a bloody *paradigm*, like any of the ancient myths that have governed our collective unconscious for this salvation in which we ourselves are to participate in anticipation of the coming divine Republic. We join with Jesus in dying—to our pride and agendas, in martyrdom as a witness to the justice of the Republic. Sharing in Christ's blood is symbolic of our dying to the bad ethics of the world and rising to new life by living the universal human ideal. That is all. Which means the power of Jesus' blood is that his loving example is what saves us from our bad existence—which the DNA in his blood bears."

Before Silas could respond, there was a knock at the door. It opened, and Helen peeked around it, saying, "It's time, Rudolf."

The man set down his emptied snifter and clasped his hands together. "Dawn breaks. And along with it, the promise of a new humanity."

CHAPTER 24

The SEPIO helicopter touched down on a frozen, neatly-manicured lawn in the middle of a vast forest half a mile west of Externsteine. Stone slabs stuck up from the ground like toothpicks in uneven rows a few yards away, making Celeste think they had probably landed in a cemetery. A building with a steep roof planted several yards to the west with a cross confirmed it.

She and Gapinski plus another operative named Gabriel from the Paris operation and Greer disembarked and ran east into the forest as the chopper lifted back into the frigid, late-December morning, the first sign of dawn beginning to crest over the horizon as it flew away toward the staging area back at a small SEPIO outpost in Münster.

Once it was clear Sebastian and the other Nous operatives had brought Silas to Externsteine, and that the area was seemingly the final staging area for Nous's plans, Radcliffe elected to send the pair and one other operative from the group at Montségur plus Greer. The other two were left to took care of securing the Nous operatives and gathering intel from the Cathar fortress castle. Understandably, Radcliffe was worried sick at Silas being taken hostage and even more apoplectic with

Nous's yet-unrevealed plans. And since the Winter Solstice had arrived, he needed his best operatives in play if they were to put a final stop to Nous's attempts at undermining the Christian faith and subverting the Church—while also rescuing their latest recruit.

As they travelled to the final leg of their mission, she kept running the Morse code through her head trying to recall the coded signal Silas sent her before he was abducted. She remembered the second and final letters were the same. *Dot, dash, dot.* The letter *R.* And she was also sure about the second one to the last: *dot, dash, dash, dot.* The letter *P.*

But was the first letter *dash, dot, dash?* Or *dash, dot, dash, dot. K* or *C?* Then she thought it was *dash, dot, dot.* The letter *D.* It might not matter if she could get the middle right. Either *dot, dot; dot, dot, dot.* Or *dot, dot, dot; dot, dot.* Either an *I* and *S,* or an *S* and *I.* Then again, it could be an *H:* four *dots* in a row.

The whole thing was a bloody frustrating exercise in mental exhaustion over the course of the chopper ride from Montségur to Externsteine. But she kept at it, praying the Lord would give her supernatural guidance.

Then all at once, it was clear. She was sure of it because the letters struck at something she had read about in the Guardian earlier in the year.

Dash, dot, dash, dot
Dot, dash, dot
Dot, dot
Dot, dot, dot
Dot, dash, dash, dot
Dot, dash, dot.
CRISPR.

She leaned back into her chopper bucket seat when the penny had finally dropped after an exhausting go at the puzzle, a grin playing across her face in satisfaction. That jolly well was it, connecting to the fascinating science editorial piece about some pigs that were bred using a procedure to splice their DNA with that of human genetic information. The article went on to paint a rather glorifying future of the gene editing tool that could one day re-wire a person genetically. It sang the hopes of mining alternative material from other genetic sources and introducing it into cells to compensate for abnormal genes, such as Down syndrome or Alzheimer's.

But then there were the darker possibilities following the tropes of science fiction novels spelling the doom of humanity —with possibilities of super-races of genetically altered and enhanced humans who would rule or exploit the non-genetically edited ones. Not only was there the thought of tampering with the human genetic code for enhancements, there was the very real possibility of terrorists using such a gene-altering technique to wipe out an entire civilization. It really would be the end of history as we knew it.

When she called Radcliffe to tell him about cracking the coded message Silas had sent moments before being abducted, he was at first confused.

"What in the blazes does CRISPR have to do with anything?" he grumbled.

"Consider this: if Nous has indeed found a Holy Grail—"

"Poppycock!" he interrupted. "The Grail is a legend, a figment of an overactive novelist's imagination—"

"That may or may not be rooted in at least some seed of a tradition stretching four- or five-hundred-years beforehand," she interrupted back. "And then there is the strong contention that Joseph of Arimathea evangelized our lands, the very man who had disposed of Christ's body coming to the shores of Britannia bearing Christianity. Perhaps he bore more than just a word. Maybe he brought a piece of the Word with him."

To say Radcliffe was skeptical was an understatement. But he granted Celeste's reasoning for the sake of argument. "Fine. Position granted. But what does it all mean, my dear?"

She had thought of that, too, when she put together the code. If Radcliffe wasn't buying the actuality of the Holy Grail, then he would be loath to swallow the potential true ends of Nous's conspiracy.

He nearly did choke, launching into a lengthened hacking cough. Partly brought on by his continued cold, partly brought on by Celeste's suggestion that one of the stolen Grails contained real blood with extractable DNA of rich genetic material that Nous was intending to splice into another person. Potentially rewiring someone with the genes of Jesus—or at least someone they claimed was the Son of God.

Trying to reason her way through it all, she said to Radcliffe, "At first, I thought the whole thing was preposterous myself. The bit about the Grail being genuine, much less bearing blood—Jesus' blood, at that! Yes, farfetched is putting it mildly. Then I wondered, why would Nous want to create a genetically replicated...well, Jesus, in the first place? But then I had a think about it: what better way to undermine the Christian faith and subvert the Church than to replicate the Savior at the center of it, casting confusion about the uniqueness of Jesus and the very purpose of his blood? And, then, if that isn't the end of it, with one replication, if they intend to mass produce some sort of rewiring serum for the whole of humanity...Well, then Lord come quickly!"

This seemed to give Radcliffe pause; for once he was without words. Then he said, "I shudder to think that there may be a milligram of truth to your conjecture, Celeste." He paused again, then blew his nose, and said, "But it seems that you have made sense of it. And considering our lad Silas sent you the word that may very well be the final piece to this godawful puzzle through coded message...I have to believe that what appears to be nothing more than science fiction is, in fact, the Church's horror feature, sprung from the silver screen and come alive at this dark hour. And on the eve of Christmas, no less, the celebration of the birth of Immanuel, the God-with-us-God who lived this life and shed his blood to pay the ultimate price in our place."

There was more silence before Radcliffe offered a final word: "Good work, Celeste. The enemy has mounted the ramparts, and they are cresting the parapet unlike any other time in the history of the Church. And you and your crew better bloody well deal the decisive blow!"

She told him they would. Moments later, they disembarked onto the frozen ground before making quick work through the vast forest at the dawn of the Winter Solstice. They came to a small frozen river as it snaked eastward, proving to be one fork to a larger one that deposited into a large pond. They crossed that branch, taking care to navigate its frozen surface until they reached the other side, and hustled to the water's edge.

When they did, they saw a series of gray stone shafts rising from the surface of Earth in a neat, single row. The first thing that struck Celeste was how similar they looked to Stonehenge, the Neolithic, man-made center of pagan worship. It was only until she looked farther on past the massive stones that she was gobsmacked by what she saw.

CHAPTER 25

Tendrils of dawn's first light began reaching over the horizon, the clear starry sky giving way to a burnt indigo that offered a morning filled with the promise for a new awakening within humanity. The Winter Solstice had arrived, and along with it the promise of a rebirthing, as well.

Borg led the party onward toward the ceremonial site, his body tingling with anticipation at what he would become. What Nous would offer the world. And what a fatal blow it would be to the Church that dared claim Jesus of Nazareth as its own.

As he huffed, steam puffing out of his open mouth through the frigid December morning, the clapboard church that stood at the center of his hometown not more than forty-five minutes away appeared in his mind's eye. The one with the ghastly wooden cross bearing that dead savior. The one that perpetuated the myth of the wonder-working power of his blood through that acrid meal named in his memory: The Lord's Supper.

He shuddered at the thought, and his mouth turned upward in disgust at worshiping the man for his death. Didn't they understand it was his life that mattered?! No wonder the earliest Christians were accused of cannibalism by the Romans, with all of that blood worship and bloodlust.

A distant memory worked its way to the surface. A ghastly hymn from the twentieth century, sung with gusto and adoration of the cross, with all of its pornographic violence. The words still sat within, nestled in his consciousness like a cancerous tumor that ate away at him. That clamorous tune still rang in his head:

> *Wärest du frei von der Last der Sünde?*
> *Macht liegt im Blut, im Blut liegt die Macht*
> *Würdest du über das Böse siegen?*
> *Wundervolle Macht liegt im Blut*

> Would you be free from the burden of sin?
> There's power in the blood, power in the blood;
> Would you o'er evil a victory win?
> There's wonderful power in the blood.

*You have no idea...*he sneered.

Of course, those pathetic, mousy churchgoers from a distant life believed that shed blood activated some magic to free humanity from sin and bring victory and the promise of a life to come. No, no, no!

A dead god is a dead god is a dead god! Nothing more.

It was only in seizing life by the horns and rising above this pathetic existence through brute force and enlightened reason that the world had any hope of salvation. And the blood of Jesus was just the antidote.

Yes, the Christ would rise again, but not by the magic of doctrine. No, no, no! It is through *science* that the power of his life-force coursing through his veins will rise to meet the challenges of humanity. The power of Jesus' blood, full of enlightenment and sublime purpose, a grounded connection with the universe and loving connection with humanity would mingle with his own—offering the world the possibility of a new Savior for a new age.

One fashioned and forged in humanity, not divinity!

They crunched onward across the frozen road. As they rounded a bend, those beautiful pillars of stone came into sharper view, the ones leveraged by his people from generations past to channel the affections of their spirits toward the universe in expectant hope.

There was a gasp behind him. He guessed it was Silas. His mouth curled upward with glee.

Good. Let him gasp. He has no idea...

WHAT IN ALL that is holy and sacred...

Rising from the frozen ground next to a large pond frosted over with ice and snow, Silas saw the rock formation that had made Externsteine famous, the sacred site of pagan Saxons thought to hold the memories of their adoration from generations past. The lawn in front lived up to that memory.

The place was deserted, except for a platform of sorts planted near the base of the natural rock formation, constructed out of roughly hewn wood and stained dark with menacing purpose. It was ringed by five torches the size of a person, with large flames giving off an acrid smell and black smoke. One sat at the base, two others near the top, and two more on either side. On closer approach, he guessed it was an inverted pentagram, symbolizing the domination of air, earth, wind, and fire over the soul, the physical and elemental over the spiritual.

Silas's stomach grew heavy with dread, and his lungs heaved hot breaths that steamed the frigid air. When they arrived, he could see the altar was circular. Then he recoiled in horror.

In the center was a cross, set in lighter wood and bent at wicked angles.

A swastika.

Borg chuckled. "Oh, don't be so disgusted. Surely a man of your learned stature would know that what the Germans twisted into a racialist, anti-Semitic symbol had long before been an ancient religious icon from the cultures and religious traditions of Eurasia, which has symbolized divinity and spirituality. Of course, it also bears a striking resemblance to another religious icon that's been perpetuated through Western religions. However, this symbol holds all of the divine promise of these pre-modern cultures for such a time as this."

"What the heck is the meaning of this place?" Silas asked with hesitation standing at the foot of the platform, breathless and confused. "What are you doing here?"

"Beautiful, isn't?" Borg said coming alongside him. "An altar combining the choicest of oak and dogwood, mingling their elemental properties in order to channel the energies of the universe for our purpose here this morning. As the strongest of the woods, oak offers a sturdy foundation that seeks a powerful guardian and liberator that's excellent for prosperity and sacrifice. It is robust and true, strongly rooted in the earth and easily channels natural life energies. While the lighter dogwood carries with it links to the warrior heroism and superhuman physical prowess of the mythical hero. The wood channels the universal magic properties of the renewal cycles of fertility, with resurrection."

The man ambled over to the altar, running a hand along its surface while walking around its circumference, grinning and taking his time as his eyes bulged with lustful expectation. He said lowly, "It will be the site of humanity's resurrection, this holiest of Earth days, redeeming what you Christians have done to the cross, with your obsession over blood and death.

For upon it we shall discover a new purpose for the blood of your Christ."

A wind blew through the pagan site, the flames flapping like flags in protest and provoking an unholy, guttural, creaking reply from the trees.

Sebastian came up next to Silas and took in a deep breath. He smiled, and said, "Can't you just feel the energy emanating from this place, everything that is sacred and holy in the universe being channeled here?"

Silas turned to him, his face twisted with a mixture of revulsion and confusion. "You know, baby brother, never in a million lifetimes would I have expected you, with all of your talk of science, to be championing the most antiscientific horse—"

Sebastian laughed. "There you go with that cursing again! Dad would have washed your mouth—"

Silas grabbed his brother by the neck of his jacket, shaking him and shoving him back so that he slipped and fell onto the snowy ground. "Don't you ever talk about Dad like that! Not under these circumstances. He loved God, loved Jesus, and banked his life—his earthly life and eternal life on that shed blood you so love to mock! He would have whipped your ass for what you've given yourself over to."

His brother narrowed his eyes and clenched his jaw. He got up from the ground and dusted himself off. "As I was going to say before you attacked me...It isn't antiscientific in the least, but the most scientific of ways to push the human race forward. What better way to cure the maladies of our pitiful race than infusing it with the blood of a bona fide prophet? And one you yourself have fancied pushing on me for at least a decade, I might add!"

"You are completely clueless! Jesus—"

Borg cleared his throat across from altar. "When you two are through having it out, how about we get on with it? Humanity is awaiting its salvation."

Silas glared at his brother before looking away.

"But first things first," Borg said, motioning toward Silas. "Come with me. I want to show you something." Before Silas could protest or question, the man walked toward the massive sandstone formations. He stopped at one in particular and glanced back. Silas walked up next to him, a guard close behind.

Silas furrowed his brow in confusion. The scene before him did not compute.

A depiction of the Descent from the Cross scene—the moment when Jesus' spent, butchered body was taken down from the cross after he had died—was carved into the side of the Externsteine sandstone. It was divided into three parts, but the largest, central portion interested Silas the most. At the center of the relief sat a cross, and to the right was a figure aiding in the recovery of Jesus' body from the object. He was lowering Christ's body toward someone standing to the left of the cross, who Silas assumed was Joseph of Arimathea. To his left was Mary, Mother of Jesus, with her hand supporting the head of her son's corpse. Opposite Mary was John the Apostle holding a book.

What is this scene doing on a set of sandstone formations in northern Germany, and at a site of pagan worship?

"You can see why I wanted to hold our ceremony at this site. Not only because of its significance in the celebration of the Winter Solstice. But also because it was just too perfect of a place to subvert the very event claimed by Christians depicted in this relief. The death of Jesus on the cross and their pathetic trust in his blood to buy them a cottage on God's celestial shores."

The significance of what had been set in motion to bring about the endgame of Nous's plot and subversion of what Christians hold dear began to press in against Silas. His mind was reeling from it all, but he felt paralyzed to do anything about it, especially with the men standing guard.

"Let's get on with it," Borg said turning back to the pagan edifice.

"Get on with what?"

He grinned, those perfect teeth shining through beneath those eyes. "Why, offer the world what Jesus himself offers, but the Church has failed miserably to leverage."

The man walked back to the altar. The guard grabbed Silas's arm and shoved him forward. He glanced back at the relief and said a short prayer.

Lord Jesus Christ, Son of God, please stop this man...

CHAPTER 26

Helen opened a black case and began setting up some equipment near the altar. A saline drip, a portable heart monitor, and a syringe with some vials of liquid. Lars was also busy with his own black case. He brought out a video camera and several black metal tubes that he began fitting together over the circular altar, creating a metal shell that extended over the platform. As Helen finished setting up her equipment, Lars mounted the camera on one of the anchoring beams of the scaffolding so that it was pointing toward the rock formation, with a cable snaking to an open laptop connected to a small satellite dish. Then he opened up a third and final case. From it, he withdrew five objects and placed them on the altar, arraying them equidistance around the edge.

The Antioch Chalice from the MET and the Nanteos Cup from Glastonbury, the stolen grails from Genoa and Valencia, and then the silver grail discovered under the ruins of the Cathar castle in Montségur.

When he was finished, Borg walked over to the head of the pagan platform, and Lars helped him on top.

"This is madness!" Silas whispered to his brother, his voice low and strained. A guard walked up behind him. His automatic rifle was slung around his shoulder and ready to use at will.

Sebastian smiled and said nothing.

Borg lay down in the center of the circular altar, his breath steaming like a smokestack from his face. He eased one arm toward Helen, and she pushed up his jacket sleeve, revealing an IV port dangling from his wrist. She connected the saline drip to him, then unzipped his jacket and connected the heart monitor to his chest, feeding the wires underneath a thick sweater. She then took the syringe and filled it with a vial of clear blue liquid.

"Are we ready," Borg said to her, his voice shaking slightly and a grin widening across his face with delightful anticipation.

She smiled back and nodded. He nodded back and sat up, crossing his legs together and staring into the camera. He said to Lars, "Activate the video equipment and implement the international live stream override-algorithm."

Lars nodded and began typing several strings of commands into the laptop. He typed another string, hit the 'Return' key, then looked at the camera. Silas could see a green indicator light flashing before turning red. A white LED light turned on, creating a ghastly, angular look on Borg.

Silas glanced at his brother, who was grinning from ear to ear. He scanned the area, from the tree line at the left to the rock formations to the pond to the tree line at the right. The guard beside him was gripping the rifle with both hands now. The second guard was standing near the camera.

He had to do something, but his options were limited.

Come on, SEPIO. Where the heck are you?

Borg began his presentation. "Greetings, fellow humans. Rudolf Borg, here. I realize we just only met a few days ago, but I have returned as a herald bearing good tidings of great joy which shall be for all the peoples!"

Silas thought it odd that Borg echoed the words from the Gospel of Luke that the angel of the Lord offered to the shepherds outside Bethlehem after Jesus had been born. He assumed he was broadcasting live on all social media channels and around the internet again, and soon it would be picked up on all the cable channels. But what would people think about the message he was bearing—not to mention the supposed cure he was peddling?

"Last we met," Borg continued, "I promised you a revolution to aid in the evolutionary progress of humanity, something to push the human race forward—No!" he interrupted himself, snapping his fingers and widening his eyes bulging with possession. "*Someone* to show us a new way forward. To show us a better way of living and being human by rising above the ignorance and bigotry, to progress our race forward by revealing to us the universal ideal in a way that makes sense to our twenty-first-century human condition."

The man pushed his greasy hair behind his ears and smiled a menacing grin with closed lips that stretched from ear to ear. He looked like the Joker from the Batman comic books Silas had read as a teenager. The very look his brother had worn.

Borg continued, "That day has arrived." He reached for something off-camera, the Nanteos Cup. He cradled it in his massive hands, peering down at it with delight and awe.

"Then he took a cup," Borg said looking into the camera, quoting Jesus from the Gospels during the Passover meal, "and after giving thanks he gave it to them, saying, 'Drink from it, all of you; for this is my blood of the covenant...'"

The man trailed off, looking back down at the broken cup, then back at the camera—that Joker grin returning. "Today, I will drink of that cup and realize the full potential of Jesus' saying, becoming the firstfruits of what I promise will be a rich harvest for all humanity!"

Silas gritted his teeth and clenched his jaw. He scanned the tree line again and the lake, looking for any sign of Celeste and Gapinski.

Nothing.

He was growing angry at SEPIO's absence. But he was even angrier at Borg's performance, and his own weakness to stop it.

"For centuries, the Church has peddled the myth that there was some sort of salvation inherent in drinking from the symbolic chalice of Christ. That it transformed into the blood that ran red down the Roman cross on which he hung." The man shook his head and smirked, his face twisting into a mixture of revulsion and eye-roll awe. "No, no, no! Understand this, my fellow humans, salvation comes not through Jesus' bloody death on the cross, but through every human act that lives out Jesus' way of life springing from that blood! Each person is their own savior, because every act of love counts as saving acts that brings the universal ideal to bear on our existence.

"We do not need saving from our sins; we need saving from ourselves! We are not bound by sin on the inside, as the Church has insisted. No, we are oppressed on the outside by bad social and spiritual systems and destructive stories that bind us to bad, regressive, harmful patterns of living. Jesus himself saw the chaotic dynamics of normal human living at work in his day and proposed a new alternative. He invites people to change the world by disbelieving old framing stories and believing a new one. This story calls all people to live life in a new way by climbing out of the pit of ignorance and bad examples, discovering the secret of enlightened living and expressing the universal human ideal of love."

He paused, lowering his head so that the angles of his face were accentuated in the dawning light. That grin appeared again, and he said, "We are called to follow in this new way by following his example that will once again walk on this earth as a fully reconstituted Savior for this new era, with the life-force of the man flowing through his veins!"

Silas went to put an end to the spectacle, but the guard butted him in his back, sending him falling hard to the ground. Then the guard was on him, restraining him. Sebastian crouched in front of him, as well. He growled, "Stop. Whatever plot that pretty little head of yours is manufacturing, just stop. Jesus *will* rise again..."

Borg was continuing his sermon, his voice rising to meet the challenge of the hour. "Jesus is the antidote, the cure because flowing through his veins was a life-force so compelling and so completing, which was instantiated in his teachings about the Republic of Heaven, a regime of living that is a radically alternative way of love. Jesus' life is what saves humanity, don't you see? Not his bloody death!"

Every fiber in Silas' being wanted to rush the camera, grab it, and implore those on the other side to accept the true nature of Jesus' power: he wasn't a Gandhi on steroids but the Lamb of God, slaughtered for the sins of the world! That blessed Christmas carol, "Hark! the Herald Angels Sing," got it right: he was born that man no more may die; born to raise the sons of earth; born to give them second birth—all because he bled out on those wicked Roman boards of execution that held his limp, lifeless body. Jesus himself said as much. It wasn't until he gave up his life after hanging on the cross for three hours that he said: "It is finished." No more sacrifice is needed! We don't need to go on striving to placate the deity through countless religious acts and good works. Jesus has brought peace between us and God through his blood, shed on the cross.

That's what he wanted to say. But that damn guard looked Johnny-on-the-spot with that rifle. He didn't have a chance.

As Borg kept at it, a quote from the English preacher Charles Spurgeon came to mind that he had burned into his memory:

> *We should shudder to think of the guilt of sin and its terrible penalty, which Jesus, the Sin-bearer, endured. Blood is all the more priceless when it flows from Immanuel's side. The blood of Jesus sealed God's covenant of grace, guaranteeing it forever. Covenants of old were struck by sacrifice, and this everlasting covenant was ratified in the same manner. Oh, the delight of being saved upon the sure foundation of God's divine agreements that cannot be dishonored. Salvation by works of the law is a frail and leaky boat whose shipwreck is certain, but the ship of the covenant fears no storms, for Jesus' blood ensures it from stem to stern.*

"Oh that the power of Christ's blood might be known and felt in us today!" Spurgeon had ended his declaration.

Indeed...

Borg leaned back against the table, making himself comfortable as the camera swung up on the track to look down on him from above.

He continued, "My fellow humans, the universe has graciously offered us a new way, a new truth, and a new life through the blood of his man Jesus, resurrected now through the modern gene-editing technology of CRISPR in order to offer the modern man the hope of transcending ourselves and our life by being empowered to establish this Republic of Heaven ourselves, as Jesus did. As the great prophet Nietzsche declared, this Kingdom or Republic is a condition of the heart —not something that 'comes upon the earth' or 'after death' as so many dimwitted Christians have claimed. And we aim to make that condition a reality."

He held the broken Nanteos Cup high against his chest, and continued, "Through the power of biogenetics, we have extracted the purity of the universe's life-force from the blood of Jesus that fell from his loving example and into this chalice, the Holy Grail. It was preserved by Joseph of Arimathea and secreted away to the Roman province of Britain, where it lay hidden for centuries, its tradition kept alive until the Medieval romance writers brought it to light. Oh yes, the Grail may be the stuff of legends, but not of myth. Today, in your hearing, is this legend realized. For I will be taking within myself Jesus' essence through gene mapping techniques, rewiring my genes into the very genes of that prophet. I will be the firstfruits of a bountiful harvest, for we will provide the same gene therapy for all of humanity—giving any and all who desire an infusion of the Christ into their lives the chance to experience the full power of what the Grail has to offer. The blood of Jesus and his very life, flowing through your veins!"

Borg nodded to Helen. She checked the syringe of blue liquid, easing its plunger to clear the remaining air. It squirted a tiny stream of liquid before she let up. She smiled and took a step toward the altar.

Silas was panicked, searching the surrounding area again.

Where are—

A sudden crack split the dawn, then three more in rapid succession.

The guard behind Silas fell, a geyser of red bursting from his shoulder.

Silas instinctively dropped himself, flattening against the frozen ground.

The man next to him was clutching his upper right arm, blood seeping out between his fingers and staining the snow a crimson hue. The woman dropped to her knees next to the altar and covered her head, sending the syringe skittering across the frozen ground. Borg was laid splayed out on the altar, helpless and defenseless.

"Borg," a woman yelled from a path running between the

two sets of rock formations. "It's over. Drop your weapons and raise your hands!"

Silas's face brightened, his eyes beaming and mouth widening into a triumphant grin.

Celeste!

He could see another larger man with a large automatic rifle stretching forward. Had to be Gapinski, wielding his weapon of choice. There was another man with him, but he was unrecognizable.

The guard at the head of the altar started to raise his weapon to offer a reply, but the ground in front of him exploded in puffs of frozen earth from rapid gunfire. He danced backward, then immediately put his hands up.

"Throw your weapon to the ground!" Gapinski bellowed. "Because there's a lot more lead with your name on it, mister."

The man obliged, and the three SEPIO operatives padded forward from their protected position toward the altar, weapons outstretched and cautious.

Borg sat upright and began to hustle down off from the darkly stained platform, but Silas launched forward to apprehend him.

"Don't even think about it, pal!" he said reaching the man. He grabbed him by the shoulders and threw him to the ground. The man landed hard on his back, but recovered and reached for his ankle, lifting his pants leg and going after a small handgun nestled in his boot.

Silas lunged for him, grabbing both arms as Borg struggled to withdraw the weapon. They slipped and slid on the frosted grass, two men locked in a struggle for their lives.

The tall man who was far stronger than Silas wrenched the weapon from his boot, but Silas held fast. Borg brought his arms up high, with Silas now on top of him.

The weapon discharged in the struggle, then again.

"Freeze!" Gapinski said coming up fast.

"Drop the weapon, Borg," Celeste joined in.

The men continued to struggle, oblivious of the two.

Gapinski held the long barrel of his automatic weapon high in the air and let it rip, the discharge echoing with angry malice for several seconds.

That did the trick.

"Alright, alright," Borg finally said, throwing the weapon to the side and stretching his arms upward.

Silas climbed over him and secured the weapon, sweaty and exhausted from the fight.

"Nice of you to drop by," he said, breathing hard.

"Thought you could use a helping hand," Celeste said, helping him up.

"And in the nick of time."

"That's the way we roll," Gapinski said.

"Wait a minute," Silas said, frantically scanning the surrounding area. "Where's Sebastian?"

Celeste and Gapinski looked at each other and scanned the open space, as well. The one guard was bleeding out; the other was lying on the ground along with Borg and Helen.

But no Sebastian.

Silas spun around and caught a glimpse of him running onto the ice-covered pond.

"Not on your life..." he growled taking off after him.

"Wait, Silas, I'm coming with you," Celeste yelled launching forward.

"No!" he yelled glancing back as he continued running after his brother. "Stay here with Gapinski and secure that psychopath Borg!"

This is between him and me.

CHAPTER 27

A wicked wind gusted through the naked trees and across the pond as Silas launched onto the ice, whipping up snow and nearly causing him to tumble forward. A raven cawed in protest, and a rabbit scampered out of his path as he plowed across the slick surface after his brother.

"Sebastian!" he called after him.

His brother slowed to look back toward Silas, giving him a chance to close the gap. He pushed faster, ignoring the fact he was trudging across ice and had no clue how thick it was. Didn't matter. He needed to reach Sebastian before he could escape. All so he could help dismantle the leadership of Nous and threat to the Church.

The thought disturbed him as he continued forward, that his brother was a key part of the upper echelons of Christianity's archenemy. Where did he go wrong with him? How could he have let that happen? What happened to turn him so bitterly against the faith?

He was within a few yards now. Sebastian glanced over his shoulder again, grunting in anger and picking up his pace to try and outrun his brother.

This isn't working...

So Silas stopped, brought out the weapon he had recovered from Borg, and fired a warning shot into the air.

Sebastian startled, hunching over slightly and throwing his hands over his head—which caused him to misplace his footing, and then lose his footing. He put his hands out for stability, but it was no use. He lost it and went down into a sprawling heap.

Silas came up fast as Sebastian flipped onto his knees and tried to recover.

"Don't even..." Silas yelled, stopping a few yards away with weapon at the ready.

Sebastian ignored him and stood, his back to his brother and ready to take off again.

Three bullets into the ice stopped him cold.

"I said, don't even think about it!" Silas yelled again. "Now, turn around. Slowly, baby brother..."

The man did as he was told, inching his feet around to face his older twin, his nostrils flared and open mouth steaming with heavy, angry breaths. "Well, you got me, big brother. Just where you've always wanted me! At the end of your line of sight."

"What the hell are you talking about?" Silas growled, his hands gripping his weapon tighter, prepared for anything.

"I've always been in your sights, ever since I left the faith two damn decades ago. But by then it was too late."

Silas shook his head, anger welling within. "All I've ever wanted to have was a conversation about why you walked away from the Church. Why you turned your back on God and the faith. I just wanted to talk—"

Sebastian scoffed and folded his arms. "Yes, Silas. That's exactly right. All you ever wanted to do was talk." He took a breath, then yelled, "All I ever wanted for you to do was listen! To care about what I was going through with my faith!"

Regret pinged Silas's gut. At some level, he knew he was right. He cleared his throat, and said, "I understand, Seba. I do. But what you don't understand is me trying to share my faith with you, what I discovered and believed, was me caring about you and your faith."

"Well, you sure didn't give a damn when we were teenagers, and Father Rafferty was *raping me*!" Sebastian's face was nearly purple with rage, and white spittle flew from his mouth.

Silas's face fell, so did his arms. His stomach dropped further.

Rape? My brother. At the hands of our childhood priest?

Silas swallowed hard, and said softly, "Wha...What are you talking about?"

Sebastian huffed and closed his eyes, as if he himself had been completely thrown off by his spontaneous reveal. His face drained of color, and he rubbed it with his hands before folding his arms.

"It started when I was thirteen. When I was still serving as an altar boy," Sebastian said, his voice trembling and eyes still closed. "One Sunday morning, I was making preparations for the Mass. And...And the man came up behind me. He grabbed—"

Sebastian stopped. He swallowed hard and took a breath, then said, "He wrapped one arm around my stomach and the other..."

He took another breath. He couldn't finish the sentence. Instead, he said, "This was the first of many episodes, lasting half a decade..." he trailed off again, keeping his eyes closed.

Silence enveloped the lake. Nothing scampered, nothing cawed, nothing rustled. There wasn't even any wind, no breeze or gusts. The world was void of anything but the bone-deep chill of the memories clawing their way to the surface from a forgotten childhood.

Silas's mind was numb, frozen and frigid from the reveal;

his gut churned from the revelation, on the verge of retching. He had no idea—none! Yes, he remembered how much Sebastian had changed. A dramatic, drastic one. Never in a million years would he have thought his brother had been abused in such a horrific way. Their father certainly didn't. Or, at least he didn't think he did...No! No way. But why hadn't their dad done something? Because he was a disengaged father who was too wrapped up in—

No! Stop.

Well, then why didn't *he* do something? He was his older brother, after all. The one who always looked after Sebastian, shielding him from bullies at school or helping him connect with the other boys when they moved to a new military base. It was he himself who encouraged Sebastian to get involved in St. James Catholic Church in Falls Church, Virginia...

I encouraged him...This is all my fault!

The questions and implications and accusations kept rolling in, a tide of regret drowning him in the middle of a frozen lake in northern Germany.

Standing on the frozen ice, Silas was overcome with sorrow for Sebastian. And love. A deep, empathetic love. He wanted to do nothing more in that moment than wrap his arms around his brother and tell him how sorry he was. Not only for what he had suffered at the hands of that man for all those years. But for how he himself had bullied him about turning from the faith. Trying to coax and convince, shame and shove him into returning back to the Church.

"Wipe that look off of your face, would you?" Sebastian snarled. "Like I'm some broken bird in need of your coddling, damaged goods that need repairing. I don't need your damn pity, and I certainly don't need your help!"

Silas startled, his eyes refocusing on his own flesh and blood. He took a breath, his throat growing thick with emotion and face quivering with anguished sorrow. "I—I..."

"You want to know, after all these years, why I left the Church? Why I turned my back on God? Why I disbelieved the lies I had been taught about his love and mercy and goodness and care and protection? Well, there you have it! The embers of my faith were smothered underneath the weight of that man of God, a vicar of Christ!"

Silas said nothing, his mouth simply hung open in disbelief and understanding, tears beginning to leave frozen streaks down his cheeks.

Then it happened.

He had let his guard down, and Sebastian took advantage.

Suddenly, the man shoved his right palm square under-neath Silas's chin, his jaw springing shut and his teeth clacking together with a wicked crunch from the full force of his powerful arm. With the other, he grabbed the barrel of Silas's gun, wrenching it from his hand in one motion with ease as Silas fell backward from the force of the blow.

He hit his head hard against the ice. The world flashed with starlight and began to dim, his head exploding in radiating pain and jaw aching from the blow. His mouth felt coppery, and he wondered if he broke a tooth but realized he had bit his tongue.

Sebastian was over him, the same Joker grin Borg offered the camera now on full display as he aimed the weapon at Silas. A giggle escaped him, and he said, "Now I've got you in *my* sights."

Silas sat, arms raised above his head. It had come to this. After all these years of bitter fighting and competition and breakdown. Him at the mercy of his brother.

He heard the click of the gun's safety softly echo off the ice toward him.

Then he heard a voice...

"Sebastian!" a woman's voice echoed, piercing the silent morning air. "This ends now!"

Silas twisted around on the ice to see Celeste aiming with purpose at his brother, her head lowered and face set as flint with one leg planted firmly in front of the other and weapon held securely with both arms forward for a kill-shot.

His eyes went wide. He sucked in a lungful of air. He could see it happening...

"No, wait!" Silas said, scrambling up from the ice as Sebastian swept his arm toward Celeste, re-aiming his own weapon at the woman instead.

Silas held up both hands and stepped forward in between the two, Sebastian picking his aim between Silas and Celeste, Celeste aiming for the man dead-center mass.

"Silas," Sebastian said, "tell your woman to put down her weapon, or I will blow her pretty little head off. Or yours, if it suits your fancy."

Celeste stepped forward, her face twisting with anger at the challenge.

Sebastian returned the stance, mirroring hers and shaking his arm with both anger and anticipation at the draw.

Silas turned so that he was perpendicular between the two, his arms outstretched in a plea to each of the people he cared deeply about to hold their fire.

He turned his head toward his brother. "Seba, don't even think about it!" Then he turned to his partner, his boss, the person he had fallen for. "And Celeste..."

"Silas, he will not walk out of here if I have anything to say about it," she said. "He helped orchestrate the theft of valuable artifacts, not to mention the subversion of the Christian faith. And he is at the top of those responsible for attempting to destroy the Church."

"Celeste, please. He has his reasons..."

"Reasons?" she shot back, her face twisting with confusion. "Whose side are you on? Now bring him in!"

This was not happening. He was not being forced to choose between his brother and the woman he loved.

Silas looked to his brother, his face etched with pain and paralysis at the choice that lay before him.

Sebastian stared blankly back, his jaw set and face ashen. He was ready to do what was necessary if Silas didn't put a stop to it.

Silas knew what he had to do. He took a breath and pivoted to face Celeste, taking a step toward her and then another with arms outstretched and back to his brother. She recoiled suddenly, sucking in a breath of frigid air, her eyes widening in surprise.

Facing her, he said, "Sebastian, a few months ago you played the family card. And I said there was no way in hell you could do that. Well..." he paused and took a breath, then said, "you can cash in that chip now."

Celeste furrowed her brow and shook her head, still training her weapon forward and trying to aim for Sebastian beyond Silas. She looked over his shoulder toward the man, who was grinning with delight. "What are you playing at, Silas?"

His face fell. He didn't want to do it, but he needed time to make things right with his brother. The only way that would ever happen was if he was still alive and free.

Silas said to Celeste softly, "We're letting him go. I have to let him go."

"What? No way! And that's an order, Silas. Step aside."

"I can't!" He closed his eyes and took a breath, then whispered, "I need you to trust me with this. Something happened to him long ago. Something I need to make right..."

She looked deep into his eyes, then glanced over his shoulder again to Sebastian before settling on Silas. Her face softened, and she lowered her weapon and nodded.

Silas sighed and offered a weak smile before turning around and facing his brother. "Go. You're free."

Sebastian said nothing, holding his pose with weapon trained on either Celeste or him. Silas didn't know which. He wouldn't have been surprised if it was the latter, given all that had transpired between them over the years.

The man finally lowered his weapon and slowly walked backward. He turned to leave, but said, "Goodbye, Sy. Until we meet again."

One side of his mouth curled upward slightly, then he spun around and took off toward the other side of the pond, reaching the tree line and disappearing into the woods.

And from Silas's life. Perhaps for good.

DAY VI

DECEMBER 24

CHAPTER 28

PUNTA CANA, DOMINICAN
REPUBLIC.

The mariachi band struck up another rousing chorus of "Feliz Navidad" as couples and families and friends, old and new-found, celebrated the eve of Christ's birth under a cloudless evening sky. A gentle breeze carried along with it the inviting scent of salt and sea, swaying palm branches and cooling the hundreds of patrons of the Punta Cana resort as they danced and ate.

The atmosphere was lively and festive, perfectly framed with Christmas lights strung throughout the plaza running down the center of the resort. Christmas trees decorated with brightly-colored streamers and small figurines flanked both sides of the open-air space. A live nativity stood to the side, complete with three sheep, two donkeys, and a cow. And, of course, Santa Claus greeted adult patrons with champagne and children with pats on their heads and trinkets. The resort spared no expense ringing in Christmas, including the traditional Christmas Eve dinner.

Tables commanding both sides of the plaza were stacked with homemade Dominican food, their aroma inviting, over-powering, dizzying. Empanadas filled with chicken and beef led the way as guests filled their plates, along with bowls full of salad containing potatoes, carrots, tayota, petit pois, onion, and a vinegar-and-mayonnaise dressing. The richly flavorful and softly textured traditional la telera bread, a Dominican staple during Christmas, filled baskets, as well as plates. Freshly roasted pork, apples still wedged in the mouths of the suckling pigs that had been roasting earlier in the afternoon, was being sliced in generous portions at four cutting stations. And grapes, apples, and Christmas sweets abounded.

Festive shouts and laughter filtered down to the beach as Silas sat against a palm tree staring out into the darkening void of water and waves, the sun slipping beneath the horizon and bathing the beach in burnt oranges and reds giving way to purples and blues above. A yacht lazily strolled across the surface in the distance. He thought he caught sight of a large fish leaping into the air, but it just as well could have been a wave. The view was perfect.

And me without a Mojito.

He chuckled softly to himself, recalling being rudely yanked from that very beach a week ago, cutting short his much needed R & R to help save the Church again from no uncertain danger. Which had pretty much been the theme of his year, the Order swooping into his life unexpectedly to beckon him to help contend for and preserve the Christian faith. And now it was his full-time gig after having been sacked by Princeton.

He sighed and leaned back against the rough-ribbed palm tree trunk, extending his legs out across the powdery sand. Not that he minded, surprisingly. He was just thankful he had another opportunity to pour himself into and make his mark on the world. Or so he hoped. He did, however, have a feeling that life with the Order as an operative with SEPIO was going to be far more unpredictable than his former life of weekly lectures, grading papers, and student arguments.

Never in a million years would he have anticipated walking into that year getting almost blown to smithereens, his mentor and second father dying in front of his eyes, saving holy relics from no uncertain peril, entering into the kind of fray he had left behind over a decade ago in Iraq and Afghanistan, discovering the Ark of the Covenant, and getting thrown into the middle of a political fight that had massive implications for the separation of Church and State and integrity of authentic Christianity.

And mostly thanks to one lady in particular.

Ahh, Celeste...

Another variable he couldn't have predicted entering into the year. Up until a few months ago, he was a happy bachelor. Just him and his cat Barnabas, living it up as he focused on his teaching and other extracurricular activities—the conference papers, journal articles, and continued research into the relics of the Church. Relationships of the female persuasion had always complicated things in the past. So he deliberately set aside the drama to prevent it from sidetracking and sidelining him from his important work. In the end, his brilliant plan had made him lonely and self-centered.

And then the Bourne who was a Bourne before Jason Bourne was a Bourne—as she had so eloquently put it—fell into his life. Or, rather, saved his life from the barrel of a gun— and on more than one occasion. There had been not a small amount of tension at points working together, but she was a dream partner in every way. Then when she nearly died, he would have moved heaven and earth to make sure she was safe and secure, back into his arms again.

Never saw that coming a year ago, but she was everything he had ever wanted in a woman, and then some. Smart and sassy. Capable and courageous. Her own person with dreams and goals and ambition. It also helped she was smoking hot with that hair and those lips and that all-too-fine—

"There you are!" Celeste said, coming up beside him. "And aren't you looking smart."

Silas startled, as if he had been caught red-handed dipping into the cookie jar.

"Oy! Didn't mean to startle you there." She sat down beside him in the sand.

He turned toward her and smiled. "You're fine. Just deep in thought."

"Really? What about?"

He caught his breath as he took in the sight before him. Her hair was unbraided and falling full over her shoulders. Her eyes were reflecting the burnt-orange sparkle of the just-set sun. Her white dress with a bright floral pattern running up and down fit perfectly.

He smiled again, and said, "Just the unexpected twists and turns of life."

"Ahh, one of those moments. Hope the twists have proven themselves to be a blessing, rather than a curse!"

He looked down at her hand, took a breath, and gently grabbed it. "A blessing, for sure."

Her eyes widened, then she grinned.

"I've died and gone to heaven," Gapinski said as he plopped down on the other side of Silas. He quickly withdrew his hand and sat straighter. Celeste shuffled her position and played with her hair.

Gapinski looked at Silas, then to Celeste. "I didn't interrupt anything, did I?"

"No, no," Silas quickly said.

"Not at all," Celeste added.

He paused, looking from Silas to Celeste again. "Good! Because I'm starved and they've got a buffet the size of a cruise ship docked over yonder filled with all kinds of Dominican goodness. So let's have at it before it sets sail," he said standing.

Silas stood, then held out his hand for Celeste. She smiled and took it. "Why thank you, kind sir."

The trio waded through the Christmas vacationers and took

their place in line. Silas handed Celeste and Gapinski a plate. Gapinski took one more.

"So, pretty nice digs, this resort has," Gapinski said as he placed three pork empanadas on his plate. "I can see why you chose it."

"Yeah, and the in-room hot tub isn't bad."

"In-room hot tub?" he said, whipping his head toward Silas, dropping a roll in the process. He quickly picked it up off the ground, wiped it on his shirt, and tossed it on his plate. "How'd you manage that? I got bupkis!"

Silas grinned. "Radcliffe pitched in a little to score me the upgrade. Said it was the least he could do, considering he cut my trip short."

"Yeah, but it was for the Holy Grail, man!"

"All the more reason to pay for an upgrade."

Gapinski scoffed and got back to work filling both plates with the festive food.

"So how are you doing with it all?" Celeste asked as she and Silas made their way together through the line.

"What do you mean?" he quickly said as he held out his plate for a nice-sized cut of pork. He nodded to the man dressed in a white uniform with tall, white chef's hat. "Muchas gracias, amigo."

"Oh, come off of it, tough guy. It doesn't bother you at all that your brother was an architect of one of Nous's most significant assaults against the Church and the veracity of the Christian faith in recent memory? That he has partnered with the Order's archenemy stretching back two millennia?"

He shrugged and continued through the line. He really didn't want to tell her what he thought. Because if he got going, he might never stop and regret what he said.

She gently touched his shoulder as he reached for a roll. He startled and recoiled away from her.

"Sorry," she said, withdrawing her hand.

He shook his head. "No, I'm sorry." He sighed as he put the roll on his plate. "Honestly, I don't know what to think. It's almost like it all was a dream, you know? Or, like, it happened to some other person, and I was just watching it all take place on the outside. Sort of numb to it all."

"Makes sense," Gapinski said. "I'll go get us a table."

Silas watched him walk away, then continued filling his plate with more food.

"If you want to talk at all, I'm here for you," Celeste said.

He turned toward her and offered a weak smile. "You have no idea how happy that makes me."

She smiled and put a stray lock of hair behind her ear, then finished filling her plate.

The two walked over to a table Gapinski had commandeered. As they sat, he took a large bite of one of his three pork empanadas, then washed it down with a glass of Dos Equis lager. He wiped his mouth, and said, "So, my man, Silas. How does it feel to have helped foil a plot to extract Jesus' DNA from the Holy Grail and infuse it into some Nous psychopath to create a pseudo-Jesus guru straight out of The X-Files—and four days before Christmas? Which, by the way, is probably the most bat-doo-doo crazy thing that's happened yet. Most missions are far from that cool. Sorry to burst your bubble on that one."

Silas chuckled. "Let's hope they're not. Because I'm finished with the Indiana Jones reruns." He took a bite of his own empanada and a mouthful of red wine. Boy, did that taste good.

"Aren't we all. But, hey, not a bad first day on the job, man. Especially since we got to lock away one of the heads to the snake, that Rudolf Borg character." He chomped into the rest of his empanada, then took another swig of beer.

"Yeah, I guess not."

Celeste looked at him, crinkling her brow. "What's the matter? You don't sound as enthused as I would have expected, this being your first official day on the job and all, as Gapinski said."

"Yeah, man. What's up? I know it's not Princeton, but at least you get to carry a gun."

Silas laughed as he finished chewing some of the slow-roasted pork, it's smoky goodness sitting well in his belly. He drank again from his wine glass, then wiped his mouth with his napkin. "Sorry, don't mean to be a downer on the night. Just exhausted is all. You know, from being interrupted from my R & R, thanks to you two."

"Yeah, sorry not sorry," Gapinski said, pouring his own glass of Cabernet and diving into a slab of pork that was falling off his plate.

"No, it's more than that," Celeste said, her head cocked to one side and eyes narrowed, as if searching him, discerning him.

Silas took another sip of his wine. "What do you mean? I'm fine, really."

"Don't sound fine. And, frankly, I wouldn't expect you to be. What with getting sacked from Princeton and your brother turning on you and all."

He smiled weakly and settled back into his chair. Her reading on him was right. And he was both uncomfortable that she could read him, that the walls he had built were either coming down or no longer working, but also comforted that she could. He sighed heavily, then grabbed his glass and took another sip.

"You're right," he offered, trying to be better at opening up. After all, these were his people now. "I guess I've been trying to ignore the fact that I was fired from the only profession that I had ever wanted, and ever was really any good at. And to top it off, my brother not only has apostatized from the faith, which is a whole other thing that I don't even want to think about. But I let him down all those years…"

Celeste set down her fork and grew silent. Even Gapinski stopped eating.

Silas hadn't noticed. He was too caught up in the moment of what he was thinking and feeling. "But the thing is, it's more than that. My mom died when I was born. Dad's dead from terrorists. And now my brother has turned against me. And literally against the Church, actively set against the Christian faith. Now I have no one!"

He threw his napkin on his plate and shoved back in his chair, gripping his armrest with one hand and his chin with the other.

Celeste said nothing and looked down at her plate. Gapinski nodded and looked to Celeste, then back at Silas, and said, "Well...you've got us. We can be your family. Me and Celeste, here. The Order, Radcliffe and Greer and Zoe."

A sudden rush of emotion seized Silas's chest. His throat grew thick, the corners of his eyes prickled with moisture. He felt silly and embarrassed at the reaction. But also grateful. Maybe he was right. Maybe they could be the family he needed—the family he thought he would find at Princeton, but never did; the family he sort of had in the Army, but lost a decade ago; the family he had been longing for his whole life.

He sat straight and sniffed, then blinked his eyes. He smiled and nodded at Gapinski, then at Celeste. "Tha—" he cleared his throat, still thick with emotion. He took a sip of water. "Thanks, man. You too, Celeste."

She smiled weakly, then grabbed his hand still resting on his armrest and squeezed it. He smiled and squeezed back, wondering what might be in store for him and her—for them, together.

"Aww, bro," Gapinski said, leaning over and slapping Silas's shoulder. "Give it here." He stood, all six-foot-four and two-hundred-and-forty pounds of him, his arms out wide and ready to give Silas a bear hug welcoming him to the team, to the family.

Silas chuckled and stood, giving in and giving one back. They patted each other on the back, and then Celeste joined in from the side, wrapping one arm around Gapinski, the other around Silas. She giggled at the spontaneous show of affection.

When they all let go, Gapinski said, "OK, I am seriously about to break out a rendition of that sappy contemporary Christian music hit from last century."

"No," Celeste moaned. "Spare us your singing."

He grabbed the half-empty bottle of wine and started singing into the head the chorus of 'Friends Are Friends Forever.'

"What in the world is this?" Silas asked, his face scrunching up.

Gapinski stopped mid-line. "Oh, no. Don't you even tell me you've never heard of Michael W. Smith's '90s hit single!"

He wrinkled his forehead. "Umm, no. I was too busy getting drunk to pay attention to the top Christian 40s, unfortunately."

"Ahh, we've got a reformed man on our hands." He continued with another few lines, working the bottle-turned-mic like it was his business, the tables around throwing them looks of equal parts confusion and entertainment.

"Alright, mate," Celeste said taking the bottle away. "No more wine for you." She whispered to Silas, "He gets like this after a few too many."

Gapinski scoffed. "So not fair! Alright, alright. This last line is for you all." He offered his best Smitty impression, eyes closed and fist holding an imaginary mic below his jaw before ending his rousing rendition of the contemporary Christian music hit.

A table two over clapped. Another booed.

Gapinski stood waving to the surrounding onlookers. "Thank you, thank you very much."

Celeste burst out laughing. She offered her own round of applause. Silas couldn't help but join in, whistling with approval. Knowing in that moment that he was beyond blessed. Far more than he could ever have asked or imagined.

Who knew what the next year held. But he was thankful that he wasn't walking into it alone.

For the first time, he was doing life with others.

With family.

ENJOY GRAIL OF POWER?

A big thanks for joining Silas Grey and the rest of SEPIO on their adventure saving the world! **Enjoy the story? Here's what you can do next:**

If you're ready for another adventure, you can get a full-length novel in the series for free! All you have to do is join the insider's group to be notified of specials and new releases by going to this link:
www.jabouma.com/free

If you loved the book and have a moment to spare, **a short review is much appreciated.** Nothing fancy, just your honest take. Spreading the word is probably the #1 way you can help independent authors like me and help others enjoy the story.

AUTHOR'S NOTE
THE HISTORY BEHIND THE STORY…

As a sucker for a good relic mystery and suspense thriller, I figured the next book was pretty obvious. And as a super fan of Indiana Jones stretching back to my early teens, here we are again on another Jones-esque quest—but obviously quite different from his adventure.

The idea of the Holy Grail has always intrigued me. And as a trained historical theologian, I've especially wondered what to make of the mythic relic. It wasn't until I dug into the history behind the legends that I really began to understand the full significance of the myth—to which I owe a debt of gratitude to Richard Barber's book *The Holy Grail: Imagination and Belief* for the meticulous research of that history and theological significance.

As with all of my books, I like to add a note at the end with some of the thoughts and research that went into the story. So, if you care to learn more about the foundation of this episode in the Order of Thaddeus, here is some of what I both experienced and discovered that made its way into SEPIO's latest adventure.

Is the Holy Grail a real Church relic?

In a word: no. However, as Rowan Radcliffe explains in chapter 8, it is true there has been somewhat of a tradition surrounding the cup Christ bore at the Last Supper. The story of Arculf and what he recounted from his visit to the Holy Land is an accurate account. Richard Barber includes this quotation in a chapter exploring "The Grail Outside the Romances," where he also lists several more contenders for the mythic chalice:

- Nothing is heard about Arculf's grail again, though there is a late-thirteenth century reference to a copy of the Grail in Byzantium.
- There is the Antioch Chalice that is indeed secured at the New York Metropolitan Museum of Art, which served as a fun opening scene for Nous's thievery. But as Silas pointed out in chapter 4, its authenticity has indeed been challenged.
- Genoa claims a vessel of the Last Supper, the *sacro catino*, a green hexagonal bowel that has been claimed to be a vessel into which Nicodemus caught Christ's blood.
- Valencia Cathedral has garnered more publicity for its *santo caliz* chalice, a simple agate cup that seems to be a genuine Greco-Roman artifact from the Near East with an Arabic inscription whose meaning is disputed.
- The Nanteos Cup, upon which this story ultimately chose to focus—both in the prologue and in the ending climax—has received a considerable amount of attention given its conspiratorial story of being secreted away in the night from Glastonbury by a band of seven monks while King Henry's henchmen descended upon the famous abbey. However

fanciful of a tale it is, there has indeed been a
considerable tradition associated with Joseph of
Arimathea and Glastonbury, as well as the Grail
itself, which the Medieval grail romance writers
seem to have exploited. The history from chapter 9
is accurate as far as the tradition goes, although
most Church historians have dismissed it, arguing
the Benedictine monk Augustine from Rome
(different than St. Augustine of Hippo) is the true
"Apostle to the English." Then again, maybe Celeste
is right: perhaps there was an actual tradition sitting
behind the legends, where this truthful foundation
was expanded upon by the Grail romances, where
he became associated with English Christianity
generally and Glastonbury specifically.

- Finally, chapters 16 to 18 about the Cathars, Otto
Rahn, and the Nazi search for the mythic Grail is
historically accurate. The Cathars were a heretical
sect of Christianity that had far more in common
with ancient Gnosticism than with the historic
Church. Rahn became attracted to studying
Wolfram von Eschenbach's grail romance and the
history of the Cathars and was fixated on the
mention of the Holy Grail being concealed in the
holy mountain of Montsalvat, which he took as the
Cathar stronghold of Montségur. And with the
support of Himmler himself, the theologians of the
New German faith who had resurrected the ancient
Germanic paganism led expeditions in search of the
mythical Holy Grail—chief among them was Otto
Rahn, the so-called real Indiana Jones. He was
deputized by Himmler's chief esotericist to conduct
research into the Holy Grail, among other
misadventures. He also wrote a few books on the

matter, one of which I used for SEPIO's research in chapter 17, *Crusade Against the Grail*. He never did find the mythical chalice, but I thought the connection with the Cathars and Nazis was too good to pass up, so I created the fictional chamber hidden in the Cathar castle from chapter 20.

It is true that the Church has disavowed any claim to the Holy Grail, writing it off as a Medieval myth devised by French and English romance writers during the twelfth and thirteenth centuries. The Gospel accounts of Jesus' crucifixion found in the New Testament do not mention anything about a chalice catching his blood, much less borne by Joseph of Arimathea. However, Monsignor D'Angelo is right that the myth has endured through the ages, nonetheless, seemingly carried along by every wind of fanciful conspiracy theory. Certainly, it is a construct of the creative imagination, but many within Christianity have viewed it as an embodiment of the highest Christian ideal and experience: the Eucharist. That was also the heart of the story that the original grail romance writers taught, as well.

What was the original story and thematic message told by the original grail romance writers?

Chapter 8 covers much of the origin of the legends surrounding the Holy Grail, which became the foundation for the mythic chalice that Jesus Christ bore at the Last Supper and that held his blood that spilled from the wound in his side. That original story was written by Chrétien de Troyes and expanded upon by Robert de Boron and Sir Thomas Malory, among others.

The grail romances, as they were known, were part of a wider set of literature in the Middle Ages on King Arthur and his knights. The French poet Chrétien de Troyes was instrumental in crystallizing the legend, presenting the Grail as a means of not only examining the chivalric ideal but also the spiritual one. This remained core to subsequent tales, in which knights search for the legendary vessel. He introduced the symbol in his final tale, *Conte del Graal*—Story of the Grail.

As the core of the story goes, a Welsh lad named Perceval undertakes a series of quests to become a knight in Arthur's court—one of which lands him at a castle where he encounters the mysterious Fisher King, who is wounded and offers a sword to the lad as a gift. Afterward, the Grail Procession commences, made up of a young man bearing the bleeding lance, later understood to be that of the centurion who pierced Christ's side; a young woman bearing a gleaming Grail made of precious materials, gold and stones and the like; and finally, a young maiden with a carving dish. Although the lad initially fails the quest for neglecting to ask the ritualistic question that would have healed the suffering king, this failure and a confrontation undressing him as an unworthy, wicked man spurs him on to devote his life to serving God and finding the Grail again. Subsequent romances would build upon this narrative, but the basic scaffolding of the story remained unchanged.

Originally, the Grail wasn't an explicitly Christian artifact, although the story was thoroughly Christian. Robert de Boron's *Joseph of Arimathea* would cement the Grail legend into an explicitly Christian symbol, specifically as the cup Christ bore at the Last Supper and the chalice Joseph of Arimathea used to catch Christ's blood at the cross. This was then connected with the tradition surrounding the man who claimed and buried Jesus' body in the tomb. As the legend goes, Pontius Pilate presented the cup used by Christ at the Last Supper to Joseph of Arimathea, who in turn was said to have collected Christ's blood from the gaping wound in his side made from the lance of the Roman soldier Longinus. Robert de Boron drew upon an

Apocrypha text in a section of the so-called *Gospel of Nicodemus* known as the *Acts of Pilate*, in which Joseph was imprisoned by the Jews after Jesus disappeared post-resurrection. In the original version, the Grail itself is not mentioned, only that Joseph's faith was miraculously sustained. However, in Robert de Boron's retelling, Christ himself appeared to the man in prison bearing the Grail and instructed him to celebrate Mass in commemoration of his death on the cross—a major feature of the grail romances.

The Eucharist has been closely bound up with the Grail. In fact, Chrétien's account climaxes when *'Perceval came to recognize that God received death and was crucified,'* as he wrote, *'And at Easter, most worthily, Perceval received communion.'* As Silas mentions in chapter 8, this is an interesting literary feature given what was happening around that time historically. From the start, early Christians took seriously Jesus' exhortation to remember the new covenant made possible through the blood he shed and the violence his body endured for our sins by drinking the cup of wine and eating of bread. Matthew recorded in his Gospel, chapter 26, this exhortation:

> *While they were eating, Jesus took a loaf of bread,*
> *and after blessing it he broke it, gave it to the*
> *disciples, and said, "Take, eat; this is my body."*
> *Then he took a cup, and after giving thanks he*
> *gave it to them, saying, "Drink from it, all of you;*
> *for this is my blood of the covenant, which is*
> *poured out for many for the forgiveness of sins. I*
> *tell you, I will never again drink of this fruit of*
> *the vine until that day when I drink it new with*
> *you in my Father's kingdom."*

Then the apostle Paul reminded early Christians of these instructions in his first letter to the Church of Corinth, chapter

11, instituting the Lord's Supper as a regular practice among the earliest followers of Jesus:

> *For I received from the Lord what I also handed on to*
> *you, that the Lord Jesus on the night when he*
> *was betrayed took a loaf of bread, and when he*
> *had given thanks, he broke it and said, "This is*
> *my body that is for you. Do this in remembrance*
> *of me." In the same way, he took the cup also,*
> *after supper, saying, "This cup is the new*
> *covenant in my blood. Do this, as often as you*
> *drink it, in remembrance of me." For as often as*
> *you eat this bread and drink the cup, you*
> *proclaim the Lord's death until he comes.*

Celebrating the Eucharist or Holy Communion was meant to be an act of declaration as much as it was an act of identification—remembering Jesus' sacrificial act on the cross through the symbols was a way to identify with his death by dying to sin and rebellion against God, while also announcing the forgiveness and new life made possible through it. And from the fourth century through the twelfth, the role and meaning of the Eucharist developed and changed considerably. A belief began to emerge that the consecrated bread and wine actually became the body and blood of Christ, called transubstantiation. This doctrine became an essential and rather dramatic ritual at the heart of the Roman Catholic Church at the time; it still is.

Throughout Church history, the meaning of this ritual has been debated: some have reacted to the Catholic belief that the elements actually transform in substance into Jesus' body and blood by insisting they remain bread and wine, but are essentially equated with Jesus' body and blood in a spiritual way to provoke and nourish faith; others insist the bread and wine (or, is often the case, Welch's grape juice) are merely symbolic natural means of remembering the supernatural event of Christ's sacrifice. Regardless, Christians have always memorialized Jesus' selfless act of sacrifice—his broken body and shed blood—by remembering that death through the breaking of bread and pouring of wine with the chalice, the grail, if you will.

Interestingly, those themes of Christ's sacrifice central to this ritual—his death and resurrection and the implication of the same for the believer with salvation and eternal life—are also central to the Arthurian romances of the Grail. Sir Thomas Malory in particular heightened the link between the Grail and the Holy Blood, portraying the vessel as an intimate part of Christ's crucifixion and entwined with the Eucharist. *'Fair sweet Lord who art here within the holy vessel'* a sick knight prayed in his version of the legend, clearly associating the relic with Christ's sacrifice on the cross for the sins of the world, of which the Eucharist is a continual reminder.

So whether the Grail is or was a real religious relic, the grail romance writers seem to have sought to draw their readers' attention to the climax and meaning of Jesus' story: his death on the cross. For as my story maintains, that is the true power of Jesus and his blood.

Why the technothriller angle extracting Jesus' DNA? Is that a thing? And why does any of this matter to his true meaning and purpose?

First: yes, CRISPR is a thing! As I was finishing up edits to this story and a few weeks before it released, the world was horrified to learn a doctor in China created the first CRISPR-edited babies with the CCR5 gene used by HIV as a doorway for infiltrating human cells completely deactivated. The CRISPR pioneer Jennifer Doudna says she was "horrified," NIH Director Francis Collins said the experiment was "profoundly disturbing," and even Julian Savulescu, an ethicist who has described gene-editing research as "a moral necessity," described the doctor's work as "monstrous."

Less horrifically, the day will soon come when we will cure someone of Alzheimer's by literally cutting out the gene variant ApoE4 that causes it, then use an alternative gene replacement to save one's faculties. However, some scientists have already mixed genetic information from two separate species, creating modern Chimeras by introducing the genetic information from one species into another. Recently, pig embryos that had been injected with human stem cells when they were only a few days old began to grow organs containing human cells. And, of course, the other option is to mine alternative genetic material from other sources and introduce it into cells, transforming existing ones into new variants using new genetic code—which I used as the basis for Nous's plot mining Jesus' "genetic material" left over in the blood from one of the chalices. The process is a bit more complicated, but it is possible. Hopefully, you were able to suspend just enough disbelief to enjoy the twist in the story!

Again, the Grail is a myth, so I'm not suggesting it's possible to mine Jesus' DNA and clone him! But as I was thinking about this story I arrived at the inevitable "What if..." questions: What if one of the supposed Grail's did have blood, and someone tried to mine it for its genetic material to create a "replica" of Jesus? And what would the religious implications be for such an accomplishment? For the faith-lives of people around the globe—to have a new genetically-replicated Jesus walking around on the earth? In essence, an incarnation of genetics, not of divinity; an immaculate conception not of God, but of man—what would that do to the faith?

Which gets me to the central theme of the story: what is the power of Christ and his blood; what is Jesus' meaning and purpose? I won't fully rehash the back-and-forth dialogue in chapter 22 and Borg's monologue and Silas's thoughts in chapter 26, but they represent two competing ideas about Jesus' power: his life of love vs. his death for sins. In our modern times, ever since the German theologian and father of liberalism Friedrich Schleiermacher, many have believed the power flowing through Jesus' veins was how he lived out the universal ideal of love—redefining even his death as a modeling death of love, not an atoning death that paid the price for our rebellion against God in our place. However, the Nicene Creed captures perfectly how the Church has understood the power of Jesus and his blood:

> *For us and for our salvation [Jesus] came down from*
> *heaven, and by the Holy Spirit was incarnate of*
> *the Virgin Mary, and became man. For our sake*
> *he was crucified under Pontius Pilate, he suffered*
> *death and was buried, and rose again on the*
> *third day in accordance with the Scriptures.*

Yes, Jesus' life of love is a good thing, one we should heed and emulate. His teachings about human dignity and justice and neighbor love have been the bedrock of Western civilization stretching back centuries. As Christians, we are citizens of his Kingdom of Heaven, the manifestation of God's will for human flourishing on Earth, and should pray that God's will in heaven unfolds on Earth, as Jesus taught us to pray. However, many have transformed that Kingdom-vision into a Republic of Heaven (the concept of which I owe to Philip Pullman, who coined it in a speech he gave that was included in his book *Daemon Voices*), which cashes out as simply humanistic progress devoid of Godly righteousness.

Here's the essential message of this book—and the good news of the Christian faith: Jesus' life doesn't save us; his death does! Even those English and French grail romance writers knew that, using the Grail as a symbol of the Eucharist—which was itself meant to remember Christ's death, his shed blood for sins. As Silas argues, this power to save isn't *in* his blood, in the genetic information that made Jesus the man of love he was and the way of love he taught. The power of Jesus is in his *shed* blood, in what he did on the cross by willingly offering himself as a sacrifice to pay the price of our sins in our place. Paul makes this clear in the first chapter of his letter to Christians living in Ephesus: "In him we have redemption through his blood, the forgiveness of our trespasses, according to the riches of his grace." Not his life, not his teachings and example of love —but through his shed blood do we find the rescue from the dysfunction, as Borg put it, that we're all so desperate for!

Jesus himself said as much: it wasn't until he gave up his life after hanging on the cross for three hours that he said "It is finished." No more sacrifice is needed! We don't need to go on striving to appease the deity through countless religious acts and good works. Jesus has brought peace between God and us through his blood, shed on the cross. And as the English preacher Charles Spurgeon rightly said, "Oh that the power of Christ's blood might be known and felt in us today!"

I'll leave you with the words of a well-known hymn of the Christian faith that partly inspired the essence of this story, "Power in the Blood," by Lewis Jones. Rudolf Borg quoted the first verse, here are the others and the chorus, which perfectly captures the essence of the true power of Jesus' blood and the reason he was born two thousand years ago:

> *Chorus:*
> *There is power, power, wonder-working power*
> *In the blood of the Lamb.*
> *There is power, power, wonder-working power*
> *In the precious blood of the Lamb.*

Would you be free from your passion and pride?
There's power in the blood, power in the blood;
Come for a cleansing to Calvary's tide;
There's wonderful power in the blood. [Chorus]

Would you be whiter, much whiter than snow?
There's power in the blood, power in the blood;
Sin stains are lost in its life-giving flow;
There's wonderful power in the blood. [Chorus]

Would you do service for Jesus your King?
There's power in the blood, power in the blood;
Would you live daily His praises to sing?
There's wonderful power in the blood. [Chorus]

May you yourself come to know, deep down, the riches of the wonder-working power that Christ's shed blood brings.

Research is an important part of my process for creating compelling stories that entertain, inform, and inspire. Here are a few of the resources I used to research the history and legend behind the Holy Grail:

- Barber, Richard, *The Holy Grail: Imagination and Belief*. Cambridge: Harvard University Press, 2004. www.bouma.us/grail1.
- Morgan, Giles. *The Holy Grail*. Edison, NJ: Chartwell Books, 2004. www.bouma.us/grail2.
- Wood, Juliette. *The Holy Grail: History and Legend*. Cardiff: University of Wales Press, 2012. www.bouma.us/grail3.
- Rahn, Otto. *Crusade Against the Grail*. Rochester, Vermont: Inner Traditions, 2006. www.bouma.us/grail4.

GET YOUR FREE THRILLER

Building a relationship with my readers is one of my all-time favorite joys of writing! Once in a while I like to send out a newsletter with giveaways, free stories, pre-release content, updates on new books, and other bits on my stories.

Join my insider's group for updates, giveaways, and your free novel—a full-length action-adventure story in my *Order of Thaddeus* thriller series. Just tell me where to send it.

Follow this link to subscribe:
www.jabouma.com/free

ALSO BY J. A. BOUMA

Nobody should have to read bad religious fiction—whether it's cheesy plots with pat answers or misrepresentations of the Christian faith and the Bible. So J. A. Bouma tells compelling, propulsive stories that thrill as much as inspire, offering a dose of insight along the way.

Order of Thaddeus Action-Adventure Thriller Series

Holy Shroud • Book 1

The Thirteenth Apostle • Book 2

Hidden Covenant • Book 3

American God • Book 4

Grail of Power • Book 5

Templars Rising • Book 6

Rite of Darkness • Book 7

Gospel Zero • Book 8

The Emperor's Code • Book 9

Deadly Hope • Book 10

Fallen Ones • Book 11

The Eden Legacy • Book 12

Silas Grey Collection 1 (Books 1-3)

Silas Grey Collection 2 (Books 4-6)

Silas Grey Collection 3 (Books 7-9)

Backstories: Short Story Collection 1

Martyrs Bones: Short Story Collection 2

Group X Cases **Supernatural Suspense Series**

Not of This World • Book 1

The Darkest Valley • Book 2

Against These Powers • Book 3

Luck Be the Ladies • Novelette

End Times Chronicles **Sci-Fi Apocalyptic Series**

Apostasy Rising / Season 1, Episode 1

Apostasy Rising / Season 1, Episode 2

Apostasy Rising / Season 1, Episode 3

Apostasy Rising / Season 1, Episode 4

Apostasy Rising / Full Season 1 (Episodes 1 to 4)

Apocalypse Rising / Season 2, Episode 1

Apocalypse Rising / Season 2, Episode 2

Apocalypse Rising / Season 2, Episode 3

Apocalypse Rising / Season 2, Episode 4

Apocalypse Rising / Full Season 2 (Episodes 1 to 4)

Faith Reimagined **Spiritual Coming-of-Age Series**

A Reimagined Faith • Book 1

A Rediscovered Faith • Book 2

Mill Creek Junction **Short Story Series**

The New Normal • Collection 1

My Name's Johnny Pope • Collection 2

Get all the latest short stories at: www.millcreekjunction.com

Find all of my latest book releases at: www.jabouma.com

ABOUT THE AUTHOR

J. A. Bouma believes nobody should have to read bad religious fiction—whether it's cheesy plots with pat answers or misrepresentations of the Christian faith and the Bible. So he tells compelling, propulsive stories that thrill as much as inspire, while offering a dose of insight along the way.

As a former congressional staffer and pastor, and best-selling author of over thirty religious fiction and nonfiction books, he blends a love for ideas and adventure, exploration and discovery, thrill and thought. With graduate degrees in Christian thought and the Bible, and armed with a voracious appetite for most mainstream genres, he tells stories you'll read with abandon and recommend with pride -- exploring the tension of faith and doubt, spirituality and culture, belief and practice, and the gritty drama that is our pilgrim story.

When not putting fingers to keyboard, he loves vintage jazz vinyl, a glass of Malbec, and an epic read -- preferably together. He lives in Grand Rapids with his wife, two kiddos, and rambunctious boxer-pug-terrier.

www.jabouma.com • jeremy@jabouma.com

facebook.com/jaboumabooks
twitter.com/bouma
amazon.com/author/jabouma

Made in United States
North Haven, CT
02 January 2024

46913351R00163